Charms and Temptation

by Beate Boeker
www.happybooks.de

Copyright 2014 by Beate Boeker
All rights reserved.

ISBN-13: 978-1499274110
ISBN-10: 1499274114

Praise for Charmer's Death

"Carlina Ashley is the owner of a luxurious lingerie store in the center of Florence. She sells a unique kind of pantyhose that don't run. Pricey, yes, but what woman wouldn't kill for something like that? But in this book, it's a question of what person WOULD kill WITH something like that, because the hose become a murder weapon and everyone who has a connection to the shop (employees, Carlina's family and her customers) is suspect. Top of the list is the store's owner, Carlina herself, who is also in a good position to uncover a few clues on her own. Of course no mystery would be complete without a dashing Commissario to aid the amateur sleuth. Then add a family of crazy Italians and this book is three parts mystery to one part romance and then gently seasoned with a dash of humor. A great read." Jayne Ormerod

"What a great story! Step into Temptation, a Florence lingerie store owned by Carlina Ashley and you'll want to remain forever--even if her clientele has a body count. This tale of a womanizer who meets his untimely demise at the ends of a pair of unique stockings hits all the right spots. There are plenty of suspects, a plucky heroine, a fabulous hero, and a setting to die for. Wonderful!" V. Ardito

Chapter 1

A shadow fell over her.

Carlina looked up from the sales counter of her lingerie store Temptation, and a smile of pure welcome spread across her face. "Is it Christmas already?"

"What a nice greeting." Trevor took off his wet raincoat and dropped it onto the low bench in front of the register. "I feel like Santa Claus, coming early." He went into the area Carlina kept for herself and placed both hands on her shoulders. "Let me have a look at you, my girl." His blue eyes shone. "You're looking well."

She laughed and removed his hands from her shoulders. "Not good enough for your standards." One of her eyebrows lifted in a half-reluctant question. "Who is it this time?"

He gave he a mischievous smile. "A ravishing redhead. She's exquisite."

"Of course she's ravishing." Carlina shook her head. "I never expected anything else." She leaned against the sales counter and pushed both hands into the pockets of her trousers. With a slight frown, she looked at him for a moment, the silence between them easy, as if they were friends, which maybe they were . . . though their friendship was unusual, to say the least. Then she surprised herself and him by asking. "Are you never going to settle down?"

He opened his eyes wide in mock surprise and pushed a tanned hand through his black hair. It was graying at the temples, but that didn't make him less attractive – on the contrary.

Carlina suppressed a grin. *He knows how attractive his arm looks when his muscles bulge like that. That's why he's wearing a tee-shirt.* She slanted a look at the rain outside, beating down on the ancient buildings of the historical center of Florence and rubbed her hands over the sleeves of her light-green cashmere sweater, glad to be warm.

"Of course I'm not settling down." Trevor's heavy signet ring blinked in the store's light. "Life would be without zest, wouldn't it?" He shook his head. "What kind of a question is that anyway? I'm your customer." He winked. "Have they taught you no manners?"

"I save them for those who appreciate them." Carlina grinned back. "I'm sorry to hear she's a redhead because I've just unpacked a delightful Christmas set in a gorgeous red color." She pointed to the shelf at her left. "It's over there. The slip ties at the side and is decorated with white feather balls. I thought of you when I ordered it."

He smiled. "Keep it for next year, Carlina. I'll find a raven-haired woman to match that set."

He called her with the nickname her family and half the town used – Carlina instead of Caroline. She didn't mind that at all, but at his words, she didn't know if she should laugh or be offended. "Do you have no shame?"

"Why should I?" He shrugged. "I'm not promising them everlasting love. They know what they let themselves in for. I'm always honest."

Carlina cocked her head to the side. "But what if they hope for more?"

"I can't help it if they choose to delude themselves." He made a move with his hand as if to wipe away the conversation. "Enough about that. How about you? Have you settled down, as you call it?" He grinned. "Or something better?"

The image of Stefano's face rose in front of her inner eyes, but she pushed it away. Even if her relationship with Stefano had developed into more than a romantic craving, which, alas, it had not, she would not discuss him with Trevor. Her feelings were too . . . private, too precious to share with this man who went out with a different woman every Christmas, as if they were Christmas trees, raised to shine for four weeks a year, discarded afterwards. "No."

"No? Just a simple no?" Trevor shook with laughter. "How can the owner of the most wonderful lingerie store in Florence, no, in the world, live like a nun?"

She grinned. "For the first part of that sentence, thank you. For the second, no comment."

He sighed. "Ah, you're hard."

Carlina shook her head. "Nowhere near as hard as you are."

"Me?" The blue eyes opened wide, mesmerizing her. "I'm not hard."

"I wonder if your many exes agree." She regarded him, thoughtful. "How do you do it?"

"What?" Trevor stroked his cheeks as if he had just finished shaving.

If only he didn't know what a determined jaw he has, and how good his chin looks when he pushes it forward like that. I would like him even better. "How do you get rid of them so easily?" she asked.

"It's all a matter of preparation," Trevor said. "I tell them from the start we're going to have some delightful weeks. Not more, not less. When my vacation comes to an end, the relationship ends, too. It's as easy as that. Every Christmas."

His words were callous, but his honesty disarmed her. *He's too charming for his own good.* "Was it always that easy?"

Trevor flinched. "Let's not talk about the mistakes of the past. It's way too nice to be back in Florence again. Now show me what you think would suit my stunning redhead."

Carlina didn't move. "What will happen if you ever fall in love?" she asked.

He turned to a black lace bra and grinned over his shoulder. "But I do, my dear. I do. Every single time."

II

Annalisa leaned against the sales counter of Temptation and glared at her cousin. "It's time to close this shop." She pronounced each word with care, as though Carlina was deaf. "Now."

Carlina tidied her desk with hurried moves. "Just a minute, Annalisa. I only need to file this invoice, and then . . . " She hated to leave stuff lying about when closing up for the night.

"You've been saying this for a quarter of an hour, and I'm bored." Annalisa rolled her eyes. "I'm also hungry, and you promised me dinner."

Carlina smiled at her. "You won't starve. Besides, do you

know that you sound like a five-year-old kid and not like an almost-twenty-year-old woman?"

"Ha. Almost twenty." Annalisa turned a strand of her long hair in her hand. "That's just the point. I'm spending my life waiting, and before I know it, whooosh, I'm twenty, past the age of all fun."

Carlina shook her head. "Dreadful. But there is a life beyond twenty, believe me. At thirty-two, I have sufficient experience to tell you."

Annalisa made a contemptuous move with her hand. "Your universe is this store."

"Quite right." Carlina looked around. Her gaze came to rest with pride on the clever storage drawers beneath each hanger that kept bras of all sizes in well-assorted rows, on the brand-new window mannequin, on the red Christmas bra and panties she had put on display today. "It's enough for me," she said. "You shouldn't underestimate how attractive a tiny universe can be if it's all in your own hands. You can manipulate it, and it's up to you to make it a success. Few things equal that feeling."

Her cousin perked up. "Yes, I see what you mean. I love the name of your store, always have." She sighed. "Temptation . . . it's perfect." Then she frowned. "But isn't it boring to deal with the same stuff year in and year out?"

"There is a lot of variety, believe me." Carlina smiled. "The lingerie industry may not advance in the same huge steps as mobile communication, but there are always changes. In a few days, for example, I'll exhibit at the Florence Christmas Fair for the first time."

"I've heard about that." Annalisa said. "Doesn't the wife of the mayor organize it?"

"Yes, Sabrina does. It's her dream to support the businesswomen of Florence, so she came up with the concept of the Christmas Fair. Do you remember my school friends Francesca, the glass blower, and Rosanna, who has that great flower shop?"

"Nah." Annalisa shrugged. "Unless you mean that tiny woman who looks like a cross between a troll and a fern?"

Carlina grinned. "That's Rosanna. Sabrina invited them both, and some others, to exhibit the crafts of Florence during the fair."

"Hmm." Annalisa looked at an embroidered bra. "But the underwear you sell isn't exactly Florentine art, is it? So how come you were invited?"

"They still had some room to fill, so Rosanna thought of me and suggested that I join, and I developed a concept for lacy underwear. The lace is from Bartosti."

Annalisa started to shake with silent laughter. "Bartosti? The big lace company? You're kidding me."

Carlina swallowed. "Stop laughing. My underwear has nothing to do with their usual lace coverings for toilet rolls. It's sexy, believe me."

"Lace coverings for butts." Annalisa shook her head. "Whatever will you do next?"

Carlina wanted to change the subject. It had taken her weeks of hard work to develop something she liked together with Bartosti, and she didn't like the idea of consumers laughing at her efforts. Hopefully other people wouldn't react like Annalisa. Maybe it had been a mistake to team up with such a traditional manufacturer.

"Can I see that super-lace-thing?" Annalisa asked.

"No." Carlina pressed her lips together. "Come to the fair on December 23rd, then you'll see it." *And don't you dare to laugh in front of strangers at my work.*

Annalisa frowned. "Aren't you a bit touchy?"

Carlina tried to get a grip. Yes, she was touchy, damn it. It was her work, her life, and this whole project was new, something she had never tried before. *Better change the subject.* "I've got something else to show you, something you'll like for sure."

She went to the tiny storage space in the back of her store. "Come here." To make more use of the limited space, she had installed two rows of shelves, one in front of the other. The front row was set on wheels that ran in guiding rails, so she could push it aside whenever she wanted to reach into something beyond or get access to the bathroom door. With a flick of her wrist, she moved the front shelf aside and reached into the cubicle behind.

Annalisa looked around. "It reminds me of a galley; no millimeter is wasted here."

Carlina laughed. "Spot on. I got in a yacht builder when I set this up. He had great ideas." She pulled out a flat cardboard box and opened it.

Her cousin chewed on her lower lip. "You know, I start to see why you find it so interesting."

Well, that's something at least. "You've seen nothing yet. Look here." Carlina held out her hand.

"A pair of nylons?" Annalisa raised her slim eyebrows. "What's so special about them?"

"They've been woven with the latest technology. They guarantee you'll have no more runs."

Annalisa's eyes widened. Her fingertips touched the soft material. "No more runs?"

"Yes. Ricciarda and I tested it." Carlina beamed at her. "It's a special way of weaving that makes sure any small hole at the toe remains a hole and won't create a run up to your hips."

Annalisa blinked. "Are you telling me one pair of nylons will now last a lifetime?"

Carlina laughed. "No. It's still a fragile material. But at least you won't have to chuck them the minute a tiny hole appears somewhere."

"Wow. That's cool." Annalisa put her head to one side. "But isn't that bad for your business? I mean, people will buy fewer nylons if they don't tear them anymore."

"No." Carlina smiled. "I happen to have the exclusive rights for these nylons in Florence. It took two months of hard negotiation before they agreed to the deal." The memory still filled her with pride. "Even if eventually the nylons will be available elsewhere, people will start to buy more expensive nylons now that they last longer, so for me, that's fine." She held out the package. "Here, take a pair. I'll officially start to sell them tomorrow, but you'll get a few hours' head start."

Annalisa's face lit up. "Wow, that's great. Thank you." She slipped the nylons into her golden handbag and looked around the storage room. "You know, I think your business is quite fascinating after all."

Carlina looked at her cousin with affection, her irritation almost forgotten. "Says the jaded almost-twenty year old who thinks she's past the age of fun."

Annalisa's smile revealed a row of pearly teeth. ". . . and starving besides."

How gorgeous she looks. Carlina made a shooing motion with her hands. "Back up. I'm done now, and we'll walk to Gino's."

Annalisa obeyed with a shudder. "Walk? But the weather is dreadful."

"It isn't raining, and after all these hours inside, I need a bit of air." Carlina turned off the light at the back, leaving on the ones that illuminated the shop window. A sharp gust of wind tore at their jackets as they left Temptation.

"Brrr." Annalisa hunched her shoulders. "Are you sure you want to walk?"

"The Vespa isn't warmer." Carlina locked the door and set the alarm. Temptation's top location on Via de' Tornabuoni was an attractive target for thieves.

Annalisa opened her eyes wide. "I'm not talking about your Vespa. Ever heard of taxis?"

Carlina took her cousin by the arm and walked her along the ancient houses toward the Arno river. Festive decorations glittered from the shop windows in the luxury stores they were passing. "Oh, come on. You're not made of sugar." She took a deep breath. "This wind is invigorating, don't you think?"

Annalisa gave her a look that spoke volumes. A sudden gust whipped up her red hair so that for an instant, she looked like a wild witch flying on a broom.

Carlina tightened her scarf around her neck. "Funny, I'd have thought there would be more people about, just a week before Christmas."

"Not at nine o'clock in the evening." Annalisa held back her hair with one hand. "Every respectable shop owner closed the door hours ago; only you insisted on staying late."

"I still had to unpack the nylons. I hope for a great pre-Christmas rush tomorrow because I put ads in several papers." Carlina dug her hands deep into the pockets of her red coat. "I'm so glad they arrived in time. They got held up in customs. I was afraid people would storm Temptation tomorrow, and I would have nothing to sell." She grinned at her cousin. "And you talk about it being boring. It's more exciting than a thriller."

Annalisa laughed. "Yeah, sure."

They reached the Lungarno Corsini and turned left.

Annalisa slanted a look at the Arno. "The water looks awful.

So gray and dirty."

Carlina leaned over the stone wall that separated the sidewalk from the steep embankment. Her gaze swept over the row of houses on the other side, taking in the mix of green wooden shutters, red tiled roofs, and the soft colors of the house fronts. Cream, faded terracotta, and soft yellow alternated, creating a mellow blend. Each house had a different height. Some were slim, crooked from age, some broad and feisty; some windows had arches, some grilles, some barren flower boxes. They looked weather-beaten, standing with clenched teeth in the icy wind, but they stood their ground, as they had done for centuries.

She smiled and turned her head to get her favorite view of the Ponte Vecchio bridge, loaded with shops. Additional rooms clung like fat beetles onto the back walls of the shops, hanging in precarious positions over the foaming water.

A feeling of tenderness swelled her heart, and she took a happy breath. "It's no wonder the tourists are in rapture whenever they see the Ponte Vecchio. It's so . . so Italian. This bridge could not stand anywhere else in the world."

Annalisa lifted an eyebrow. "Must be because you're half American. I see nothing special in it. It's decrepit, that's what it is."

Carlina shook her head. "You only think so because you were born here. Isn't it fascinating to think how unique it is because it grew with time and was constantly adapted to changing needs? Another bulging room added here, another layer of paint there, peeling off again, revealing the bridge's age, and so making it irresistible?"

Annalisa eyed her. "If a bulging something and a peeling layer of paint is making me irresistible, then by all means, let's buy a pot of paint." She linked her arm through Carlina's and dragged her away from the stone wall. "Come on, get over your romantic moment. It's freezing, and even if you're enjoying your fling with poetry, that doesn't mean I have to get pneumonia."

Carlina followed her cousin with a grin. "I wonder what it takes to make you feel romantic."

"Easy." Annalisa looked like a smug cat. "A bottle of golden champagne, a brand-new pair of flaming diamond earrings, and a whirlpool with rose leaves."

"A whirlpool with rose leaves would get clogged up

immediately."

Annalisa gave her sharp glance. "Now who's unromantic? Really, Carlina, I wonder about you. You start to rhapsodize over an old bridge that's falling apart and give me a cleaning woman's remark when it comes to whirlpools." Her high heels clattered over the uneven stone slabs. "Besides, they don't. I tested it."

Carlina stopped dead. "You tested it? Who has a whirlpool? And who was stupid enough to throw rose leaves into it? Don't tell me Tonio treated you to a day in the spa. It's not his style at all."

Annalisa lifted her chin. "Tonio is history. Has been for ages."

Carlina blinked. "You mean five days."

"How do you know?"

"Six days ago, he had dinner at our house, and it didn't look then as if he was history."

"Oh, well." Annalisa conveyed Tonio to the past with a careless shrug. "I fell in love. It's different this time." She turned away and crossed the street to reach the restaurant.

I've heard this before. Carlina followed her without a word.

"You don't need to be so disapproving," Annalisa gave her cousin a defensive glance. "He's older . . . and . . . and different. He's not a boy."

"Hmm." Carlina held open the door to Gino's restaurant. "Come on in. You can tell me all about it while we're having dinner."

Twenty minutes later, Carlina inhaled the aroma of the rabbit ragout with gnocchi in front of her. "Just the right dish for a cold winter night." She savored the first bite in silence and smiled. "The first bite is always the best, don't you think?" Her cousin didn't reply, but Carlina didn't notice, filled with happiness. "I guess it's because your taste buds are not yet used to the treat they get."

Annalisa sighed and continued to nibble on her lettuce leaf. "Don't tempt me."

"Why didn't you take the ragout as well?" Carlina frowned. "You're not too fat."

Her cousin clenched her teeth. "It has to stay that way. I have to be perfect."

Oh, oh. Carlina blew onto her ragout to cool it and slanted an inquiring glance at her cousin. "The new lover is very demanding?"

"He isn't." Annalisa speared a piece of lettuce with her fork. "But I have a plan. A big plan. That's why I won't take any risks." She took a deep breath. "I want him to marry me."

Carlina dropped her fork. "What?"

Annalisa finished her confession in a rush. "He's rich, and handsome, and . . ." she gave a wistful sigh, " . . . so experienced. After him, I can't ever go back to those young guys." Her face twisted. "Besides, he needs to settle down."

Her cousin swallowed. "Does he know that?"

"Not yet." Annalisa's face clouded. "I tried to give him a little hint, and he reacted a bit . . . strangely." She shook herself. "However, there are ways to overcome that. I don't believe him at all when he says it'll be over after the holidays. After all, he's never met a girl like me before." She pushed back a strand of her red hair.

Something sharp pierced Carlina. A man rich and handsome, here for the Christmas vacation, her beautiful cousin with red hair . . . She gasped and sat up straight. "Don't tell me your lover's name is Trevor?"

Annalisa's mouth opened. "How do you know?"

"Madonna." Carlina blinked. "Drop him, Annalisa. Right now."

"Are you crazy?"

"You won't reform him, I promise." Carlina's voice rose. "He'll leave you heartbroken."

"No, he won't." Annalisa crossed her arms in front of her magnificent chest and gave Carlina a fiery stare. "I can do it. I know I can."

"Not a chance in . . . " Carlina broke off. It wouldn't help to get Annalisa's back up. The more she protested now, the less Annalisa would come to her when she needed help.

"How do you know so much about him anyway?" Annalisa asked.

Carlina met her eyes. *I have to tell her, even if it sounds brutal.* "Whenever he's in town, he buys underwear for his current lover."

Annalisa flung her fork next to her plate. "You're lying."

"No." Carlina wanted to hug and shake her at the same time. She bit her lip, all her feeling of well-being gone. "I wish you hadn't met."

"How can you say that?" Annalisa flashed her an angry look. "He's the best thing that's ever happened to me. For the first time, I feel alive. You might just as well wish that I should be dead."

Carlina's throat was dry. "I'd rather wish he was dead."

III

"Are you still awake?" The text message flashed green through Carlina's darkened bedroom like an extraterrestrial presence, landed in a tiny capsule on her bedside table.

Carlina smiled, slipped her arm from underneath the leopard print bedspread, grabbed her cell phone, and called Stefano. "Barely," she said instead of a greeting.

"I'm lucky then," he said.

She could hear the smile in his voice and tried to picture him. His light eyes and lean face usually looked so harsh but were transformed when he smiled.

"I just wanted to ask if you'd have time to have dinner with me tomorrow," he said.

Her heart did a somersault. She had not seen him for weeks, no, months.

"I know it's a lot to ask." He sounded nervous.

Garini nervous?

He said, "You'll be exhausted from the Christmas shoppers at Temptation."

A thousand thoughts zigzagged through her brain. She had the nylon launch tomorrow. She would be dead on her feet by the time the day ended. She would look like a scarecrow. She didn't give a damn. "No, that's fine." She smiled. "As long as I can sit the whole evening."

He laughed. "I think I can arrange that."

She didn't want him to hang up. She wanted him to laugh again. It went straight through her, warm and strong, like fire. "Are you sure your lovely boss won't throw another body your way the minute you want to leave?" His boss had done just that, twice. Okay, so maybe it was normal for a police inspector from the homicide department to come across bodies all the time, but the timing had been rotten.

"I told him half the city of Florence could be murdered in their beds, and I would still take the evening off." His voice held the faint ironic note she had somehow gotten addicted to.

Carlina chuckled. "What a dramatic way to put it."

"His words, not mine. Whenever a case isn't solved quick enough for his taste, he asks me if the citizens of Florence are still safe in their beds. He claims it's the mayor who's saying it, but I know better."

"How do you know that?" Carlina stretched and wriggled her feet. *I will see him tomorrow.* Her body tingled to the tips of her toes with joy.

"The mayor has changed, but the question is still the same."

Carlina laughed. "I see."

"Honestly, I feel bad about standing you up so many times."

"It's not your fault. Of course you had to be with your father after he broke his wrist." It had taken him a full month to get better. She had counted the days.

"I knew you would understand that. I've never met anybody with such a fierce family loyalty." His voice teased her.

"Well, tomorrow, we won't cancel, come hell or high water. Family and murder be damned." As she said the words, a faint feeling of fear crossed her heart. Had she challenged destiny? Carlina shook herself. Nonsense. She had a date with a busy man. That was all.

He laughed. "It's a deal. Shall I come to your house at eight?"

"Yes." That would give her enough time to take a shower and dress, even if the store was open later than usual. Thank God Florence still stuck to traditional opening hours.

"Sleep well, Carlina."

"Good night."

She snuggled underneath the covers with a happy sigh. She would see him tomorrow. She could also ask his advice how to protect Annalisa.

All would be well.

Chapter 2

Carlina woke early. Everything inside her hummed with expectation. She put on a pair of the new nylons in black, a short skirt that twirled around her when she moved, and combined it with a soft sweater that had fake leopard fur at the end of the sleeves and at the collar. She smiled when she looked into the mirror. She looked like a cat, a purring, happy cat.

She downed a cup of strong coffee, then ran downstairs, an hour earlier than usual. Her hand touched the smooth wood of the railing that curved from the top floor of the house, where she had her apartment, past her mother's apartment, where everything was quiet, thank God.

Two floors down from her apartment, she stopped for an instant and laid a package with a pair of nylons in front of her cousin Emma's door. Emma would know it was a thank-you for the help she had given her during the pre-Christmas cleaning at Temptation.

Still humming, she ran down the last flight of steps and reached the ground floor where her great-uncle Teo lived. He came out of his apartment just as she opened the heavy wooden front door.

He was a head shorter than Carlina, and his white hair stood up in wisps, but he was dressed with care as always, his trousers sharply creased, his white shirt immaculate. "You're early today, Carlina."

She gave him a kiss on his leathery cheek. He smelled of aftershave. "Yes, I have a special promotion today. It's very exciting."

He nodded. "I know. The indestructible nylons, right?"

Carlina laughed. "Yes. How well you remember everything I tell you." *He looks so wistful. He must be lonely now. It seems so long ago that we had these awful murders, and yet, it's only a few months. I really have to find something to keep him occupied.*

"Of course I remember the unbreakable nylons." He smiled at her. "Have a good day, my dear, and tell me all about it tonight."

"I won't be home tonight," Carlina said. *I hope.* "But I'll tell you later, all right?"

His rheumy eyes sharpened. "So that's why you've been humming all the way down."

She turned so quickly, her skirt swung out. "You're way too clever, Uncle Teo." She winked and waved at him. "Have a good day!" The door closed behind her with a bang, but it opened again immediately.

Uncle Teo stuck out his head. "Are you going to tell me everything?" He put special emphasis on the last word.

She grinned over her shoulder. "Of course not!" Then she hurried to her Vespa.

As she still had time, she stopped at the bakery around the corner from the Basilica di Santa Trìnita and bought a cardboard box of flat Copate biscuits for her assistant Ricciarda and herself. The almonds and sugars would give them quick energy if the day should prove to be too hectic for lunch, and the wafers on the top and the bottom of the biscuits would protect their hands from becoming sticky. The perfect pick-me-up if she ever saw one . . . though she might not need them today; her high level of adrenaline could carry her through the whole day . . . or so it felt. Carlina still hummed while she opened the door of Temptation.

With a smile, she hung up the sign she had prepared for the shop window. 'Mai più smagliature!' it said, 'No more runs!'.

A minute later, Ricciarda arrived. She, too, wore a short skirt and a pair of the new nylons Carlina had given her. Carlina smiled. They had not discussed it, but Ricciarda knew the best way to show a new product was to wear it . . . which usually was out of the question.

"You look great," she said.

Ricciarda smiled back. "So do you." Her black ponytail shimmered in the winter morning light coming through the window. "Shall we bet how many nylons we'll sell today?"

Carlina laughed. "God, I have no clue. I've never done this before. Twenty pairs? Twenty-five?"

"Forty at least." Ricciarda stretched out her hand. "The one who wins will buy the other a box of Copate biscuits."

Carlina shook her assistant's hand. "Deal. But guess what?" She grinned. "I already bought us a box."

"Perfect." Ricciarda went behind the sales counter and exclaimed in surprise. "What are these?" She pointed at four shiny bags, filled to the brim.

"They'll be collected later on by a courier from the Garibaldi Hotel." Carlina's smile came out lopsided. Yesterday, when she had sold Trevor all the lingerie, she had felt nothing but happiness. Today, after having learned that Annalisa was going to wear them, things had shifted so much, she was unable to relive yesterday's triumph.

Her assistant lifted an eyebrow. "Wow. It looks as if you had a great day yesterday."

"Sort of." Carlina shrugged. "Trevor is back in town."

Ricciarda bent over the bags and looked inside. Her black ponytail slid over her shoulder and touched the embossed golden Temptation logo on the bag. "Trevor? Do I know him?"

"Not yet. His name is Trevor V. Accanto, and he's a fabulously rich American who comes to Florence every Christmas."

Ricciarda turned from the bags and concentrated on aligning some hangers. "Does he always buy that much underwear for his wife?"

Carlina suppressed a sigh. "It's not for his wife."

"Oh." Over her shoulder, Ricciarda gave Carlina a startled glance out of blue eyes. "One of those, is he?"

"Hmm." Carlina said. "But charming."

"They usually are." Ricciarda's voice was dry.

"Yes, more's the pity." Carlina went to the tiny storage space at the back of the store to get more gift bags. She needed to refill the gap in the front that Trevor's shopping spree had left.

"I wish it wasn't like that." Ricciarda said from behind her.

"You wish men weren't charming?" Carlina bent down to pick up the bags and turned back to the front of the store.

Ricciarda gave a snort. "No. I wish the charming ones didn't have so much power over us." Her voice held a bitter trace.

Surprised, Carlina stopped in her tracks, her arms full of glossy shopping bags. She had not employed Ricciarda for long, but so far, her assistant had never shown the slightest sign of being opposed to charming men. On the contrary, she knew precisely how to deal with them, how to make them feel welcome without overstepping boundaries. Maybe she had sounded so disapproving because she was a convinced Catholic and had strict moral standards? Carlina didn't know what to say. She wasn't close enough to Ricciarda to ask personal questions, and maybe she had only imagined that bitter note in her voice.

Ricciarda looked around. "We're all set, aren't we?" She sounded her normal self again, and the moment was gone.

"Yes." Carlina said. "But if you really think we'll sell forty pairs today, I'll unpack a few more boxes in the back. Just to be prepared."

She disappeared behind the curtain that separated her storage room from the store. It was still quiet, and Ricciarda would manage in the front.

Carlina took a folded footstool from the hook on the wall, opened it and sat down. Then she pulled the box of nylons close and slid it open with a box-cutter. She moved with routine, filling the slots in the shelf, assorting them by size. Her thoughts went to Stefano Garini as if pulled by an elastic - whenever she didn't pay attention, they snapped back to him. She liked him. A lot. And she could read in his eyes that he liked her too. At least it seemed like it whenever he stopped for a short chat at Temptation.

It seemed incredible that they both lived in the same town, so close together, and never managed to meet properly. As bad luck would have it, his father had broken his wrist the very day after Stefano had found her grandfather's murderer. That's how she had met him. How long ago it seemed. Carlina remembered her erratic grandfather with a pang. It would be the first Christmas without him. *Better concentrate on Stefano and their date tonight.* They would have had their first date weeks earlier if she hadn't gone on vacation, booked ages ago. November was a slow month at Temptation, and she had spent three weeks in sunny Martinique, thinking about him more often than ought to be allowed. When she came back, he was in the middle of a stressful murder investigation, working day and night. Then he had gone on vacation, visiting his sister and skiing in Switzerland. And now, finally, they were both back in town, and tonight, she would see him. Maybe she should suggest going somewhere out of town, to avoid any of her family members littering Florence. It would be awful if they ran into her mother or one of her zillion cousins. They were so curious, they would stick to them without shame.

Tonight. Tonight. Suddenly, she recognized the tune she'd been humming all day long. West Side Story. God, she was smitten. She cut up the empty box and stuffed it into the garbage can. She heard Ricciarda laughing, then a low murmur of voices. She'd been so deep in her thoughts, she'd never noticed the first customer had arrived.

Carlina pushed the curtain aside and froze. It was Trevor. He bent forward, his handsome face close to Ricciarda's upturned face. She smiled at him as she piled four bras and matching slips onto the counter. Of course, she had no idea who he was. They looked like an advertisement together, for family shampoo or chocolate or something.

Annalisa's determined face rose in front of Carlina's inner eyes. She shuddered. *I don't want to talk to him.* She stayed where she was.

"I won't take these with me," Trevor said. "Just add them to my bags over there. I told the receptionist at the Garibaldi Hotel to send a courier before noon."

Ricciarda's eyes widened, and she stared at Trevor as if she had seen a ghost.

Carlina started forward without thinking. "Hi, Trevor. I didn't see you come in."

"Carlina!" He turned to her and kissed her on both cheeks. "What a charming, raven-haired assistant you have."

Carlina felt sick. "Yes, she's very good." She tried to give Ricciarda an encouraging smile, but her assistant's eyes looked glassy.

Talk. Make him talk. Distract him. "How come you're about so early?" she asked.

"I had planned to take a run along the Arno, but when I passed your store and saw it was open, I decided to say hello."

Now she noted he was wearing trainers and a sportive outfit. He sure didn't look his age. "How nice." She hoped her smile didn't look as fake as it felt.

"Why are you here so early?" He winked. "No reason to stay longer in bed?"

"We're having a promotion today." Carlina felt as if on autopilot. "For run-proof nylons."

"Yes, Ricciarda told me." He flashed a thousand watt smile into Ricciarda's direction who still stood as if made of marble. "But I don't buy practical things. They're not romantic enough."

"It doesn't matter." Carlina swallowed. "She already has one pair."

"What?" Trevor frowned.

"Annalisa is my cousin." Her eyes held his.

His eyebrows soared. "Oh. I see."

"Yes."

Nobody moved. It was so quiet, Carlina could hear the soft jingle of a metal hanger moving in the warm air coming from the radiator. Something between them shifted. It felt as if their friendship was cut into a million tiny pieces, blown up into the air, and when it settled again, it showed a picture that was unrecognizable, nothing like it had been before.

Then Trevor smiled.

For an instant, Carlina glimpsed the old picture, but the change had been too complete, too drastic. They could not go back, never return to their easy banter.

"Are you going to impersonate the enraged mother now?" he asked.

"No." Carlina bit her lip. "I . . . I'm just asking you to be careful."

"To be careful?" His tone mocked her. "Just what do you mean, my dear?"

"I mean . . . " Carlina swallowed. "Annalisa is very determined." *Determined to hurt herself, if only she knew.*

A smile crinkled around his eyes. "I've dealt with determined women before."

". . . and young." She met his eyes, willing him to understand, willing him to agree that Annalisa was too young to be a Christmas fling.

"I know." Trevor touched Carlina's arm. "Don't worry. I've got it all under control."

She shivered. It sounded like famous last words, though to be honest, if anybody had things under control, it was Trevor, and Annalisa would be the one to lose. Annalisa would be destroyed, and she saw no way to stop it.

Trevor turned on his heels, waved at them both, and left.

Ricciarda swallowed so hard, Carlina could see it. "You're right," she said. It came out as a croak. "He *is* charming."

The ringing of Carlina's phone interrupted them. "Excuse me." She fished her phone out of her handbag and checked the display. Uncle Teo. *Now what does he want? We only talked an hour ago.* Carlina pressed the green key. "Uncle Teo? Is everything all right?"

"Of course, my dear." Uncle Teo sounded cheerful.

Carlina couldn't suppress a smile, half-exasperated, half tender. *He's a curious old bat.*

Uncle Teo said, "I was just wondering if you could pass on a message to Signor Garini tonight."

I have not told you whom I'm meeting. Carlina didn't answer.

"Carlina? Are you still there?" A clanging sound told Carlina that her great-uncle had started to shake the phone.

"Yes, I'm still here. What is your message?" There. That was a good compromise. He could get it out of his system, and she had not offered any information.

"Can you remind Signor Garini that he said I could work for the police some time? Do some investigations?"

The mere thought of Uncle Teo tracking criminals caused a shiver to run down Carlina's back. "When I see him, I'll tell him."

"Oh, are you not going to see him tonight, then?" Uncle Teo sounded disappointed.

"Uncle Teo." Carlina made sure her voice was patient. "I'm not a teenager anymore. You don't need to screen my every move."

"But I'm not doing anything of the kind!"

She could see in her mind how he drew himself up and squared his shoulders as he said that.

"I'm just asking you to pass on a message. Will you, dear?" The question ended on an anxious note that got to her.

"I will."

"That's great. Thank you." He sounded his usual self again.

"Bye, Uncle Teo." She hung up, shaking her head. She had to find something to make him happy, and soon.

II

"Is that you, Garini?" Cervi poked his head out of his office door.

Stefano Garini suppressed a sigh. He should have tiptoed past the office of his boss. "Yes?" His voice made it clear how reluctant he felt to obey the summons.

"Come in for a moment."

Oh, no. Garini glanced at his watch. Almost one o' clock. Seven hours before he could see Carlina. Surely Cervi wouldn't manage to destroy his plans yet again?

The office smelled of Cervi's aftershave, something cloying and sweet. The air was spent, stifling and dry from the radiator. Stefano tried to breathe through his mouth.

"Sit down." Cervi made a tired move with his hand toward the leather chairs around the mahogany desk in the center of his office. With a sigh, he lowered himself into one chair and fixed his subordinate with a resigned look. "A man has been found strangled in the Basilica di Santa Trìnita."

Stefano clenched his teeth. He knew where Cervi was leading, but this time, he was going to put up a fight. "Have you told Sergio?"

Cervi shook his head with a glum expression. "He called in sick this morning. A heavy cold."

Again! Stefano made sure his voice sounded even. "You promised me the next case would go to him."

Cervi shrugged. "I can't drag him out of his bed by his hair, can I?"

Stefano narrowed his eyes. What amazing luck Sergio seemed to have. Every time a body dropped somewhere in the city, he was sick. Or maybe it was the other way round: He was sick so often, it wasn't surprising that a few murders coincided with his illnesses. "How about Paolo?"

Cervi shook his head. "Paolo is on vacation." His face was impassive. "A cruise in the Caribbean. It has its advantages if you have a rich wife."

Look who's talking. Stefano suppressed his sarcastic thought and straightened. "I have worked on the last four cases without pause. I told you I would leave tonight at six, and I'm afraid I can't cancel it again."

"You're forgetting your vacation a short time ago."

Stefano swallowed his reply. It wouldn't go down well to mention Cervi's extra-long vacation every summer, stretching from mid-July to mid-September. With Sergio ill and Paolo on vacation, he knew he couldn't refuse to take on this new case. *Damn.* He clenched his teeth. "I'm taking up this case, but I have to get off at six o'clock tonight." That would leave enough room for last minute delays. He didn't want to keep Carlina waiting.

"Just what is so important tonight anyway?" Cervi's gaze focused with interest on Stefano's face. He looked like a vulture waiting for prey.

Stefano met his gaze and didn't reply.

Cervi chuckled. "Like that, is it? A woman, no doubt." He leaned back and folded his arms in front of his chest. "If you had wanted a nine-to-five-job, you should have become a clerk."

Or I should have applied for your position.

Cervi's face lost all trace of a smile as if he had heard Stefano's thoughts. "There's no choice, Garini. You have to do it."

I know that, idiot. Stefano made sure his face didn't show his emotions. "Fine. As long as I can put the investigation on hold after six tonight."

Cervi leaned forward. "What if something decisive happens tonight? Will I tell the mayor that you had to take time off to schmooze with your girlfriend?"

Stefano got up. "You may tell him I suddenly fell ill and that you couldn't very well drag me out of my bed by my hair."

Cervi's face turned red.

Stefano continued without heat. "And now you'd better tell me all about it."

Cervi jumped up. "Talk to Gloria. She took the call."

"Fine." Stefano turned to the door.

"Remember, Garini." Cervi's voice followed him out of the room. "I want a written report every two days. Starting tomorrow."

III

Gloria bent forward so her impressive cleavage would hang

right in front of Garini's eyes. "The call came fifteen minutes ago. What took you so long? Didn't Cervi find you?"

Stefano closed his eyes for an instant. "Tell me what it said."

"A couple of tourists stumbled over a body in a corner of the Basilica. The priest is watching over the body and waiting for you."

Fantastic. A murder inside the Basilica and tourists involved, a few days before Christmas. What wonderful headlines for the sensation-seeking press. Stefano sighed. "Anything else?"

"No."

At least no Mantoni was involved. Stefano shuddered as he thought back to the case last autumn, when Carlina and half her family had been suspects. A thought chilled him. It was possible that the priest was part of the Mantoni family. But no . . . he couldn't imagine anybody of that exuberant and crazy family taking holy orders.

Fifteen minutes later, Garini stopped his motorbike in front of the Basilica and frowned. A faint rain drizzled down and made the cobblestone pavement treacherous and slick. His assistant Piedro should have arrived by now and closed the church to the public, but he was nowhere to be seen. No surprise there.

He pulled open the heavy wooden door and stepped into the basilica. A current of cold air, redolent with the smell of incense, made him shiver and shrug deeper into his heavy leather jacket. At the altar, he could make out a few people standing around, but in the dim light, details were smothered. The candles at the altar flickered as he approached the sober group, and the sound of his steps echoed through the vast church.

A thin man, almost as tall as Garini, detached himself from the group and went toward him with measured steps. "I'm afraid you can't come any closer, my son." His long fingers plucked with a nervous move at the sleeve of his black cassock.

Stefano pulled his identification out of his pocket and held it out to the priest, though he knew it was too dark to make it out. "I'm Commissario Garini from the Homicide Department."

The priest clasped his hands together as if in prayer. "I'm Padre Balli."

Good. No Mantoni. "Padre." Garini inclined his head. "Please close the door of the church and then explain the situation to me."

The priest gave a start. "The door? Oh, yes of course, I forgot." He hurried away, his wide habit fluttering at the edges like the wings of a hectic bird.

Garini went to the altar. Close by, he was able to discern the two people standing next to it. A woman with gray hair like a helmet and a square form stood with her feet planted apart as if she expected the ground to rock beneath her feet any minute. The slight man next to her seemed insignificant in contrast. To their left, a dark shape lay on the stone floor, half-concealed by the shadow of the wooden benches.

Garini turned to the priest who had come back. "In a few minutes, the police team will arrive, but I need some light first."

"Yes, yes, of course. I'm sorry." Padre Balli shook his head as if wondering how he could have forgotten to illuminate his church to celebrate the occasion of murder and hurried through a door at the left of the altar. A click, and two weak spotlights flickered to life. Their irresolute light only seemed to enhance the darkness in the rest of the vast church.

"This won't do." Garini frowned. *Where is the forensic team? Have they gone Christmas shopping?* "Do you have a stronger light?"

The priest looked startled.

Why is he so nervous? Is it a reaction to the murder? I'll have to ask him later. Aloud, Garini said, "A bigger lamp, maybe?"

"I . . . I'll check." The priest disappeared through the side door and returned with a floor lamp. It had a yellow silk top with tassels that swung to and fro as the priest presented it.

It looked so incongruous that Garini had to suppress a smile. He took the lamp with one arm and placed it next to the body. The priest plugged in the cord, and a mellow light illuminated the dead man on the floor. His body laid slumped between the first and the second row. From where they stood, they could only see the back of his head. He was covered by a dark coat with an upturned collar, but that was all Stefano could make out. If he investigated the details now, he would overlook too much. This meant he had to wait for the camera team and their strong lights and first had to concentrate on the witnesses. It wasn't an ideal situation as he needed more light to see their faces clearly, but at least they weren't half-hidden behind a bench. He turned to the couple at his side. "Who found him?" he asked.

"I did." The stout woman said with a gravelly voice.

The small man next to her looked at his feet as if he found the brilliance of this black patent leather shoes fascinating.

Now that the light had improved somewhat, Garini could make out his short-cropped hair. It covered a head that reminded him of a racing horse – an elegant bone structure, not an ounce of fat, the skin stretched tight over the bones.

The Commissario frowned. At first, he had assumed that the two were a couple, but somehow the slight man didn't suit the practical woman next to him. She was a tourist, that much was obvious from the sturdy pair of shoes to the guide to Florence sticking out of a serviceable pocket of her shapeless coat. The small man was more difficult to place.

The priest returned to the little group like a silent bird.

Stefano took out a small notebook and a pencil. Where was Piedro with the tape recorder? "Please tell me your names."

"Gertrude Asseli." The stout woman said.

Now Garini could place her accent. She came from the German-speaking part of Switzerland.

She continued without being asked. "I'm from Zurich, on vacation in Florence, and we called you," she checked her watch, "thirty-two minutes ago." Her face twisted in disgust. "I have to say you took your time."

Garini turned to the small man. "And you?"

Ms. Asseli gave a snort. "I found him on top of the body."

Both the priest and the slight man flinched.

"I beg your pardon?"

"Oh, he fainted when he saw the body and fell right on top." Ms. Asseli's voice was filled with contempt.

Stefano turned his back to her. "Could you please tell me the story in your own words, Signor . . . ?"

The man twisted his cap in his hands and swallowed so hard, it shook his whole body. "Morin. I'm Leopold Morin from Paris." His Italian was perfect, his voice low and cultivated. "I teach Italian at the university of Nanterre."

"I'm a teacher, too." Gertrude Asseli cut in. "I teach biology and geology." Her complacent smile revealed teeth as large as sugar cubes.

Stefano looked from one to the other. "So you know each

other?"

"Oh, no." Leopold seemed shocked, and the look on Ms. Asseli's face showed that for once, they shared the same feelings.

Padre Balli shook his head in a sad way like a man who doesn't understand why his kids don't get along.

"I . . . I came to church to pray," Leopold said.

Garini narrowed his eyes. It sounded as if Leopold was picking his words with care. Or was he making up a lie? But he'd had enough time to concoct a story. Thirty-two minutes, to be exact. No, maybe less. Gertrude had not yet explained how long it had taken her to shake life into the senseless Leopold.

"I went to the front, my eyes on the altar. I'm afraid I was a bit distracted due to . . . the beauty of the church, and it was dark. When I stepped into the pew, I stumbled and fell." He shivered. "I must have hit my head because the next thing I knew, Signora Asseli was trying a mouth-to-mouth-resuscitation on me." He looked revolted.

What a cruel fate for the fastidious man in front of him. Garini hoped nobody noticed his twitching lips.

"It was my duty as a citizen," Gertrude Asseli stated with satisfaction.

"Did you move the body?" Garini asked.

Ms. Asseli shrugged. "I'm sure Signor Morin flattened him when he fell on top." It sounded as if the Frenchman had the shape of an elephant instead of being a bundle of bones.

"But you did move him too, my child," the padre said, his hands clenching and un-clenching into nervous fists.

"What?" Ms. Asseli rounded on him.

Padre Balli took one step back but stuck to his guns. "When Signor Morin had woken up and had sat down over there," he nodded at the opposite pew, "to recuperate, you lifted the head of the dead man."

"Well, of course I did." Gertrude shot him a furious look. " I thought he might be in need of help, and it's my duty as a citizen to come to the help of those who need it."

Poor victims. Stefano scribbled down the words as fast as he could. How he missed his tape recorder. His assistant Piedro was supposed to bring it. "And did you try the mouth-to-mouth resuscitation on him?" Stefano slanted another look at the body on the floor. The victim's feet pointed toward them, and in the yellow pool of light, the stitching in the leather soles – a sign for high quality shoes - was clearly visible. Gertrude Asseli must have scrambled right over him. Damn.

"Of course not." Ms. Asseli looked as if she had expected better powers of deduction from a member of the Florence homicide department. "It was obvious he was dead."

Stefano went to the other end of the pew, slipped between the first and the second row and knelt next to the body without touching anything. Now he could see the distorted face, the black tongue. Strangled with a black scarf. He touched the material with his fingertips. Gossamer thin, silky. Not a scarf, something different. He knew the material, but for an instant, couldn't place it.

"It's a pair of nylons." Ms. Asseli's voice boomed through the church. The hollow sound magnified in the vast dome and echoed from the walls.

Garini's stomach lurched. Carlina had mentioned a special launch of nylons today. For an instant, her face with the cat-like eyes appeared in front of his inner eye. *Stop being a fool. She isn't the only woman with access to nylons in Florence.* He straightened.

A booming knock made the priest jump. He hurried up the aisle to open the door.

Garini watched the arrival of his force without moving. *Finally.* The camera team took over. As soon as the strong lights had been installed, Stefano watched the scene like a hawk and walked all around the victim, taking in every detail. From the position of the body, it was possible that he had knelt when he was attacked from behind. A clean way for the murderer to avoid the victim's hands and fingernails. *Damn.*

Someone plucked at his sleeve.

"I would like to leave, Commissario." Leopold's brown eyes looked like a puppy's. "I feel the need to wash."

"To wash?" The cold seeped through Garini's coat into his bones. A need for a fire he understood. But water? The flash-light of the camera illuminated Leopold's scared face for an instant.

"Yes." Leopold took a trembling breath. "I was in touch with a dead man, besides, . . . " his voice petered out, but the look of loathing in Gertrude's direction spoke volumes. No doubt the

attempted   mouth-to-mouth   resuscitation   would   remain   a
nightmare in his memory.

"I'm afraid I need to know a few more things before you can
leave," Garini said.

Leopold stiffened. "Yes?"

Garini took him by the arm and went toward the side, out of
Gertrude's hearing range. "Are you here on vacation?"

The lean face in front of him quivered. "Yes."

"Why did you choose this church to pray?"

The Frenchman lifted his hands. "I don't know. I was . . . en
passant . . . I took a notion to pray."

"Are you a Catholic?"

"Mais oui." Morin looked at his shoes.

Another flash-light filled the church like lightning.

"Do you know the victim?"

"Non!" It came out as a shout, muted by fear.

Garini made sure his face didn't show what he was thinking.
Maybe Leopold was nervous because he had covered a body
with his full length. Part of his reaction was understandable. But
this seemed a bit over the top. "Is there anything you think you
should tell me?"

"I need to wash." Morin got more nervous by the minute.
"Please."

"He didn't want to stay." Gertrude's voice came from behind
Garini, "but I told him not to budge. It's our duty as a citizen to
assist the police."

Stefano clenched his teeth and turned his iciest stare on her.
"I will come to you in a minute, Signora Asseli. Please let me
finish my conversation with Signor Morin first."

Gertrude grunted and stomped back to the priest who still
stood next to the altar, wringing his hands.

Stefano asked to see Morin's passport and noted the number
as well as the address of his hotel and his cell phone number.
"How long do you plan to stay in Florence?"

"Until the twenty-seventh."

Another week, covering Christmas. "Are you here on your
own?"

Leopold shifted his weight from left to right. "Yes."

How odd. Alone over Christmas in a foreign town. "Have you
been to Florence before?"

"Oh, yes, quite often. As an Italian teacher, it's only natural."

"I see." Garini narrowed his eyes. "If you should feel a sudden need to leave before this date, do contact me." Garini made sure his gaze fixed in a stern way on Leopold's face. "We are closely working with the police in other European countries, so a flight would not serve any purpose."

Leopold looked as if he wanted to run out of church as fast as his feet could carry him.

His feet. Something irked Stefano about Leopold's feet. ""You wear uncomfortable shoes for a tourist," he said.

"I like these shoes." Leopold placed a black woolen cap onto his short hair and pulled it forward until he all but disappeared beneath it.

"But surely sneakers would be more comfortable for the ancient cobblestones of Florence?"

Leopold shuddered. "I abhor sneakers. They are so . . . uncultivated."

"I see. "Stefano nodded. A victim with hand-stitched leather soles, a suspect with shiny patent leather shoes, and Gertrude Asseli with no feeling for beauty at all but an overdeveloped sense of duty. What a mix. "I might need to speak to you again, Signor Morin. Please inform me if you wish to leave town."

Morin nodded, turned on his heels and shot from the church like a man released from the gallows.

The padre followed him with billowing habit to open the door.

Garini watched the Frenchman leave with a frown. The church seemed to get colder every minute. He couldn't feel his toes anymore, though he had put on shoes with thick rubbers soles this morning. He shook his head. His mind seemed to be stuck on shoes today.

He turned back to the victim, illuminated in bright light. The camera team was done. Their pictures had fixed his exact position from every angle. It was time to pull the dead man out of his position between the heavy pews, otherwise Stefano could not get to him.

"Ciao." An insouciant voice came from behind Stefano.

Stefano swiveled around and took in his young assistant with the gelled-up hair. "Piedro. You took your time."

Piedro shrugged and didn't meet Stefano's eyes. "My bike

broke down and--"

It always breaks down on your way to work. "Not now." Garini cut short his subordinate. "Help me get the body out from between the pews." Together, they shifted the heavy man until he was stretched out in the aisle.

Stefano knelt down on one side, his hands skimming over the body. The woolen coat felt think and warm; the lining was silk. A broad chest, muscled arms, and a flat stomach spoke of regular workout. A fit man in the end of his fifties. His sweater was pure cashmere, the white shirt thick cotton, the cuff links heavy gold. A fountain pen with a golden nib stuck in his shirt pocket, and a titanium signet ring graced the left hand. It showed the entwined initials TA. Stefano went through the victim's pockets and pulled out a wallet. One platinum credit card, four gold credit cards. Nine hundred Euros in cash.

Garini suppressed a whistle and pulled the driving license from the wallet. The victim's name was Trevor Vincent Accanto. A rich American, strangled inside the famous Basilicata just before Christmas, a fainted Frenchman on top, a redoubtable Swiss woman by his side, and a nervous padre hovering over the whole. *Damn.* The tabloids would be delirious with joy. He pulled his thoughts back and addressed Signora Asseli. "How long did it take you to make the call after you had found the dead man?"

"Nowhere near as long as it took you to come here," she said.

Piedro snickered.

Garini didn't twitch a muscle. "Can you narrow it down a bit more?"

"Not more than ten minutes. I knew it was my duty to inform the priest right away, and the minute I turned around to look for him, he already came from the vestry." She nodded at a side door behind the altar.

Garini turned to the padre who had kept quiet in the background. "Do you corroborate that statement?"

"What?" The padre gave a start. "I . . . ", he plucked at the sleeves of his habit with nervous fingers. "Yes, I think that's about right."

Garini fixed him with a hard stare. "Can you swear to this in front of a jury?"

Padre Balli paled. "I . . . I think so."

Gertrude Asseli pulled herself up. "Are you insinuating that I'm telling lies, Commissario?" Her voice made it clear she thought this an insult.

Stefano met her gaze without blinking. "Let's just say I find it interesting that you are trying to steer everybody involved in the direction you wish to take."

Her face turned blueberry red. "How dare you?" With her anger, her accent got more pronounced.

"This is a murder investigation, Signora Asseli. I am here to find a murderer, not to keep everybody happy. Do you wish to add anything to your statement?"

The Swiss woman pressed her lips together.

"No? Then please give your name and hotel address as well as the number of your passport and cell phone to my assistant. You may leave afterward." Garini nodded at Piedro. "Don't forget to note how long Signora Asseli plans to stay in Florence." He turned his back on them and gave the pathologist at the side a sign. He had watched the proceedings with the interest of a curious terrier. "You can start, Roberto."

"When did you say the call came in?" Roberto opened the victim's eye and focused a small light on it.

"Ten to one." Garini answered.

Roberto nodded. "So the victim was found at twelve forty." He added in a low voice, "Remind me to invite you when my mother-in-law plans to come the next time. She's a similar battleship as the Swiss lady, and I'd be happy if you could annihilate her to dust in the very same way."

"If you think that was tough, you've never met a Mantoni." The words slipped out before Stefano could stop them.

"Oh?" Roberto's eyes lit up. "Who are the Mantonis? Do I know them? Is there really a human being that can't be intimidated by you? I want to meet her!"

Stefano shook his head, annoyed at having told the curious pathologist more than he wanted. That wasn't like him; as a rule, he had himself much better in hand, but then, the Mantonis had unnerved him, and they still did. If only he could see Carlina tonight. Technically speaking, her last name was Ashley because of her American father, but her Mantoni mother, and her close link to the rest of the family, all living in the same building, made her a true Mantoni. Not as crazy, definitely shaped in a different mold, but special. She went under his skin in a way no woman had ever done. She even--

He gave himself a little shake and forced the thought away. "Can you tell me when the victim died?"

Roberto gave an exaggerated sigh. "Closed as an oyster, as always." He shrugged. "Well, if you insist on talking shop, I can tell you he died after twelve, taking the low temperatures here into account."

"Anything else?"

"So far, no. I'll check him in detail when I have him at home."

Stefano suppressed a wry smile. *I wonder if he also talks about the morgue as his home when speaking to his wife.*

Gertrude Asseli stomped up to them, with a scared looking Piedro trailing behind. "You will hear from me, Commissario."

Garini made her a little bow. "I am looking forward to it, Signora." He turned back to the victim's wallet in his hands. Maybe he could find out where he had stayed in Florence. A wad of receipts filled the second compartment, and Stefano took them out and held them at an angle, so he could see the print on the flimsy paper. From the look of it, the American had created the annual high volume of Christmas business for the industry of Florence single-handedly. Louis Vuitton, Ferragamo, Dior, Boss . . . The American had spent astonishing sums with machine-gun-like speed. The latest receipt was from 11.27 AM. Stefano frowned and lifted his head. "Search the church, Piedro. He must have had shopping bags with him." Once again, he returned to the wallet. One receipt was crumpled and had gotten stuck inside. He pulled it out with care and smoothed it. The Temptation logo jumped off the paper and froze him. This morning, at 09.48 AM, the victim had been in touch with Carlina. *Damn.*

"Em, excuse me?" Padre Belli appeared next to him and hovered like a sad-looking crow.

"Yes, padre?"

The padre wrung his hands. "I . . . when will you take the . . . the body away?"

"Within the next hour." Stefano looked up. "We're almost done here."

Padre Belli nodded. "That's good. We have to prepare for the choir lessons soon, and I don't want to keep people waiting." He turned aside.

"One moment, please." Garini said.

"Yes?"

"Do you know the victim?"

Padre Belli's gaze fluttered to the dead man's face for the fraction of a second. His mouth twisted. "I . . . I find it hard to tell."

"His name was Trevor Accanto. He was American."

The padre shook his head. "No, my son." He seemed relieved. "I did not know this man."

"And yet, he came here to pray."

Padre Belli shrugged. "That happens all the time. Tourists come to admire the building, and quite a few of them stop and pray for some moments. I think it's important to have an open church, to allow people easy access to God. The Church has to be here, for the people." He said it with a slight vehemence in his voice, as if he had had to defend this point of view often in the past. Then he looked at the floor, and his shoulders drooped. "Though I did not think a murder would happen here - ever. How can people do such a thing in the very presence of God?"

Garini preferred not to answer that question. "Did you know Signor Morin or Signora Asseli before?"

"No." The padre shook his head. "As I said, we often have tourists stepping in for a short time."

"Did anything about them strike you as unusual? Did they say anything out of the ordinary?"

The padre lifted his thin shoulders. "No. They did not like each other, but then, why should they?"

Why, indeed. Garini decided to change track. "Can you tell me why you're so nervous?"

The padre gave a start. "Me? I'm nervous?" His hand continued to pluck at the sleeve of his cassock in an unconscious movement.

"Decidedly."

Padre Belli swallowed so hard that his Adam's apple moved visibly. "Well, I . . . I wonder if the murder has desecrated our church. I will have to talk to the bishop and get information."

"It's not the first time that murder was done inside a church." Garini said without inflection.

Startled eyes flew to his face. "What do you mean, my son?"

"I'm sure there's an established procedure."

The padre's nervous fingers relaxed. "Oh, do you think so? It would speed up things. I've been wondering, with Christmas only one week away, if we can continue to use the church as always . . . " He looked at the body on the floor. Sorrow combined with pity etched lines onto his kind face. "It's not right to kill, my son. Find the murderer."

"I will."

Garini turned away. He was inclined to believe that pure chance had led the padre and the two tourists to the scene of crime. First of all, he had to learn more about the victim and the people who were close to him.

"I could not find any shopping bags anywhere." Piedro appeared from the dark. "Maybe they were stolen?"

Garini frowned. "But why kill the man on top of that?"

"Maybe the victim saw the thief taking the bags, and the victim grabbed him, and there was a fight, and--" Piedro sounded excited as he colored in the details.

"Piedro." Garini made sure his voice remained even. "Don't invent an exciting story without any basis whatsoever. From the position of the victim, it is clear that he was strangled from behind. If you are busy stealing several shopping bags and are being attacked by the owner, is it likely that you take the time to pull out of a pair of nylons, dance around him and strangle him from behind?"

Piedro frowned. "No."

"Exactly. If you want to solve a murder, every puzzle piece has to fit. You can't re-shape them to make them fit, just because they would go beautifully with your pet theory."

Piedro sighed. "But what happened to the bags?"

"We'll find out. There has to be a solution."

Chapter 3

Stefano Garini hurried through the frosted glass doors of the luxurious Garibaldi Hotel and took a deep breath. The warm air inside the magnificent lobby smelled of flowers and perfume. The big chandelier high up in the center of the hall glistened. Its light was reflected in hundreds of dark-red Christmas balls decorating the magnificent Christmas-tree to his right.

Stefano's shoulders relaxed. Of course a man like Trevor Accanto would stay in the Garibaldi Hotel. Where else? And how lucky for him because he would not have to deal with some suspicious hotel owner but his old friend Peter. He crossed the lobby with care. The ancient mosaic beneath his feet filled him with reverence. At least some things produced by humankind were beautiful. When he reached the reception desk, he smiled. "Buongiorno, Anna."

"Stefano!" The dark-haired woman with the stylish bob held out both her arms and kissed his cheeks. "How wonderful to see you!" She spoke Italian with an American accent.

"How is little Linda?" he asked.

Anna smiled. "Cheeky and chaotic. She has taken after her father."

He laughed. "And where is Peter?"

"In his den." Anna inclined her head toward the door behind the reception. "To what do we owe this unexpected pleasure?"

His smile faded. "It's not good news, I'm afraid. One of your guests got himself murdered."

Anna blanched.

"Don't worry. It's got nothing to do with you."

She swallowed. "Who is it?"

"Trevor Accanto."

Her gray eyes widened. "Oh, my."

"You don't sound too surprised."

Anna took a deep breath. "I . . . I'm shocked."

He leaned against the reception desk. "Yes, but not surprised. Why not? What can you tell me about him?"

Anna looked over his shoulder into the vast lobby. "I don't think we should discuss this here. The guests might overhear us." She stepped aside. "You'd best go in and talk to Peter directly."

He didn't take his gaze off her. "Anna. Relax. He was strangled at the Basilica Santa Trìnita today, and I have to find the murderer. I do not believe for one second that it had anything to do with you or Peter."

She lifted her thin shoulders. "I know. I just can't help remembering--"

He touched her arm. "That was years ago. If you know anything, you have to tell me."

Again, she looked beyond him into the lobby and lowered her voice. "Trevor Accanto was a rich American with Italian antecedents. He came to Florence every Christmas."

He frowned. "Why Christmas, when it's cold and uncomfortable? Why not summer?"

She shook her head. "I don't know." She swallowed. "Every time, he was accompanied by a lady. A beautiful lady."

"What was her name?"

Anna sighed. "You got me wrong. It wasn't one lady. It was a different one every year. Every single one was stunning . . . but they never signed the guest book."

He took a deep breath. "So you're telling me I have to deal with dozens of beautiful and unknown ladies as suspects?"

Anna nodded. "I'm afraid so."

He fought the feeling of being overwhelmed. "What happened to the ladies when he left?"

Anna shrugged. "They disappeared, too. All but one."

"Yes?"

"It was last year. She was French, I believe. He called her Suzanne. When he had left, she came back and tried to trick us into revealing his home address in the States." Her face twisted. "We couldn't tell her anything, of course. I felt so sorry for her." She took a deep breath and lowered her voice even more.

Garini bent forward to understand her low murmur.

"Then she tried to break into the office." Anna looked at her fingers. "Peter caught her."

Stefano frowned. "Why didn't you go to the police? You never even mentioned--"

She shook her head. "We discussed it, but we felt it wouldn't help." She took another deep breath. "Ever since, I've had a hard time being friendly to Mr. Accanto. He was quite ruthless when he wanted to drop a woman, you know." She shrugged. "A ruthless charmer."

"Have you ever seen her again, that Frenchwoman called Suzanne?"

"No." Anna shook her head again. "I've been afraid that she might come back this Christmas to make a big scene, but fortunately, she hasn't shown up."

"I see." Stefano straightened. "Thank you, Anna. I'll talk to Peter now."

She nodded. "You do that. I'll get you a cup of coffee."

Stefano went past Anne through the door into the back office area. He crossed a small office with white walls and attractive wall hangings made of colorful brocade, then opened the door to another office behind. The floor was covered ankle deep with files. In the middle of the chaos, his friend Peter sat behind a desk and munched an apple. He jumped up. "Stefano! I've not seen you for ages. How is your sax?" His Italian still held a faint British note.

Garini smiled. "I don't have enough time to play. And your trumpet?"

"Ditto." Peter shrugged. "With Linda, we have less time than ever."

"I can imagine." Garini eyed a chair laden with files. "Do I sit down?"

Peter cleared the chair with no respect for the longevity of the files. "Of course. Take a seat." He went back to his desk and sat down. "What happened? I don't believe this is a social call."

"It's not, unfortunately." Garini shrugged. "Your guest Trevor Accanto was murdered today at the Basilica di Santa Trìnita."

Peter took a deep breath. "Oh, no." He looked at the door. "Does Anne know?"

Garini gave him one of his rare smiles. "If I didn't know you, I would think you're acting crazy." He leaned back, stretched his legs, and folded his hands behind his head. "However, with your history, I know you're more or less normal, and to answer your question, yes, Anna does know, and I've already explained that she has nothing to fear. The situation is completely unlike the one when I got to know her."

Peter frowned. "Are you sure?"

Anne appeared in the door, carrying a tray with two golden cups and a fragile saucer with wafer-thin chocolate cookies. The fragrance of strong coffee filled the room. "I thought you might need something nice." She looked at her husband. "Has Stefano told you?"

"Yes, I have." Stefano said. "And I repeat that you don't need to fear anything."

She gave him a smile that looked a bit like a child collecting its courage.

Stefano turned back to Peter. "Now tell me all you know about Trevor Accanto."

Peter took a cup of coffee from his wife and balanced it on a pile of paper, then took the saucer with the cookies and pushed it toward Garini. "Thank you, love." He smiled at his wife, concern and love etched into his face. "Don't worry, dear."

"I won't." Anne passed the second cup to Garini and left without a sound, closing the door behind her.

Peter leaned back in his chair and sighed. "All I know about Trevor Accanto." He shrugged. "I can say it in one sentence: He had it coming."

"Why?" Garini took a sip of the fragrant coffee and balanced the cup on his knee. The pile of paper on the desk looked way too wobbly to support the cup.

"I lost count of the women he had with him. Every Christmas he appeared, and every Christmas it was another."

"So he was a regular guest." Garini looked at the creamy swirl inside his cup of coffee and the white plume spiraling from it. "Since when?"

"We'd have to check the register for that," Peter said. "At a guess, I'd say he has been coming to the Garibaldi Hotel for four or five years already, if not more."

"Besides his obvious taste for beautiful women, what was he like?"

Peter looked at the ceiling as if collecting his thoughts and brushed back his dark hair with one hand. "That's the funny thing about it; you had to like the guy. He was courteous, correct, and generous. He told you what he expected, but he was never unfair or unreasonable." He sighed. "I wish I could say that of more of our guests." He put his head to the side and looked at the apple core perched precariously on a cardboard file. "Anne said he was a charmer, and she was right. Everybody loved him."

"One didn't. He was strangled with a pair of nylons."

Peter reared back. "Geesh. Isn't that difficult?"

Garini lifted his eyebrows. "What makes you think so?"

"Well, nylons stretch like crazy."

"You've got something there." Garini narrowed his eyes. "I'll give it a try."

"I wish I could see that." Peter grinned.

Garini frowned in thought. He didn't like the sound of this story. Too many suspects and too much money made a bad mix. "What about this year? Who was he with?"

"A redhead," Peter said. "A stunner, of course, but I don't know her name. She was Italian, though, and if I'm not much mistaken, she was also a native Florentine."

"How do you know?"

Peter shrugged. "Experience. You can tell at one glance what country people come from if you run a hotel, and if you run it a little bit longer, you can even tell which area of that country. I once had a short conversation with her while she waited for Mr. Accanto."

"Have you seen her today?"

Peter frowned. "I . . . yes, indeed. She left the hotel around ten."

"Was she with him?"

He shook his head. "No, she was on her own, but that wasn't unusual. He always went for a run in the morning, and usually, the ladies didn't join him."

"Was she upset?"

"Oh, no." Peter shook his head. "She was humming and swinging her handbag. I'd say she was in a great mood."

So this morning, everything was still normal. Garini stared into space. "Did anything strike you as extraordinary this year?" He bent forward. "Anything that was different to the years before?"

"No." Peter didn't hesitate.

"Is there anything else you can tell me?" Garini looked at his friend without blinking. "Anything at all, even if it doesn't seem to be related?"

Peter frowned. "If you ask me, last year was different. If he had been killed a year ago, I would have said that we have an immediate suspect. The woman he had with him at the time was called Suzanne, a Frenchwoman. She came back after he had left and made a scene." He looked at Garini with the expression of someone who had a confession to make. "Did Anne tell you that she broke into the office?"

"Yes."

Peter avoided his eye. "She seemed devastated. We were sorry for her, but we couldn't help her."

Garini swallowed his reproach. "Do you have her address?"

Peter shook his head. "I seem to remember that she came from Paris, but that's hardly surprising. She left her address and asked us to forward any news we had of Trevor Accanto, but of course we threw it away."

"What a pity." Garini sighed. "Anything else?"

Peter looked at his fingers for a moment. "Not at the moment, no. But if I think of something, I'll let you know."

"Thanks." Garini emptied his cup and got up. "Could you please show me Mr. Accanto's room now?"

"Sure." Peter got up. "We just need to get the master key from the safe."

"Master key?"

Peter led the way back to the lobby. "The master key allows us to open the safe in each room. Our guests program their own code into it, but they usually forget it right away, and then we need to open the safe for them, of course only while they are present." He took a slim, black key from the safe behind reception and closed it again.

"I've checked our register." Anne came up to them and held out a piece of paper to Garini. "This is Mr. Accanto's home address in Florida. He didn't put anything into our office safe, but he may have used the one in his room."

"Very efficient, thank you." Garini took the paper and stowed it away in his jacket. "Can you also check how often he stayed with you?"

"I've already done that." Anna smiled. "He has been staying with us for the last five years. This was his sixth time at the Garibaldi Hotel. He always came in the middle of December and stayed for four or five weeks."

"Hmm." Garini frowned. "Did you ever have the impression that he came for work?"

"No." They both said at the same time.

"He came for pleasure," Anne added. "That much is sure."

Garini frowned. "I wonder why he doesn't come in summer."

Peter looked at him. "I asked him that once. He said his uncle's birthday was in December, and because he was so attached to his uncle, he made it a rule to come every winter."

An uncle. It was the first time someone had mentioned family. "Did that sound convincing?"

Anne and Peter exchanged a glance. "Difficult to say," Anne finally said. "But on the whole, yes, I can imagine that he would do that. He was a curious mix of being caring and dropping people."

"Do you have the uncle's name or address?"

"I'm afraid not." Peter shook his head. "He just mentioned him once, in passing." He made a move with his hand. "Let's take the stairs. Mr. Accanto always had the Boccaccio Suite."

Peter led him to the curving stairs covered by a thick carpet in a muted red color. The smooth wood of the polished walnut banister glistened. As they climbed the stairs, the chandelier light from the lobby and the soft piano music receded, but the atmosphere of luxury remained. They passed an arched window with a fragrant flower in a slim vase. Garini smiled. "You're surrounded by beauty."

Peter nodded. "I am, but if you have the responsibility of keeping it up, it pales a bit." He pointed at a massive wooden door. "This is the Boccaccio Suite."

"I wouldn't want to enter this by force." Garini eyed the heavy hinges.

"You'd not get far unless you came with a battering ram." Peter smiled. "They built things to last in those days." He took a heavy brass key with a curlicued top from his pocket, inserted it into the lock, and turned it.

"Nice touch." Garini said. "A plastic card would rather destroy the feeling."

Peter opened the door and held it open for Garini to enter.

When Stefano looked up, the words dried in his mouth. He was in the most perfect room he had ever seen. With their entrance, several hidden spotlights had gone on and filled the room with a warm glow, evening out the cold winter light filtering in through the high windows. The floor and the high stone walls were bare, giving the room a medieval touch, but this austere effect was mitigated by rich brocade wall hangings in muted colors of red and gold. A matching material had been used to drape the four poster bed at one side of the room. A desk with a comfortable looking leather chair in front looked as if it had come straight from the library of a castle. On the opposite side, the wall was covered with a wardrobe made of polished wood. It stretched across the whole wall like an elaborate wainscoting. To their right, another heavy wooden door stood half-open and revealed a glimpse of a state-of-the-art bathroom in the background. "I'm impressed."

Peter smiled. "It's our best room, and Mr. Accanto always booked it for his whole stay."

"Can I search it now?"

Peter made a move with his hand. "Feel free. Do you want me to stay?"

"Yes, please, if you don't mind. I'd like to have a witness." Garini started with the polished desk made of gleaming walnut wood and opened the top drawer. A laptop of the latest generation fitted snugly into it. "I'd like to take this laptop with me, so someone can go over the contents. I'll give you a receipt."

"Sure." Peter sounded a bit uneasy. "Will you have to keep it long? I'm not sure how the heirs will react."

"We won't need it more than a few days." Garini looked up. "Do you know anything about the heirs? We've just contacted the US, and I hope they'll soon come back to us."

"No, I don't know about any heirs or Mr. Accanto's family in Florence." Peter sighed. "This uncle he once mentioned never came to the hotel, if he exists at all." He looked around. "I guess we'll have to move his stuff to a storage room until someone will come and claim it."

"Yes, you should do that, and I'll keep you updated about the heir." Garini opened another drawer and found a fountain pen that looked as if it had cost his yearly income. "Nice." He opened it and wrote one word on the creamy colored notepad of the hotel. The pen slid over the paper without a sound, leaving a rich trail of royal-blue ink behind. Next to the pad, Garini discovered an ink bottle with a historical looking label. "Do you provide this as the finishing touch of atmosphere?"

Peter shook his head. "No, but it's a good idea. I'll suggest it to Anne. Mr. Accanto always signed with a fountain pen. He used several different types." He put his head to the side. "I've not often seen him use that one, though."

"I remember he had one in the pocket of his jacket, not quite as heavy." Garini lifted the ink bottle and checked the contents. "It's half empty, so it does indeed seem as if he used it regularly."

"Does it matter?"

Garini shrugged. "Probably not. I'm just trying to take in every detail to get an idea about the kind of man he was."

"He was a man who combined the last word in technology," Peter nodded at the laptop, "with a traditional fountain pen that had to be filled by a piston mechanism. So what does that tell you?"

Garini smiled. "It tells me that he did not use the fountain pens as status symbols."

Peter lifted his eyebrows. "You have to explain that."

"If it had been a status symbol, he would have had only one pen in his possession, from the best-known brand in the world, and it would probably have dried out by now. Instead, he had several fountain pens of different brands with him; they all write like butter, and he did not go for the easy cartridge system but used the more complicated but charming version of a piston mechanism."

"So?"

"So I have to adjust my picture. Mr. Trevor Accanto was a connoisseur. He did not go for the obvious; he cherished quality."

Peter grinned. "I could have told you that. He stayed at the Garibaldi Hotel, after all."

"All right, all right." Garini held up a hand. "But it tells us something about his character. If I had found a plastic ballpoint pen in there," he pointed at the desk, "I'd have known it was placed there by someone else."

Peter opened his eyes wide. "Now I see."

Garini looked around the room. "Actually, this room looks too clean to be lived in."

"Oh, that's because the cleaning personnel has gone through it. I know that it didn't look like that this morning."

"No?"

"No." Peter shook his head.

"How do you know?"

"Because I heard Viola complaining." Peter went to the phone next to the bed and typed in a number. "Viola? Would you come to the Boccaccio Suite for a moment? Thank you." He turned to his friend. "She'll tell you herself."

"Thanks." Garini used the time to lift the mattress and peered underneath. "Nothing."

The door opened. "Here I am, Signor Grant."

Viola gasped as if she had been running. She leaned against the door-frame while catching her breath.

Her figure reminded Garini of gnocchi - soft and white and round. Even her hair was fluffy.

"Is it true that the American was killed?" Viola swallowed.

"I'm afraid so," Peter said. "This is Commissario Garini who'd like to ask you a few questions."

Her brown eyes widened until the whites showed all around. "But it's got nothing to do with me!" She lifted both hands as if to avert a blow. "I didn't touch him; I hardly knew him. Why do I have to answer questions?"

"Because you might have valuable information that can lead us to the killer," Garini said.

"Oh." She gave him a measuring glance, then drew herself up. "I see. What do you want to know?"

"Did you clean this room today?"

"Yes, I did." Viola rolled her eyes. "And a real hassle it was. That red-haired lady threw all her clothes around, and every morning, I had to pick them up. She always had tons of shopping bags lying around, and wrapping material, and I never knew what to do with it." She spread her hands. "Some ladies get real angry if you clear away the shopping bags, from the big brands, that is."

"How about Mr. Accanto?" Garini asked.

"The American, him, I didn't mind so much. He always

cleared his stuff away."

Garini didn't take his gaze off her. "Where did you put all the stuff from the red-haired lady?"

"In here." Gloria went aside and slid open the wooden door at the furthest end of the wardrobe. "I hung it all up, though I knew she would throw most of it on the floor, and I'd have to do it again tomorrow."

Garini froze. The wardrobe was stuffed full with female apparel, but he couldn't tear his gaze away from the glossy shopping bags, all neatly folded. With one step, he was next to the wardrobe and picked up the top one with the distinctive logo of Temptation. *Carlina's store.* His mouth went dry.

"She had so many of those bags," Viola sighed. "But it's such an expensive store that I didn't dare to throw away a single one."

Garini clenched his teeth. *Damn.* He had hoped Carlina would only have a slight connection to this case, and now it sounded as if the rich American had even been a regular customer.

"In the mornings, Mr. Accanto often went shopping on his own and later surprised his . . . friends with the results." Peter explained. "The bags were all directly delivered here. I think some of them are still downstairs at this moment."

With an effort, Garini dragged his thoughts away from Carlina. At least he now had an explanation why the rich American didn't have a single shopping bag with him when he was killed at Santa Trìnita. He focused on Viola. "Did you notice anything unusual about Mr. Accanto or his friend this morning? Anything, even if it doesn't seem to be related to the murder?"

Viola pushed her lower lip forward and frowned. Then she shook her head. "No, I don't think so."

"Did you empty the paper bin this morning?"

Viola drew herself up. "Of course I did!"

"But you didn't notice anything unusual?"

She shook her head. "Nah. Some paper, a tissue, stuff like that. Nothing special."

"And in the bathroom?"

Viola frowned. "The bathroom bin was empty. I remember because I found an empty bottle of shampoo on the floor, and the cellophane wrapping of a new one." She sniffed. "That red-haired lady dropped everything right where she stood. She didn't put no things where they belonged."

"Thank you." Garini nodded. "If you should later think of anything, just contact Mr. Grant, so he can get in touch with me."

"Fine." Viola looked around the room. "What will happen to all the stuff?"

"We'll lock it up until the heir comes to claim it." Peter answered.

"Even the women's clothes?"

Garini and Peter exchanged a glance.

"Probably not." Garini answered. "Once we know the red-haired lady, we can ask her to collect it. Technically, these things belong to her."

When Viola was gone, Garini continued with the wardrobe and quickly worked his way through the female clothes. He found two pairs of nylons and placed them on the bed. "I'd like to take those with me," he said.

"Right." Peter looked at them with a sober expression on his face.

The next wardrobe was filled with Mr. Accanto's clothes, rows and rows of expensive suits. Even if someone had bound Stefano's eyes, he would still have been able to tell that he was touching the most expensive clothes men could make. The materials felt thick and smooth at the same time. He turned out the pockets and checked the deepest recesses of the wardrobe, but he did not find anything, not even a stub of paper. "Mr. Accanto must have been a very tidy man," he said.

"Yes, he was very organized," Peter said. "I've never seen him out of his depth."

Garini closed the wardrobe. "Could you open the safe for me now?"

"Sure." Peter slid yet another wooden door aside and revealed a well-stocked bar. Next to the gleaming bottles was a metal box, set directly into the stone wall. He turned the key and pulled the door open. "It's empty." His words sounded hollow.

"Damn." Garini clenched his teeth. He had hoped to find another lead, anything to give him a better indication about Trevor Accanto, his business, his interests, possible motives for murder, but all he had found was the confirmation that Mr. Accanto had been a regular customer at Temptation . . . and that was something he could well have done without.

He finished the search by checking the bathroom, but it did not reveal any further secrets.

Chapter 4

Carlina pushed a strand of hair from her hot face as she handed yet another bag with the distinctive Temptation-Logo to a customer. What a successful day. And tonight, she would see Stefano. She smiled to herself and turned around, just to see him standing at the entrance to her tiny store.

For one frozen instant, she wondered if her wishful thinking had conjured up an illusion, then she knew he was here in person. Tall, his lean face serious, but his eyes . . . had she ever thought his eyes cool? They looked at her in a way that made her feel as if she was the most beautiful woman on this planet. Her throat dried out.

"Carlina."

"Ciao." She went toward him on legs that felt too wobbly to be her own. "Did I miss the time? We said eight, didn't we? At my house?" She checked her wrist watch. It was a quarter past seven, much later than she had thought, but not late enough to make him come and look for her at Temptation.

Now she stood directly in front of him, not knowing how to greet him. They had seen little of each other in the last weeks, but their phone calls had created an intimacy that suddenly made her shy. A little hesitant, she smiled up at him. For some reason, the small scar next to his mouth made him irresistible.

When he bent forward, her heart stopped, but he only greeted her as if she was a good friend, briefly touching her cheeks with his. He smelled of leather and soap, his cheeks cool and a bit scratchy. She suppressed the urge to throw her arms around his neck.

"You're not too late." His voice always held a faint ironic trace. "I'm early. I wanted to consult with you on something, and I thought it might be easier at Temptation, but I see that you're busy. Should I come back later?"

Carlina checked the room. The last customer was still in conversation with Ricciarda, but she could tell they would soon be done. "No. If you're willing to wait ten minutes, I can close the shop."

"Sounds good." Garini leaned against the sales counter, his hands deep in the pockets of his black jeans. He looked out of place, surrounded by all the feminine underwear, and yet, so sexy she found it hard to look away. With an effort, Carlina turned her back on him and started to tidy up the store, her hands flying. It looked as if a herd of buffaloes had trampled through it, but it had been worth the trouble. Her sales had exceeded her highest expectations. If the last customer would buy one pair, she would end up with fifty-two pairs of nylons sold, a record she wanted to celebrate in style tonight, with Stefano, even if she felt as if some of the buffaloes had trampled across her as well.

"I take it the nylon promotion did well?" Stefano's gaze rested on the golden display next to the sales counter that looked like an ice-cream cone. It was usually filled to the rim with special offers, but today only one limp bra remained inside.

"Very well." Carlina could feel a triumphant smile stretching to her ears. "I'll tell you all about it later." She didn't want to brag with customers within earshot.

Ricciarda came to the sales counter with a curious look at Stefano. Wisps of hair had escaped her ponytail and her blouse looked crumpled, but she treated the customer in front of her with unchanging friendliness.

She's a treasure. Carlina gave her an encouraging smile. When the last customer had left, she closed the door and leaned against it with a happy sigh. "What a success!" She handed Ricciarda the whole bag of Copate biscuits which they had never had the time to touch. "You won our bet. They're all yours."

Ricciarda smiled. It looked a bit exhausted, but sincere. "Thank you, but I think we can share them tomorrow. We both deserve them."

"I think you've never met," Carlina turned to Garini. "This is Ricciarda Fazzolari, who has worked for me these last two months. Ricciarda, this is Stefano Garini." She omitted his title and any other explanation because she did not know how to refer to him. A friend? Were they friends? It was hard to say.

Garini took one sharp look at Ricciarda, but he didn't seem to be impressed with her clear skin and the deep-blue eyes. Then again, you could never tell what Garini thought.

Carlina took one hundred Euros out of the cash box and put them into an envelope, then handed them to Ricciarda. "A bonus for the good work today. You did a great job."

Ricciarda's face lit up. "How nice. Thank you." She fished her handbag from behind the sales counter, opened it, and stored away the envelope. "Oh, I just remembered; your mother came to the store today while you were out for lunch. I'm sorry I forgot to mention it earlier."

Oh, no. From the corner of her eye, Carlina could see that Garini's mouth twitched in anticipation. She knew exactly what he thought of her family. "Did she say what she wanted?"

Ricciarda frowned. "I admit I didn't quite get it, but then, I had a customer, and I may have been too distracted."

Garini's smile grew more pronounced.

Carlina wanted to give him a hard nudge with her elbow but managed to control herself.

"Oh, now I remember." Ricciarda's frown cleared. "She said the cards spelled danger and money for you, and she wanted to make sure you were safe."

"What cards?" Garini sounded as if he had to ask in spite of himself.

Carlina suppressed a sigh. Sooner or later she had to tell him. "Mama took up fortune telling."

"Madonna." He blinked.

Carlina decided to overhear his remark. "It soothes her and gives her the feeling that the universe is following certain rules."

His ironic gaze came to rest on her. "Does this mean she has given up walking around with a cushion?"

"No," Carlina said. "She still carries around a cushion. But she has now decorated it with golden stars."

"Interesting."

Carlina felt she had to defend her mother. "A cushion has many practical uses."

"Yes, but not if you take it shopping." Garini pushed his hand through his hair.

"You have to see the cushion as a little idiosyncrasy." Carlina said. "I mean, if you have to be a bit crazy, walking around with a cushion is at least a harmless form of craziness. It doesn't hurt anybody."

"Harmless?" Garini lifted his eyebrows.

She met his incredulous gaze straight on. "Completely harmless."

He shook his head. "So now she tells fortunes? Whatever will she do next?"

Carlina smiled. "It's quite entertaining, really. She told my cousin Ernesto that he would soon be baptized with fire, and when a friend at the Internet café dropped a cigarette onto his head, she claimed that had been exactly what she had foreseen."

"She could have made it clearer," Garini said. "How did she learn it?"

"She bought a book." A giggle escaped Carlina. "It's called 'The future in ten days'. It took her twenty, but she says she's now on top of the game. I find it quite amusing."

"You would." His gaze came to rest on her, and the expression in it made her catch her breath. "And now she has foreseen money and danger for you?"

Ricciarda laughed. "Well, the money part at least is true."

Carlina jumped. She had forgotten Ricciarda's presence. "I'll clear this up tomorrow, Ricciarda." She smiled at her assistant. "You can go home straight away. I won't stay long, either."

Ricciarda smiled. "Thank you." She went to the door and opened it. Over her shoulder, she said, "I don't think you need to worry about that danger forecast from your mother. Didn't she foretell too, Carlina, that you would marry next year and have five sons? Quite a feat for twelve months." She grinned and waved at them as she closed the door behind her. "I'll see you tomorrow."

Carlina could feel herself going bright red. *Great. Just great.* "Interesting enough," she said with as much composure as she could muster, "destiny as predicted by my mother always coincides with her dearest wishes. For some reason, the cards don't dare to contradict."

He gave her one of his rare smiles. "How prudent of them."

"Hmm." *If he continues to look at me like that, I'll melt right in front of his eyes.*

"I came early because I need your professional advice," Stefano said.

Carlina blinked. Professional advice? What on earth could he mean? He didn't want to buy a bra, surely?

He zipped open his heavy leather jacket and took out a pair of battered nylons. "Can you tell me anything about these nylons?"

Carlina touched them with her fingertips, but one look had been enough. "Sure I can," she said. "These are run-proof nylons. They are exclusively sold in Florence by yours truly, who started selling them this very morning with immense success." She grinned at him, but when she saw the bleak expression in his face, the happy grin slid from her face, and a cold feeling of dread filtered into her heart. "What's the matter? Why do you look like that?"

He closed his eyes for an instant. "Damn. I'd hoped there would be no direct connection."

"What do you mean?" Carlina wanted to shake him.

Stefano pressed his lips together. "These nylons were used to strangle a man today."

That did it. Her knees, already wobbly from the way he had looked at her, decided to give in completely. She tumbled and would have fallen if he hadn't caught her arms with both hands. For an instant, she wondered if she should pretend to be weaker than she was, just to prolong the delicious feeling of being in his arms, when she heard his voice.

"I'd forgotten that nasty habit of yours."

Carlina straightened with haste and gave him an indignant look. "It's not a nasty habit. I'm just not used to people shooting bad news at me without any consideration for my feelings." She took a step back and straightened her skirt.

His eyes narrowed. "Do you want more consideration for your feelings?"

The question hung between them, and all at once, she knew they were not talking about a bit of friendliness, about being polite. He was asking if she wanted the truth, if she was prepared to be a partner on equal terms, discussing things the way he discussed everything, open, occasionally ruthless, but always honest. Carlina swallowed. She did not want to be wrapped in cotton wool, did not want to be treated like a weak female, or even worse, be protected from nasty things by being kept in ignorance, but she didn't dare to tell him right now. It was too . . . intimate. "Well." She squared her shoulders. "For a start, it would help if you made sure I was seated the next time you spring something nasty at me."

"I think you should sit down now."

She blanched. "What? Is there worse to come?"

He didn't reply.

"Listen, Garini, I've had a long day, I'm tired and worn out and starving, and--" to her horror, her voice broke, "I've been looking forward to a relaxed evening, but it looks like that's not on the cards anymore."

His mouth twisted. "I'm afraid not." He reached out his hand and caressed her cheek with one brief move of his thumb. "I'm sorry."

She turned away with an abrupt move, so he wouldn't see the tears in her eyes.

"Can you close up?" he asked. "I still think we should go somewhere and have dinner."

"Right." In silence, she straightened the worst disorder and closed Temptation.

The wind had calmed down, and now the rain fell as if it was a curtain, straight and clear, with a continuous pattering sound. "Nasty weather." Carlina hunched her shoulders.

"The car is over there."

"You have a car?" Carlina was surprised. "I've only ever seen you with a motorbike."

"I prefer the bike," he said as he led her down Via Tornabuoni and opened the door of a medium-sized Fiat, "but the car was free, so I took it from the pool."

As she buckled up, he asked, "Do you wish to go home first, to freshen up?"

She shook her head. The danger of running into her mother was too big, besides, all her happiness at seeing him had been smothered by a lump of dread. She wanted him to tell her the worst, but not before she'd had something sustaining to eat.

They left Florence, and soon, the little car climbed the hills, but she didn't pay attention to where they were going. Her throat hurt with suppressed tears. She had been so much looking forward to this evening, and now Garini had retreated into his professional shell, hard and cynical, a shell she had hoped he wouldn't put on anymore when she was around. What on earth had he meant when he said there was a connection between her and the murder? Fifty-four women owned these nylons in

Florence. No, maybe not that many, after all, some had bought two pairs, one even three. Did he want her to list the names of all her customers? Was that why he had come to her? She tried to push the thought from her mind. She was supposed to tell him something. What was it? Ah yes, now she remembered. "Uncle Teo wants me to remind you that you've promised him some sleuthing job." She decided not to mention that his other mission had been to find out if she was really dating Stefano Garini tonight.

"Oh." Garini shifted the car into a lower gear as they mounted a hill. "Do you want me to do that?"

Carlina sighed. "I'm not sure. On the one hand, the mere idea of him trailing someone happily and totally unprofessionally makes my blood run cold. On the other hand, he's very lonely."

"He is?"

"Yes." Carlina pressed her lips together. "I often wish I could offer him a job myself, but an old man like him in a lingerie-store . . . he would scare my customers away."

"I can imagine." There was a smile in his voice.

"However, at night, when I come home, he often waits for me, and he wants to know every single detail of my day, he's so bored. Also, it's the first Christmas without his brother and his wife, and that's so difficult. I'm sorry for him."

Garini glanced at her once again but didn't reply. "We're here." He parked the car beneath a gnarled olive tree, its arms bare of leaves, and got out.

Carlina followed him, shivering in the cold wind. "Where are we?" She looked around. The building in front of her looked like a barn, but the door had been replaced by huge glass panes, and golden light spilled out, welcoming her in.

"The restaurant is called Da Marco. Marco once helped me in one of my cases." He smiled at her. "He only started up last week, so it's still a bit of a secret."

She had to return his smile in spite of her misgivings. "Secret enough not to be known to my family, you mean?"

He grinned. "I didn't say that."

She couldn't suppress an answering smile. "At least admit you had it on your mind."

"Of course I had." He shrugged. "After all, you once told me your mother had six brothers and sisters and just as many cousins, and now I expect members of your family to pop up at every corner of Florence."

"What a dreadful thought." She laughed.

He grinned and held open the door for her to go through.

She ordered potato soup because she was too exhausted to chew, and because she needed something warm and comforting and easy. It came with thick slabs of fragrant bread, sweet butter, and tasted so aromatic, she licked off her spoon with a contented smile. "No wonder it's called vellutata di patata, velvet of potatoes. It's like a caress, only inside." She lifted her head and met his gaze straight on. "Now tell me your worst. Do I gather that you need to trace fifty-four nylons all over Florence and the one who can't show hers is the murderer?"

He frowned. "Why fifty-four?"

"Because I sold fifty-four pairs today."

Stefano closed his eyes for an instant, his face set like a mask.

"I'm sorry." Carlina wanted to wipe away the expression on his face. "In fact, there are less because some women bought two. I could--"

"Did you sell them early or late in the day?"

She stopped short. "What? Oh, late. It was such a strange day. I opened the store with so much expectation; Ricciarda and I even had a bet going on how many pairs we would sell, and then . . . nothing." She shook her head. "I felt dreadful. All those negotiations, the money spent on the advertising . . . and the effect was zero. At ten to twelve, when we had sold only one pair, I decided to go for an early lunch. I still had to run to the bank before they closed." She frowned. "What? Why do you look like this?"

His face was wooden. "Go on. What happened then?"

She had the feeling that every sentence was drawing a noose tighter around her neck, that he didn't want her to go on, on the contrary, but she had to continue, as if destiny was pulling her forward, toward a goal she did not want to reach. "Well, when I came back, everything was still dead. Ricciarda had sold only one slip from the special offers. It was disheartening. So I sent Ricciarda out for lunch and started to clean the--"

"When was that?"

"What?"

"When did you come back from lunch?"

Carlina frowned. "Around one, I believe. I treated myself to a nice lunch at the Trattoria delle Stelle, to make up for my lost hopes."

"And when did Ricciarda come back?" He was in true interrogation mode now; he had even taken out a notebook and scribbled down unreadable things.

"Around two, I believe. No, maybe earlier, say, half past one." Carlina shrugged. "I can't tell; I don't clock her time. She's a great employee, reliable, and willing to work longer if there are customers; that's why I don't control her times that much."

His light eyes scanned her face. "And how many nylons had you sold by the time Ricciarda returned?"

"None."

"None?" He almost shouted the word.

Carlina bit her lips. "No. It was crazy, but the customers only started to come by three. I remember because we were discussing at a quarter to three if I should send Ricciarda home early, and we said we would wait until three, and then, as if they'd heard that we were discussing it, they came in hordes."

He pressed his lips together. "So until a quarter to three, you had only sold one single pair of these brand-new nylons that you would recognize everywhere and could not ever possibly mistake for any other brand?"

She swallowed. "Yes."

"Did anybody else have access to these nylons?"

"No."

"You gave no one a pair before today?"

"Well, yes, now that you mention it, I did. Of course I am wearing a pair, and I gave some to Ricciarda, so we could show them off today, and then I gave one to Annalisa, but that's all."

"What about the woman who bought them in the morning? Do you know her?"

"No." Carlina shook her head. The expression on his face frightened her. "She paid in cash, so I can't even look up her name."

Garini looked like thunder impersonated.

"Why is that so very bad?"

"Because," he reached out and gripped her shoulder in a vice-like grip. "The victim was strangled with your special nylons between twelve and one forty today."

"Oh, Madonna." She could feel the blood draining from her face, leaving her with an unreal feeling, as if she was floating.

He shook her. "Pull yourself together, Carlina. You can't faint now."

She stared at him, her eyes wide. "Are you telling me I'm a suspect?"

"Technically, you are." His hand was still hard on her shoulder, but she could feel the warmth from his fingers through her sweater.

"But?"

"But nothing." He spoke through clenched teeth. "I'll try to get out of this case tomorrow."

She felt cold. "I don't think that's necessary, Garini. After all, if I have no connection to the victim, it's ridiculous to suppose that I'm a suspect."

"You know him."

Her eyes widened. "What? I've heard nothing. It's impossible." Then she remembered that she had switched off her phone during the afternoon rush. "Who is it?" Her mouth was dry.

He clenched his teeth. "It's Trevor Accanto."

"No." Her voice didn't obey her. Her lips formed the words, but no sound came out. "I don't believe it." The lights of the restaurant receded. She saw Trevor's handsome face, his laughing, blue eyes in front of her inner eyes. He had been so alive this morning.

Garini was watching her like a hawk, his hand firmly keeping her in this universe. "I came to see you at Temptation because I saw the receipt in his wallet. When we searched his hotel room, we found several bags from Temptation."

"Not Trevor." She couldn't take it in.

"How well did you know him?" Garini sounded cool and official.

"I--" Something slid into her consciousness. Annalisa! She shook off his hand and jumped up. "I have to go."

With one smooth move, Stefano stood at her side. "Wait. What's up?"

"I'm sorry, but I really can't stay."

He took both her arms. "Carlina, please. Could you stay and

explain first what's going on?"

Impatience shook her. "I need to go. Really."

"Why?" His light eyes scanned her face.

"Because . . ." Carlina broke off. Should she tell Garini that Annalisa had been Trevor's last lover? Why put her under suspicion? Maybe he would not find out. They had only been going out for five days. Telling him would put her into danger. It was needless and dangerous. *Nonsense,* a voice inside her replied. *You know Garini looks deeper than the surface. He doesn't go for the obvious solution, just because it's easy. If he did that, he would have arrested you last October when you were his best suspect.*

His eyebrows lifted, and he loosened his hold on her. A wry smile touched the corner of his mouth. "Are you aware that your face betrays every single thought?"

Carlina squared her shoulders. "So what did I think?"

"You know something relevant, and you're afraid of telling me, probably because, as usual, you wish to protect someone from your family."

Her jaw dropped. "Right. Do I still need to go into details?"

"Please."

She couldn't help it. If he looked at her like that, and asked for her help, instead of commanding or threatening, she had no stand. Carlina dropped back onto her seat. "Trevor was a most charming man." She frowned as she looked at his immobile face. "You know, with you, it's the exact opposite."

"You mean I'm not charming?"

"I mean I can never tell what you think. Never."

He smiled. "You'll learn."

Something warm sizzled through Carlina. "It would take decades."

Their eyes locked. "We've got time, don't we?"

The moment hung between them, like a glass ball, fragile; warm light reflecting in a rainbow of colors, until Carlina realized she had stopped breathing. With an effort, she returned to the topic at hand. "I got to know Trevor some years ago. Four, maybe five. He's a rich American who comes to Florence every Christmas. And every year, he takes up a new lover."

Garini nodded. "I've heard about that. It's an interesting habit." His voice was ironic. "Do you know how he achieved that?"

Carlina shook her head. "I've no idea. A combination of charm, money, attraction, whatever." She shrugged.

"And how did he get rid of them?"

Of course Garini got to the point with his swift speed that used to terrify her. Funny, she wasn't terrified anymore. She wanted to stop and analyze her change of feelings, but she had to reply first. "He told me it was all a matter of preparation, of telling them from the start it was nothing but a fling."

"Hmm." Stefano watched her. "And how did you get to know him?"

Carlina smiled. "It's obvious, isn't it? He was my best customer, and we chatted for a bit whenever he came into the store."

"I see." He frowned into space, then focused his gaze again onto her. "Now tell me which Mantoni family member is involved."

She flushed and stared to play with her spoon. The warm light reflected in the shiny surface as she turned it in her hands. "It's Annalisa. She . . . she started an affair with him about a week ago."

Again, his feelings didn't show, if you didn't count a certain tightening in his jaw. "So she was the beautiful redhead Peter mentioned."

"Who's Peter?"

"Peter Grant is the manager of the Garibaldi hotel." He shook his head. "Don't tell me Annalisa accepted her lover's terms."

She looked up with one swift move of the head. "How do you know she didn't?"

"I had the pleasure of meeting her at the last investigation that involved your family. She's quite--" he broke off, then continued as if he had wanted to use a different word, "willful."

Carlina bit her lips. "She wanted to convince Trevor to marry her."

"Had she proposed to him yet?"

She flashed him an angry look. "Stefano! It's not a joke!"

"I'm not joking." He shook his head. "I just happen to know Annalisa."

She sighed. "Apparently, she had mentioned the subject, and he had not reacted the way she wanted him to."

"I'm not surprised."

His words were so low, she almost missed them. "Very funny." Carlina pressed her lips together. "But to go ahead and kill him is not the right way to achieve that particular aim. You can't marry a corpse."

"True." He put his head to one side. "But what about jealousy? Maybe she didn't want him to find a replacement."

Carlina shook her head. "He usually stuck with one woman during his vacation. If she had killed him next year, I might have understood. But not this year, not while she still stood a chance to marry him. It doesn't make sense." She bent forward. "Don't you see? Annalisa was the lucky one this year; she had no reason to kill him."

"Yet." His voice was dry.

"I think you should look at his discarded lovers. I doubt they all felt serene and happy about it. Even if prepared, it must have been difficult to give up a man like Trevor."

Stefano frowned. "What made him so special?"

Carlina scratched her head. "It's hard to say. He was quite good-looking, but that was not it. He had charm, too, and an easy way of talking with everybody. He could flirt without making you feel dirty, without being clumsy, with a light touch that made you laugh even if you didn't believe a word." A sudden tear rolled down her cheek. Surprised, Carlina wiped it away. "He had a lot of taste, too. His lovers were all stunning."

Stefano blinked. "So every woman he met fell in love with him?"

His words were even, but Carlina sensed a tension. *Nonsense. You're imagining that. Garini wouldn't be jealous of a dead American.* She smiled a bit. "You can enjoy being with someone without falling in love. Besides, I didn't approve of his morals." For some reason, it was important that he should know, even if it came out way too stiff.

"Did you tell him so?"

"No." Carlina shrugged. "I don't have the right to judge the morals of my customers. It's not my business, just as it's not my business where they work and how they earn their money."

"What about the other women who knew him? Take your assistant, Ricciarda. Did she like him as much as you did?"

"She didn't approve of his morals either, that much is sure."

Carlina remembered their conversation. "But she liked him nevertheless." She sighed. "That was Trevor all around. You had to like him, in spite of everything."

"Why are you working with Ricciarda? What happened to your other assistant? What was her name, again? Elena?"

Carlina sighed. "Yes. Her mother died, and Elena decided she had to travel the world to find herself. The last mail I got was from Calcutta. That's why I put up an advertisement and got Ricciarda."

"So Ricciarda is not related to you?"

Carline smiled. "No."

"Great. I'll arrest her immediately."

"Stefano!"

He smiled. "I'm joking. I thought it's easier if she's not from your family, but I forgot that you get just as protective about your staff."

"She's a great assistant, and I really need her with Christmas just a few days away. So don't you dare take her in." She lifted the spoon and shook it in his face.

He caught her hand. "I'll do my best."

His hand was warm and held hers firmly.

Their eyes met, and Carlina caught her breath. She wanted to hold this moment and remember it.

The smile faded from his eyes. "Please be careful, Carlina. This murderer is ruthless. He killed his victim in a public place, inside a church, for heaven's sake, and that should tell you something."

She frowned but did not pull her hand away. "Do you think the murder was premeditated?"

"I'm not sure. As I said, it's risky to kill someone inside a public church. On the other hand, if he went there often, it might have been observed. Do you happen to know if Trevor was religious?"

She couldn't suppress a giggle. "I shouldn't think so. After all, his morals hardly fit any religion I know."

"But people are multi-layered. They can cling to a bit of religion and blend out other parts."

Carlina gave a snort. "It's called hypocrisy."

Stefano frowned. "I need to find out more about Trevor. How did he become so rich, do you know?"

"His father owned several factories, and he inherited the lot."

"What kind of factories?"

Carlina smiled. "Rubber factories." She pushed back her chair and got up. "I really need to go, Stefano. Annalisa needs me."

Stefano gave the waiter a sign. "I'll join you." It wasn't a question.

She threw him a doubtful glance but didn't say anything until he had paid the waiter and they were back in the car. Shivering in the cold, she said, "I think it might be better if I first talked to Annalisa on my own."

A streetlight illuminated his set jaw for a fleeting moment. "I'm sorry, but I have to butt in."

She closed her eyes. "Didn't you say you want to give up this case?"

"Yes. Tomorrow. I can't do it today."

Carlina bit her lips. "Listen, Garini, I really don't think it's a good idea if you talk to her right now. She'll be frantic."

His voice was cold. "Stop this. I can't change the rules for you."

It felt like a slap to the face. Carlina hugged herself. Of course his work would come first, as always. Why did that surprise her?

In silence, they covered the rest of the way, back to the historical center of Florence. In silence, they passed the piazza di Santa Croce, the basilica watching over it, basked in soft light. In silence, she opened the heavy wooden door to the family house in Via delle Pinzochere and let him in. "Everybody will be having dinner at my aunt Benedetta's, on the first floor."

He didn't reply.

Carlina grabbed the smooth wooden railing to support her as she mounted the steps. She felt like leading the enemy to a secret camp.

He followed her without a word.

She opened the door of her aunt's apartment with her own key, feeling his disapproval though he didn't say anything. One master key opened every lock in the house. To her, it felt practical. To a man like Garini, it was lunacy.

An enticing smell of fried mushrooms and a babble of voices billowed into her face. Carlina opened the door to the kitchen.

"Ciao."

The babble stopped.

Carlina looked around. Her mother's henna-red hair had fallen out of the ponytail and framed her face like irresolute flames. She had her cushion in her lap, gripping it with both hands as if it was a life-line, crushing one golden star in the process.

Oh, no. Major crisis. In general, her mother only carried the cushion with her if she left the house. If she kept it with her while going to her sister, one floor down, things were bad indeed. Carlina tried a smile and looked at her aunt Benedetta, seated next to her mother. Benedetta's usually smiling face was grave, and her mouth, though bright with lipstick as always, drooped. She was much younger than her elder sister Fabbiola. Two of Benedetta's children still lived with her, Ernesto, a seventeen-year-old, and Annalisa. Annalisa wasn't there, but Ernesto sat next to his mother. His red hair stood up, spiked with gel, and he had the delighted expression on his face when a catastrophe happened that didn't involve any of his own misdeeds.

Benedetta's eldest daughter Emma had married a few months previously and lived with her husband Lucio in an apartment on the same floor. Both were seated at the lower end of the table. Lucio, his arm around Emma, had been talking in a soothing voice to Uncle Teo, who headed the table but now twisted around to stare at Carlina like all the others.

Carlina blanched. "Where's Annalisa?"

"Carlina! Where have you been?" Fabbiola tried to thrust back a strand of henna-red hair without success.

Uncle Teo's white eyebrows lifted. "You are bringing your young man for dinner? Fast work, Carlina."

"But that's the Commissario." Ernesto's face lit up. "Are you hot on the trail of the killer?"

"Carlina!" Emma stretched out her arms to her older cousin as if she wanted to be hugged. "Isn't it tragic? Poor Annalisa."

"Have you eaten?" Benedetta jumped up.

"We don't know," Lucio said with a concerned look at his young wife.

Carlina blinked, not knowing what he referred to.

"Thank you for answering the question." Garini gave a

meaningful glance to Carlina as if he wanted to say he had not expected a sensible answer from any Mantoni anyway. He advanced into the room and addressed Lucio. "Do you know how long Annalisa has been missing?"

Benedetta lifted both hands. "She has not been home for two days!"

Ernesto rolled his eyes. "That's not unusual."

His mother shot him a dark look. "Just what are you trying to say, Ernesto?"

"Santa Maria, nothing." Ernesto shrugged. "But she's been out and about with that lover of hers for a week, and she's become stuck-up, too, faster than you'd believe. As if she was a Queen or something. I'd say there's no reason to panic."

"But the lover has been murdered today." Uncle Teo's voice sounded calm.

"How did you learn about that?" Garini cut in, in control of the situation.

Carlina swallowed. She did not want Garini to interview her family. She had wanted him to become a friend, to become used to her crazy family step-by-step. Now they were all suspects again, and he eyed them with the same precision and accuracy as a scientist eyed a dead bug.

"The cards told me." Fabbiola sighed so deep, her whole body shook. "This morning, the knight of death towered over the house."

Garini gave her a look of acute mistrust.

"I heard it on the radio." Uncle Teo nodded, as if to affirm his memory. "I came up to talk to Benedetta, and we called Annalisa on her cell phone."

"You told Annalisa on the phone that Trevor was dead?" Carlina felt sick.

"No, we told her to come home urgently."

Garini took out a notebook. "When was that?"

Uncle Teo scratched his head until his white wisps of hair stood up. "It was the six o'clock news."

"So Annalisa came home right away?" Carlina pulled out a chair and pushed it in the general direction of Garini before she dropped onto hers.

"No." Benedetta and Emma said at the same time.

Benedetta continued. "We met her in town because she was

still at Giulietta's."

"Who is Giulietta?" Garini frowned.

"Giulietta is a cousin once removed," Carlina replied. "She's also a hairdresser. I assume Annalisa had her hair done?"

"Yes." Benedetta nodded. "She was in the middle of a special procedure that could not be interrupted."

"She had her hair dyed." Ernesto clarified with a grin.

His mother ignored him. "So we decided to meet Annalisa there."

"Did you all go together?" Garini sounded fascinated, no doubt envisioning a hysterical family meeting at the hairdresser's.

"Yes." Benedetta nodded. "That is, Fabbiola, Lucio, Emma, Ernesto and I went. Uncle Teo stayed here."

"Annalisa had a fit." Ernesto said, as if Annalisa was a three-year-old who had thrown a tantrum. He tilted his head to the side and frowned in thought. "Though not as bad as the day when she tried to die her hair blond, and it looked like straw."

"Ernesto!" His mother rounded on him. "How can you be so unfeeling?"

He shrugged. "It's not me who's unfeeling."

"What happened then?" Garini sat on the chair and continued to scribble into his notebook.

Lucio pressed his wife closer to his side. "She stormed out. And that's the last we saw of her. She has not come home."

Benedetta wrung her hands. "I'm really worried. Her hair was still wet, and it's so cold outside."

Carlina patted her shoulder in a comforting gesture. *Annalisa's wet hair is our smallest problem right now.*

"We tried to call her, but she turned off her phone." Emma huddled against Lucio's arm.

I want to huddle against someone, too. Carlina shook her head in wonder. Where had that thought come from? She stole a look at Garini's immobile face out of the corner of her eyes. If she yearned to be huddled by Garini, she could wait a long time. *Better try a lamppost; it'll be more accommodating.* She pulled herself together. "Have you contacted Annalisa's friends?"

"What friends?" Ernesto asked. "The ones she left behind her when she started in her new, exalted life?"

"Now that's enough." Benedetta got up. "Help me to clear the table, Ernesto. Do you want to eat something, Commissario?"

"No, thank you; we have eaten already."

Fabbiola lifted her head. "I know. I saw love and happiness for you this morning."

Garini looked startled. "For me?"

"For my daughter," Fabbiola said with dignity. "I have not yet laid the cards for you, but if you wish, I can do so right away." She pulled a pack of cards from her voluminous skirt.

Carlina chortled. Stefano's face had become more wooden than normal, but she knew what he was thinking. "I think he doesn't have the time for that, Mama. We'd better go and look for Annalisa right away."

Stefano lifted his eyebrows. "We?"

"Yes." Carlina fixed him with a belligerent stare. "Believe me, you'll get more out of her if I'm with you."

"I'll come with you, too." Benedetta dropped the dirty plates in the sink with a clatter and turned. "Annalisa will need her mother."

"And me." Fabbiola got up and fixed her trusted cushion underneath one arm, preparing for battle. "The cards told me to stick to my loved ones today."

Carlina couldn't quite suppress a nervous giggle.

Stefano threw her an exasperated glance and got up. Then he looked at Fabbiola. "I think you, Mrs. Mantoni-Ashley, should stay in the house and become the center of operations."

Fabbiola straightened her back and gave him a regal nod.

Carlina lifted her eyebrows. *How clever he is.*

He turned to Benedetta. "And you, Mrs. Mantoni-Santorini, should prepare a warm soup for Annalisa. She will need it as soon as she comes back."

Benedetta looked thoughtful. "I guess she will."

"Maybe I should go with you," Emma said. "I'm Annalisa's eldest sister, after all."

Garini shook his head. "If Annalisa wants to get in touch with you, she'll try your apartment."

"That makes sense." Lucio got up and pulled Emma with him. "Let's go downstairs."

"Where will you go?" Uncle Teo frowned at Garini while Lucio and Emma left the kitchen. "I believe you shouldn't take Carlina with you, this late at night."

Carlina clenched her teeth. "Uncle Teo, I'm old enough to look after myself."

"I'll return her safely." Garini took Carlina's arm and propelled her to the door. "We'll be in touch."

"You're a great manipulator." Carlina said as soon as the door of the apartment had shut behind her.

"I doubt it'll last long. Let's get out of here before they recover and join us."

"I'll quickly run upstairs to get a thicker jacket. I'll be back in a second."

Carlina ran to her apartment, taking two steps at a time. Where could Annalisa be? Ernesto wasn't far off the mark. Annalisa had many superficial friends, but who would she turn to when in trouble? Had she turned to anybody? Maybe she was walking through the city, alone, confused, drenched by the cold rain? *Hardly that.* Carlina shook her head. *Don't become melodramatic. Annalisa is not that kind of girl.* She opened the door of her apartment and went to her wardrobe without turning on the light. She knew the way, and a bright beam from the stairs spilled into her apartment. She stretched out her hand to take the warm coat off the hanger, when, from the corner of her eye, she saw something move. A dark figure unfolded from the sofa and advanced in her direction.

Carlina screamed.

Chapter 5

"Shhh, Carlina."

The whisper stopped her mid-scream.

"It's only me."

"Annalisa!" Carline took her cousin by the shoulders and shook her. "How are you? Why are you hiding here? Everybody is so worried!" Her knees trembled from the shock.

Annalisa stared at her with wide open eyes, as if she had never seen her cousin before. "Trevor is dead."

Carlina's eyes filled with tears. "Yes." She pulled her cousin into her arms and hugged her tight, but Annalisa stood stiff and unyielding. Carlina frowned. What had happened to her cousin?

"Did you kill him?" Annalisa's voice sounded hoarse.

Carlina's arms dropped, and she took one step back. "What?" *I must have misunderstood.*

Annalisa crossed her arms in front of her chest. "You said you would kill him."

"What?" This time, Carlina almost shouted it. "I said what? Have you gone crazy?"

Annalisa shook her head. "No. You said so. I remember exactly."

"Never! I never said I would kill Trevor." Carlina stared at her cousin. It was too damn dark to see. She switched on the light without taking her gaze off Annalisa. Had she gone crazy? Had the shock transformed her, given her the idea that she had to revenge Trevor's death?

The bright light blinded her for an instant. She narrowed her eyes and checked with a quick gaze that Annalisa had no weapon.

Nothing.

Unless Annalisa decided to strangle her with her bare hands, she was safe. "Annalisa, listen." She bent forward. "I liked

Trevor. I didn't harm him. I never said I would kill him."

"Yes, you did." Annalisa pressed her pretty lips together. "At the restaurant. You said you wished we had never met."

"That doesn't mean I wanted to kill him!"

"But when I said you might just as well wish I was dead, you said you wished he was dead. My Trevor. Dead." Her voice trembled.

"Oh, that." Relief washed over Carlina. "Yes, I may have said that, but I never meant I would kill him. Of course I didn't! Come on, you must know that."

"You didn't like me being with him. You said so." Annalisa looked at her cousin with mistrust.

"Of course I said so! I would be a funny cousin if I liked you falling in love with a fifty-something who has a different lover every Christmas."

Annalisa pressed her hands over her ears. "Don't talk like that! I don't want you to say such things about him. He was a Saint!"

"Hardly." Carlina's voice was dry. A thought zigzagged through her brain. "Was Trevor religious?"

Annalisa shrugged, her mouth in a pout. "I don't know. He wanted me to go to church on Sunday, to listen to a concert, but we overslept." Tears can down her face. "Oh, Carlina, we had so much fun. I can't believe he's dead." She covered her face with her hands and started to sob.

Carlina stood in front of Annalisa with hanging arms. She didn't dare to hug her again, besides, how could she hug her, minutes after her cousin had asked her in all sincerity if she had killed her lover? She shook her head. How little they knew each other. "Annalisa?"

"What?"

"What did you do today during lunch time?"

Annalisa lifted her tear-stained face. "Are you asking me if I have an alibi? I didn't kill him! How dare you ask me that?"

Carlina swallowed. "You'll have to answer anyway. Garini is here."

"What?" Annalisa stared at her. "Garini? That computer-like policeman without feelings? I hate him!"

"It doesn't matter what you think of him," Carlina realized her voice had taken on a hard edge. "But tell me something else.

Do you still have the nylons I gave to you yesterday?" Had it only been yesterday? It seemed like a year.

"What?" Annalisa looked as if she had never heard of nylons. "What nylons?"

Carlina lowered her voice. "The run-proof nylons."

"I . . . yeah, I'm wearing them."

Carlina bent forward and checked the nylons her cousin was wearing beneath her short skirt. Her throat went dry. "Those are not the nylons I gave to you."

Annalisa opened her eyes wide. "What do you mean? Of course they are." She frowned. "Don't tell me you can distinguish different types of nylons at a distance of one meter."

"I can if they have the wrong color." Carlina said. "The nylons I gave to you were black. These are brown."

Annalisa made an impatient move with her hand. "How can you harp on about nylons the very day Trevor died? You're so unfeeling, Carlina."

"Because . . ." Carlina closed her mouth with a snap. Maybe it was better not to tell Annalisa. Garini would be furious if she gave confidential information to a suspect. If it was confidential. He hadn't actually said so, had he? No, better not say anything. "You put them into your handbag, didn't you? And you stayed the night with Trevor, is that right? Then you should still have them inside your handbag." She looked around the room. "Where is it?"

"I don't believe this." Annalisa's voice rose to a hysteric pitch. "Why are you obsessing about my nylons?"

Garini's voice came from the open door. "Because Trevor Accanto was strangled with a pair of run-proof nylons."

They both whipped around.

"What?" Annalisa lifted both hands as if to ward off a blow. She closed her eyes and swayed.

Carlina jumped forward and steadied her.

"The tendency to faint at bad news seems to run in the family." Garini's voice was dry. "Please tell me where you spent your day, Signorina Santorini."

Annalisa opened her eyes. "I won't tell you! I want an attorney!"

"That's fine." Garini sounded relaxed. "If you wish, I can invite you to the police station where we can wait for your attorney together. Do you think you can convince him to come within the next half hour or will we have to wait longer?"

Annalisa hid her face in Carlina's shoulder. "I don't want to talk to him!"

Carlina bit her lips. "You have nothing to hide," she said. "Just tell him the truth."

Her lovely cousin lifted her head. "He wants to frame me. I know he hates me!"

"Stop that!" Carlina shook her cousin. "He's a professional. He has to ask these questions, and you have to answer. Feelings don't enter the game." *Certainly not with Garini. I've never known a man who has himself so well in hand, more's the pity.*

"Annalisa!" Benedetta charged through the door, closely followed by Fabbiola, Uncle Teo, and Ernesto. "I heard your voice!"

Carlina released Annalisa.

Benedetta hugged her daughter, but as she was a head smaller than Annalisa, she only managed to put her arms around her waist. "Are you all right? Where have you been? Come downstairs! I'll make hot soup for you, that'll make you feel better."

"I laid the cards for you, my dear, right after I heard the terrible news." Fabbiola put an arm around Annalisa's free shoulder. Together, the three now looked like a misshaped bug with too many arms and legs. "The cards spell happiness for you, very soon. A dark stretch for some time, but nothing to worry about."

Carlina bit her lips to stop smiling. How like her mother to call a murder "nothing to worry about", just to make them feel better.

"I can't believe you find that funny." Garini said in a low voice.

He was getting way too used to reading her face.

Ernesto was watching his sister with detached interest. "Did you kill him, Annalisa?"

Annalisa turned on him with a hiss. "Of course I didn't! How dare you say that? I loved him! He was the love of my life, my--"

"I'm sorry to interrupt," Garini said. "But I still need to hear your answer to my question, Signorina Santorini. Where did you spend the day?"

Annalisa shot him a dark look. "I was shopping."

"Where?"

"In . . . in the city. Do you want to know every shop I saw?"

"Yes." His face was imperturbable. "I also wish to know when you started, when you stopped, and where you had lunch."

"Maybe she can make a list and give it to you tomorrow." Uncle Teo's voice was deep and calm. It had a soothing effect.

"Yes. That's a good idea!" Benedetta gave Stefano a hard look. "My daughter is exhausted. She needs to rest now."

He acknowledged her words with a brief nod. "Give the list tomorrow morning to Carlina before she goes to Temptation. I'll see her during the day."

Carlina gave him a quick look. She was going to see Stefano tomorrow? It was the first time she'd heard of it. What did he mean?

He was looking at Annalisa. "One other question before you go, Signorina Santorini."

"What?"

"Where is your handbag?"

"It's there." Ernesto pointed at Carlina's sofa. "Underneath the cushion with the leopard print."

With one swift move, Garini was by the sofa. "Do I have your permission to search your bag?" he said.

Annalisa rolled her eyes. "Oh, hell, you're getting on my nerves."

Benedetta shook her head, scandalized by her daughter's manners. "Annalisa!"

"Yes or no?" Garini said.

"Yes, for heaven's sake!"

He held it out to her. "Please take out everything."

Annalisa grabbed her bag and dumped the contents onto the low table in front of the sofa. "There."

A bunch of keys fell with a clatter onto the wooden top, followed by an address book, a patent leather planner, a makeup bag, a jewelry box, a lipstick, a pink purse, and when she gave the bag a final shake, a powder compact rolled out of the bag, opened and spread a thin film of powder over the whole heap.

"No nylons," Garini said.

Annalisa shrugged. "So I took them out. I can't recall, really,

I can't."

"Annalisa." Carlina put her hand onto her cousin's arm. "It's important. Try to think. Where have you seen them last?"

She pursed her mouth. "I don't know."

"Think." Carlina bent forward. "Can you remember unpacking them?"

Annalisa frowned. "Yes. I wanted to put them on, but then Trevor--," her voice trembled. "He wanted me to wear this skirt, and it's brown, so I took them off again, and then . . ."

"Yes?"

"I can't recall. I dropped them somewhere, I believe."

"So they should still be at the hotel?"

Annalisa shrugged. "Yes."

Carlina swallowed. "We can check that out."

Garini lifted his eyebrows. "We?" he said under his breath.

Carlina could feel her face going hot.

"In fact, I have already checked the hotel." Garini pulled two tights from his pocket. "Can you tell me anything about these nylons?"

Annalisa and Carlina both gave him a startled look.

"Nylons all look the same." Annalisa shrugged. "How on earth should I know if these belong to me or not?"

Carlina took the nylons and stretched them between her fingers, then checked the labels. "They were not sold by me." Her voice was quiet. "It's another brand."

Garini fixed Annalisa with his light eyes. "These were the only nylons we found in the hotel room. Are you sure you can't give me any idea about the whereabouts of the pair which Carlina gave to you as a gift?"

Annalisa crossed her arms in front of her chest. "Heavens, if you absolutely want to know, I guess they got torn, and I threw them away."

"However, these nylons don't have runs. How come they were torn so quickly?" His voice was calm.

The Mantoni Clan held its breath. For once, the silence was absolute.

Carlina looked from one to the other, perturbed. Where was this leading?

Annalisa lifted her shoulders as if she was freezing and hugged herself. "I dare say you don't know anything about it,

Commissario," she gave him a dark look, "but in certain situations, panties are only in the way, and it may just be that Trevor removed them a bit too impatiently."

Carlina gave her cousin a warning look. *Don't try to provoke him!*

Garini didn't twitch a muscle. "I see. I'll note your statement in the report, and you can sign it tomorrow."

Benedetta blinked and roused herself as if she had woken from sleep. "Enough talking," she pulled her daughter to the door. "Annalisa needs to rest. Buona notte, Commissario."

The gang trooped out of the room.

Garini turned and looked at Carlina.

She couldn't read the impression on his face. "That remark about fainting being in the family was pretty nasty." Carlina hunched her shoulders.

"If she had fainted for real, I wouldn't have said anything," he said.

"How on earth do you know she didn't?"

"That admirable blush on her cheeks never paled." His voice was dry. "You, however, turn green before you faint."

"What a nice comment." Carlina shook her head. "Thank you so much."

A smile settled in one corner of his mouth. "Would it help if I said it's a very fetching green?"

"Not at all." She couldn't help it, she had to grin.

"Listen, Carlina, I--"

"Yes?"

"I'd give anything not to be in this situation." His mouth tightened. "I'm unable to treat all suspects in this case equally."

She caught her breath. "You think you know who killed Trevor?"

"No." He shook his head. "I think I know who didn't."

"Oh." She could feel her face going hot. "I see." She heard her mother's voice, floating up through the open door, talking about happiness to come, then Uncle Teo's measured steps, going downstairs. She lifted her eyes, only to see that his gaze rested on her, a curious expression in them. Was it tenderness? He didn't look like the cynical Garini she knew. What if he gave this case to his colleague tomorrow? At least he knew her family, knew that their eccentric behavior didn't mean they were murderers. He would look deeper; he would not accept the obvious solution just because it was served on a silver plate. Besides, she would be closer to the case, could help to protect Annalisa, and she would spend time with him, time he would not usually have for her. "Would you--" She broke off. Madonna, this was hard. "Would you mind awfully continuing with this case?"

The tender expression on his face receded and left it wooden. "Why do you ask?"

"I . . . I know you're fair."

"I should hope my colleagues are, too."

She looked at her hands, cramped around each other. "Yes. I guess they are. But it would be more comfortable with you."

His eyes narrowed. "Because you think I would overlook any irregularities in the behavior of your family? I don't condone murder, even if it would protect the Mantonis to look the other way."

"I didn't mean that!" Her throat ached. How could he get her so wrong? How could he believe that she would want him to be corrupted? Didn't he know her well enough? Didn't he know that she would lose all respect for him? She straightened her shoulders. "I think you should go now."

"Cuckoo!" Fabbiola peered into the room. "I thought I would tell the lovebirds that it's time to call it a night."

"For heaven's sake, Mama!" Carlina glared at her mother. "I'm not seventeen anymore."

Fabbiola wagged her finger at them and opened her mouth, but before she could say anything, Garini interrupted.

"You're quite right. Good night." He nodded at Carlina as if she was an acquaintance he'd just met at the station, brushed past Fabbiola, and hurried from the room.

Damn. Carlina felt like crying.

"My, he was in a hurry, wasn't he?" Fabbiola frowned. "He's an odd man, to be sure."

Carlina looked at the cushion underneath her mother's arm and at her flowing, lilac garment, sprinkled with silver stars. "Yes," she said tonelessly. "Very odd."

Chapter 6

"Can I talk with you for a minute, Signor Cervi?" Garini knew Cervi didn't like to be addressed before ten o'clock, but he had no choice.

Cervi looked up from his desk where he had been staring at a single piece of paper, covered with fine writing, and frowned. "Place the report onto my desk." He spoke in a low mumble as if he was still half asleep.

"I did so two hours ago." Stefano pointed at a folder next to Cervi's elbow. "It's about the case."

"What?" It was more a grunt than anything else.

"I need to be taken off the case."

That got him. Cervi lifted both eyebrows, a sign of extreme activity at this time of the day. "Why?"

"Because I know the involved suspects personally."

"What?" Obviously, Cervi had not yet managed to overcome the stage that only covered monosyllables.

Now was the moment to introduce the clinching argument. "I fear the mayor would suspect foul play if the public learns that I have personal connections to the case. That's why I suggest we ask Sergio to take over. He's back in the office today." Even if Sergio was half-dead and sniffing, but at least he was back.

Cervi stared at him. "The mayor?"

A distinct improvement. Two words in a row, even if slurred together. Stefano remained standing though he would usually have taken a seat uninvited. "You remember the scandal two summers ago, when the mayor suspected that we had treated the Leonetti brothers better than deserved because you knew them personally? I wish to avoid the same situation."

A pulse started to beat in Cervi's neck. "The Leonetti brothers."

Three words. Way to go, Cervi. "I could go through the case with Sergio. It only started yesterday; he'll be on top of all the facts in no time at all." *Wake up, Cervi. Say yes.*

"Why?"

"Excuse me?"

"Why you wanna stop?"

Stefano bent forward and spoke slower. "Because I am personally connected to some suspects. It doesn't look good."

"Who?"

Damn. He'd wanted to avoid that. "Carlina Ashley."

"Who's that?"

Stefano lifted an eyebrow. He was not going to answer a question that sounded like an insult.

"C'm on, Garini." Cervi glared at him. "Who's that girl? What does she have to do with you?"

"We're friends."

"Oho." Cervi leaned back, and a slow grin spread across his face. "Friends, eh? You can't stop investigating cases only because friends are involved, Garini."

Stefano balled his right hand into a fist. What a dirty grin his boss had.

Cervi shrugged. "If I stopped working under those circumstances, I couldn't take on a single case."

As if he has a zillion friends in town. "I still think it would be wise to put Sergio onto the case, Signor Cervi."

Cervi shook his head. "Can't do that. Would be different if she was your lover." He bent forward. "Is she?"

Garini clenched his teeth. What if he said yes?

Cervi chuckled. "If you can't even answer that question, it shouldn't be too difficult to stay neutral. I say go right ahead with the case." He lifted his index finger. "I expect you to be professional, though, don't forget that. We can't offer the mayor grounds for funny thoughts."

Garini left Cervi's office with his teeth clenched. As he walked down the corridor to his office, he made a conscious effort to unlock his jaw, but it felt as if his muscles would splinter. *Damn that man.*

"Signor Garini!" The breathless voice came from behind him, accompanied by the sound of trampling feet.

"Buongiorno, Piedro." Garini didn't slow down.

Garini's assistant broke into a gallop to keep up with his boss.

"I have checked the backgrounds of Signora Asseli and Signor Morin, as you told me. It was a bit difficult, as the French number you gave me only led to someone who refused to speak Italian."

"How surprising, seeing that you called Paris. Why didn't you try English?"

Piedro shot him a surprised look. "English?"

"Yes. You've heard of English. It's the language spoken all over the world whenever international communication is necessary."

"Er. I don't speak much English."

Garini stopped and looked at his assistant. "Do you want me to book you a course?"

Piedro looked horrified to the tips of his gelled-up hair. "A course?"

"Yes. Language lessons. I can get you on a free course, once or twice a week, after work. Every six months, you take a test to check how much you've learned."

Piedro swallowed. "Ugh. I mean, great. I . . . did you say it's after work?"

"Yes." Garini made sure his face didn't show his feelings.

"Oh. I see. Well, I managed to find someone in Paris who spoke Italian."

"Congratulations." Garini resumed walking.

"And there's no report whatsoever on Leopold Morin."

"That's what I expected." Garini opened the squeaking door of his office and went in. "Anything else?"

"They also checked the Internet. It seems students say he's a bit of a dry stick but not too bad overall."

"That all about him?"

"Yes."

Garini waved Piedro in the direction of a wooden chair and sat down behind his desk. "What about Gertrude Asseli?"

Piedro swallowed. "She's well known in Zurich for complaining to the police about all kinds of things." He lifted both shoulders. "In fact, they laughed at me and asked me to arrest her, so she would not return home. I did not think that was funny."

"What things?"

Piedro pulled a battered notebook from his jacket and looked at his notes. "The left-hand neighbors listen to music that's too loud, the right-hand neighbor does not clean up after his dog, the town does not sufficiently light up the parking space in the shopping center, and the zoo does not clean the cages correctly besides feeding the monkeys with bananas."

Garini frowned. "Are you sure you got the last bit right?"

Piedro nodded. "They spoke Italian with a funny accent, but I understood them well."

"But that doesn't make sense."

"What?" Piedro double-checked his notes. "Well, I . . . I'm not so sure. They laughed all the time." He frowned. "I had the impression they were laughing at me, but I don't know why."

"Did they give you any additional information about that monkey-banana-incident?"

Piedro looked at his notebook as if he hoped it would start to speak to him. "They said something I did not get, but you once told me to write down everything, even the things that don't make sense."

Garini curbed his impatience with an iron hand. "Yes?"

"She read a book about nutrition. But she didn't file a report about that, so I don't see why they mentioned it."

"Maybe it was a modern book about the correct nutrition for monkeys, and it said that bananas are not good for monkeys."

"Oh." Piedro's face lit up. "Yeah, that's what they said. They talked too quick to write it all down, so it sort of slipped my memory." He eyed his boss with something like respect.

I can't believe I'm discussing monkey food. Stefano shook his head.

"I don't know why she filed so much." Piedro once again frowned at his notes. "They didn't say."

"No doubt she sees it as her duty as a citizen to report everything she considers to be wrong."

Piedro nodded with glassy eyes. It was the look he always had when he stopped following a conversation.

His attention span is shorter than a squirrel's. Garini suppressed a sigh. Why had Cervi given him his own son as an assistant? To survey what he was doing or to drive him up the wall in exasperation? "Thank you for that information. Now type up all these notes and send them to me before lunch."

Piedro's face fell. He nodded, got up in slow motion, and left the room with drooping shoulders.

No doubt he thought being a policeman is chasing criminals at gunpoint all the time. Garini shrugged. He couldn't help it that life was different. If only Piedro was a bit quicker to add two and two together. Then he could give him more interesting jobs. But his assistant even managed to botch the least important things, like checking up on Morin and Asseli, which had been more of a routine than anything. Nothing linked them to the case, nothing but being at the wrong time inside the Basilica. Garini got up. He had to talk to Carlina again, and he didn't know if the feeling inside him was dread or excitement. It was a new feeling, something he had never felt before. Drat the woman.

II

Garini stopped his motorbike at a red light and pushed up the protective shield from his helmet. The air felt like liquid ice, but a light-blue sky, thin and translucent like a veil, took away the feeling of oppression he had felt yesterday. The feeble winter sun played on the sand-colored stone of the little café to his right. A few hardy souls had even taken seats outside, well wrapped up in mufflers and coats. Tourists from the north, no doubt. No self-respecting Italian would sit outside in weather like that. An old man, wrapped into so many clothes that he looked like a woolen ball, sat close to the sidewalk and blinked into the light. The look he gave passing people was intense, filled with the sort of hunger that shows loneliness.

Garini frowned. He knew this man. It was Teodoro Mantoni, Carlina's great-uncle. Suddenly, he heard Carlina's voice. "It'll be his first Christmas all alone."

A horn rang out, and a voice from behind him shouted. "Have you fallen asleep on that bike of yours? Stop dreaming, man! The light is green!"

Garini gave a start. On an impulse, he turned right and stopped in front of the café. He locked his bike, took off his helmet, and went to the table where Carlina's Uncle Teo sat immobile like a woolen statue.

"May I join you, Signor Mantoni?"

Uncle Teo looked up. His eyes widened, then he smiled.

"Signor Garini." He got up and shook Stefano's hand. "What a pleasure to see you. Can I invite you for a cup of coffee?"

Very bored. "Thank you." Stefano was glad he was wearing his heavy leather jacket because a chilly wind took away any effect the winter sun might have had. He took the seat offered.

"Is everything all right?" Uncle Teo's eyes focused on Stefano with surprising sharpness. "With Carlina?"

Stefano felt a bolt going through him. "What about Carlina?"

"She seemed down this morning."

Not more down than I. But he was not willing to discuss his relationship with Carlina, even if there had been anything to discuss. "You once offered to help me with a case," he said. "And I would like to take you up on that offer."

Uncle Teo sat up straight. "Yes?"

The waiter appeared and Garini ordered a coffee. As soon as the waiter was out of earshot, Garini continued. "There's a suspect in the case I'm working on. His name is Leopold Morin. He's French."

"Yes?" Uncle Teo leaned forward. "I speak French."

"You do?" Garini smiled. "That's good, but you won't need it."

"No?" Uncle Teo's bushy eyebrows lowered with disappointment. "Why not?"

"Because I want you to remain invisible. Just check out where he's going, and what he's doing. Follow him if you can, check when he comes to the hotel, and when he returns." That should keep him occupied for some days, covering Christmas, and it was a job where he could not come to harm.

"Do I call for you when he does something suspicious?"

"No." *There won't be anything suspicious.* "Just note what he does, and send me a report--" Garini stopped. He had wanted to say "whenever you want", but that didn't sound convincing enough. Uncle Teo was an intelligent man. "Send me a report every two days." *God, I sound like Cervi.*

"Will do." Uncle Teo nodded.

"Your coffee." The waiter slid the coffee in front of Stefano with one swift move.

"I have two other people on the job as well, so it'll be enough if you cover him from morning till one o'clock." Shadowing people could be exhausting, and Stefano did not want Uncle Teo to have a breakdown. If he was lucky, Leopold Morin did not leave his hotel before nine o'clock. "You will not see these other people, though."

"All right." Uncle Teo's eyes started to sparkle. "Do I call you to report where he is when I leave my post?"

"Yes. If you don't reach me, just leave a message. I'll pass it on."

"Good." Uncle Teo bent closer. "How do I recognize this Frenchman?"

"He stays at the Albergo di Armonia on the Borgo Santi Apostoli. He's very thin and small and has virtually no hair. Outside, he wears a black cap and a dark coat, oh, and he likes patent leather shoes. You should have no difficulty to recognize him."

Uncle Teo nodded. "Do you have a picture of him?"

"In the office." Garini lifted his cup and took a cautious sip. The coffee was scalding hot. "I'll get in touch with my assistant and ask him to give it to you when you call at the police station."

The old man waved a nonchalant hand. "That's not necessary. Just give the picture to Carlina, and she can pass it on to me."

"Carlina should not know of this." Garini placed the cup back onto the saucer with a rattle. He had spoken before he knew it.

"Oh?" Those rheumy eyes held a distinct glint. "You quarreled?"

"No." Garini bit off the word. He didn't offer an explanation.

"Let me give you a bit of advice." Uncle Teo tilted his head to one side, his eyes sharp. "She's a great girl. A woman, I should say. Very loyal."

That's just the problem. Garini tossed back the rest of the coffee, scalding his tongue, and got up. "I have to go. Thank you for covering this case, Signor Mantoni." He placed some coins onto the table. "I'll call my assistant in a minute, so he'll be prepared for your visit."

"One moment, young man." Uncle Teo held up his hand. "Don't let a good thing slip through your fingers."

"I won't." Garini clenched his teeth, turned on his heels and went to his bike. What on earth had come over him? Out of sheer compassion, he had asked a civilian to take up a needless job, and all he got in return was a stupid admonition. He felt incensed for Carlina. They all behaved as if she was on the shelf, in danger of passing the 'best before' date. Didn't they have eyes in their heads? Had they no idea how alluring she was with her irrepressible smile and those freckles on her nose? If only she wasn't so loyal, so bent on protecting her family and friends. If only he had gotten out of the case, then he could have stood by her side, could have helped her without any conflict, without being torn between reason and instinct. As it was, he had to remain neutral, had to keep her at a distance. It was difficult enough as it was, with his feelings jumping up and down like yo-yo. He was not used to being in such a state. He was used to being in control, to having his life well in hand. Drat the woman.

III

"I say, I think I need a bigger size after all. These Italian things are all too small." The petulant voice of the English lady in the changing cabin could be heard in every corner of Temptation.

Carlina caught five bras which came sailing over the partition. Why hadn't the English lady noticed she needed a bigger size before she tried on half the inventory? "I'll get you a larger size." She turned on her heels and caught a commiserating glance from Ricciarda who was busy explaining the new nylons to a customer, managing at the same time to listen to the conversations going on around her.

With an answering smile and a slight shrug of her shoulders, Carlina turned to the shelf that showed the model the English lady had liked from the start, but just as she picked up the larger size, Annalisa stormed into the store.

Her hair hung in lank streaks down to her shoulders, and her face was so pale, she seemed translucent. "Carlina!"

"What's the matter?" Carlina's voice sounded sharper than she wanted. Cold fear flashed into her heart. Had anything happened? Did Garini want to arrest Annalisa?

"I can't stand it at university anymore. They all look at me, and they whisper, and . . ." she covered her face with her hands, her whole body shaking.

Carlina placed a hand on her cousin's shoulder and steered her to the storage room in the back. With one fluid move, she took a folding chair from the wall, placed it on the floor, and pressed Annalisa onto it. "Sit down. I'll be with you in a moment."

"I say, am I going to wait until New Year before you'll bring me the size I need?" The British lady put her head through the slit in the black curtain and held it close below her chin. Her head now looked like a disembodied member with improbable curls, floating through the room. Her mouth turned down at the ends, forming the most malcontent shape Carlina had ever seen.

"I'm coming." Carlina passed her two bras. "I've taken two different sizes, so you can check which one fits best."

The head disappeared as if someone had sucked it inside the changing room. "I say, do I look like an elephant? How dare she bring me such a huge bra?" The mumble wafted through the curtain, all too clear to hear. Now even Ricciarda's customer lifted her eyebrows in surprise.

Damn. I hate it when people poison the atmosphere like this. Carlina hurried back to her cousin and knelt down next to her. "What's the matter?" She spoke low enough so the customers would not be able to overhear them.

"I . . . I just can't stand it. Life is so empty, so useless without Trevor. I feel left over and discarded."

Carlina stroked her cousin's red hair. "Yes." She swallowed. "I can imagine how difficult it is."

"How much is this bra?" The English accent penetrated even into the back of the store.

Carlina squeezed Annalisa's arm for comfort and turned back to the changing cabin. "Which model is it?"

"I say! The one you gave me, of course!" Ms. Malcontent snapped.

Ricciarda's customer gave an embarrassed smile, stopped the conversation, and hurried from the store without buying anything.

Damn. Now Mrs. Malcontent had driven her away. Carlina swallowed her anger. "It's a special Christmas-offer and--"

Stefano Garini appeared behind the glass door of Temptation. The black leather jacket and the scowl on his face gave him a menacing air that grew more pronounced as he opened the door and entered together with a gust of icy wind.

Carlina's voice petered out.

"Well?" The English head appeared in the slit of the curtain, the eyes hard. "What about the price?"

Carlina pulled herself together. "It's forty-nine Eu . . .,"

Annalisa gave a high-pitched scream. "I haven't done it! I swear!" She jumped up and clutched Carlina's arm. "Carlina! Don't let him arrest me!"

Mrs. Malcontent's eyes widened. "That's a ridiculous price, I say . . ." her head swiveled to Garini. "Are you a police officer? I say you should arrest them for over-pricing products."

Garini ignored her. "Can I talk to you for a moment?" He looked at Carlina, his face immobile.

"Yes."

"I say, how dare you walk away? You have enough customers, so you can treat them like dirt?"

Ricciarda took a step forward. "If you need anything, I'll be happy to be of assistance."

"Carlina!" Annalisa pulled at her cousin's arm. "Don't leave me!"

Carlina detached herself with a reassuring pat on her cousin's arm. "Don't worry. I'll be right back." She smiled at Ms. Malcontent, "Thank you for understanding. It's an urgent matter." She grabbed her coat from the hook in the storage area, mouthed a "thank you" to Ricciarda, and rushed outside.

Garini followed her. "What is Annalisa doing here?" His scowl deepened.

"She came for comfort." Carlina closed the zipper of her coat and turned up her collar. "Is that a problem?" *Why does he scowl at me like that? Is he still angry because of the things I said yesterday night?*

"I think you should keep your distance," he said.

"She's my cousin!" Carlina lifted her chin, prepared to go to battle. *He doesn't understand the concept of family at all.*

"Yes, and she's also the number one suspect in a murder, with motive, means, and no alibi. Try to be a little bit rational." His lips pressed together into one thin line as if he wanted to say much more and had trouble keeping it back.

Her anger rose up like a geyser, suffocating her. "Listen, Garini, I'm not a child. I know what I'm doing, and I know my family very well."

"Fine." He snapped off the word. "But are you aware that

Annalisa would never move a finger to protect you?"

Carlina blinked. She knew Annalisa well enough to recognize the strong streak of egotism in her, but she also knew how much her younger cousin had struggled after the early death of her father. Having lost her own father at the age of thirteen, she knew what Annalisa had gone through and had developed a strong protective instinct. She decided it was safer not to reply to Garini's question. "What do you want?"

"Did you really threaten to kill Trevor during your dinner with Annalisa?"

So he had overheard their conversation yesterday. Carlina drew herself up. The sharp wind crept underneath her coat with chilly fingers. *Attack is the best form of defense.* "I didn't think you would snoop behind doors."

"I didn't snoop." His jaw clenched. "I heard you scream upstairs. Do you think I would stay downstairs, waiting for the sound of your body falling to the floor? Of course I rushed to your apartment right away."

Carlina frowned. "I didn't hear you."

"You wouldn't have heard a walrus; you were so intent on each other."

"Oh." Carlina swallowed. "But still you listened to our conversation without making yourself known."

"True." Garini nodded. "I remembered you wanted to talk to Annalisa by yourself."

"Ha." Carlina gave a derisive snort. "Am I supposed to believe that?"

Without warning, his face broke into a smile. "No. Would you?"

His smile did things to her she couldn't control. With a stern hand, she suppressed an answering grin. All anger evaporated. "Would I what?"

"Would you not have grabbed the opportunity to listen, if you had been in my place?"

Carlina opened her mouth and closed it again.

"Admit it." A spark of amusement lit his eyes.

"Oh, well." Carlina shrugged and smiled at the tip of her feet to avoid smiling at him.

"You haven't answered my question." His voice was soft.

She wasn't fooled. "I said it without meaning it. You know

how it happens; you're angry, and you say you will kill someone, but of course it doesn't signify anything. It was part of the situation." She tried to read his face but couldn't tell if he believed her. Maybe he never threatened to kill anybody unless he meant it. With an inward sigh, she pulled a piece of paper from the pocket of her jacket. "Here's the list."

He frowned. "What list?"

"The list where Annalisa spent her day yesterday. You asked her to make it by this morning and to give it to me."

"Thanks." He stretched out his hand to take the paper, and his fingers touched hers for an instant. "You're cold," he said.

"Yes." Carlina said. "Can I go inside again?" She turned back to her store.

The English lady came out with a swagger. She had a bag with the Temptation logo in her hand.

Well done, Ricciarda.

"Not yet." His hand stopped her. "Can you give me a full list of the women who had a pair of your special nylons by one o'clock yesterday?"

She sighed. "But I told you already."

"Let's just make sure."

What was he trying to say? That he wanted more suspects? She bit her lip. "I . . . I don't think I have forgotten anybody." With a frown, she tried to recall the conversations she'd had when giving away the nylons. She remembered how she had joked about it with Ricciarda, how delighted Annalisa had been, how much the first customer had liked the soft feel of the material.

He interrupted her thoughts. "So far I have only four people on my list. You, . . ."

Of course he mentions me first.

". . . your assistant Ricciarda, one unknown woman who bought one pair of nylons during the morning, paying in cash, and your cousin Annalisa."

Carlina nodded. "That's it."

"Are you sure?"

"Yes." She thought back and frowned. "Oh, no, I forgot. There was another. It was stolen."

"What?" He towered over her. "When did you learn that?"

"This morning." Carlina bit her lips. "We counted everything twice, but it seems one pair is gone."

"Great." Garini closed his eyes for an instant. "I thought we only had to find one unknown woman, but now we also have to find an unknown thief."

"I'm sorry." Carlina shook her head. "I--"

"Ciao, Carlina!" Emma's voice trumpeted across the street.

Carlina jumped. "Emma!"

Her cousin crossed the street right in front of an Alfa Romeo that stopped with screeching brakes. She didn't even look at it. The fur she wore looked more expensive than the car next to her. With its fluffy bulk, it made her long, slim legs seem even longer in contrast. "Bit chilly for a rendezvous, isn't it?" Emma winked at the Commissario.

"At least we're not wearing next to nothing." Carlina pointed at Emma's short skirt. It covered only half of her thigh, and her high heels prolonged her legs by another nine centimeters.

"But Carlina, I wanted to show off my new nylons!"

Carlina caught her breath. *Damn, damn, damn.* She had forgotten Emma. She had tried to recall everyone by going back to every conversation involving the new nylons, but of course she hadn't talked with Emma. Instead, she had only placed the parcel in front of her door, and it had completely slipped her mind. Carlina was aware of Garini's unmoving body next to her, but she didn't dare to look up. He would never believe the lapse had been unintentional.

"New run-proof nylons?" His voice was low, dangerous.

"Yes!" Emma's happy voice filled the street.

Chapter 7

Carlina wondered if she should faint. No, better yet, fly. Fly away and never return.

"Em." She cleared her throat. "I forgot Emma."

His face was hard. "Sure." His voice was dripping with irony.

The expression in his eyes made her quake. Hot fury mingled with something else she could not quite define. Carlina's throat hurt. She had botched it. Her friendship with Garini was at an end before it had started. "I have to go." Her voice sounded like a goat's. She turned on her heels and hurried to the sanctuary of her store.

As she burst through the door, Annalisa and Ricciarda looked up from their intense conversation.

"Carlina, Ricciarda just had a great idea!" Annalisa's cheeks had returned to their usual rosy color. "She said I could help with the preparations for the Florence Christmas Fair!"

Carlina swallowed.

Ricciarda laughed and held up both hands. "I didn't say that, Annalisa!" She gave a lopsided smile to Carlina. "I just mentioned that we have plenty to do to prepare for the Christmas Fair and thought that maybe Annalisa could help."

"Don't you think it's a cool idea, Carlina?" Annalisa gave her cousin a hug.

Carlina returned the hug half-heartedly. She felt too overwhelmed to take a decision. Her mind was still on the forgotten nylons, and on Garini, fuming with anger, behind her. She felt as if she had turned her back on an angry tiger. Any second now, he would follow her without a sound and would breathe liquid fire down her back – or he would turn away and never be seen again. She had no idea what was worse.

"Say something, Carlina!" Annalisa frowned. "What's the matter with you? Did the Commissario say something nasty?

He's awful; I told you so."

"I'm all right," Carlina said with an effort. She hung up her coat and went aside to rearrange a hanger that was already in a perfect position. In doing so, she managed to look sideways toward the door without being too obvious.

Nothing.

He had left.

A sharp pricking behind her eyelids made her blink.

"So, what do you say?" Annalisa was almost hopping up and down with impatience. "Ever since you said it's your universe, and that you can do anything you want, I have thought that I would like to work at Temptation, too. And if you have so much to do right now, then it would fit perfectly well, wouldn't it?"

"Yes, of course." Carlina wondered if she would ever see him again.

"So that's fixed, then!" Annalisa beamed at her. "When shall I start?"

Carlina blinked. "What?"

"Shall I come back tomorrow at ten? I still need to clear up a few things today."

Carlina nodded. Garini was gone, and he would not return. Whatever she did, it didn't matter.

II

The yellow streetlight reflected with a sick yellow hue from the wet cobblestone pavement. Garini shivered and pulled his leather jacket closer. Was the ground wet or frozen? It felt treacherous beneath his feet. Thank God he only had a short way to go before he reached his apartment. His steps echoed from the scarred walls around him. Nobody was around at this time of the night.

But stop.

A woman appeared from the side and hurried along the street, away from him. Now she turned her head and cast a frightened look over her shoulder. The yellow light gave her face a ghastly pallor.

Stefano's heart contracted. Carlina? What was she doing here, in the middle of the icy night? He opened his mouth, but no sound came out. He felt sweat breaking out, creating a cold film on his forehead. Why did she look so scared? He hurried to catch up with her, but the distance didn't lessen. Had she broken into a run? Was she scared of . . . him?

His mouth turned dry. He started to run. She had nothing to fear from him. Didn't she know that? He tried to shout, but his words came out as a whisper, frozen in the air, not even reaching his own ears.

A black Mercedes overtook him with a vicious hiss. It raced through a puddle, and a jet of icy mud and water covered him to his hips.

Carlina! Finally, he came closer.

The Mercedes stopped with squealing tires. A door opened without sound, gaping like the entrance to a dark cave, and a man in a dark suit jumped out.

No!

The man clamped his hand over Carlina's mouth.

She kicked at his legs but missed.

Garini pulled his gun, but didn't dare to shoot. "Police! Stop!" His feet pounded the ground. Fear clawed at his throat. He was too far away.

Carlina crumbled.

The man caught her, threw her into the car like a limp reed, and jumped in. The car accelerated with a deafening roar.

Garini fired at the tires, but his bullets seemed to have no effect at all.

The kidnapper leaned out of the open door. His masked face turned to Garini. A laugh, loud enough to be heard in spite of the motor, filled the cold air. A victory sign, then the door closed with a bang.

"Carlina!"

His own shout woke him. Hands clammy with sweat, Garini kicked at the bed cover that had twisted around his legs. A nightmare.

Relief mixed with anger filled him. A dream. How dare his subconscious play him a trick like that? He got up. His knees still felt as if filled with custard. *Damn.* She had lied to him, had pretended to forget Emma in her list of nylon-owners, protecting one of her family again. She had no right to disturb his night like that. *I can't trust her.* Her omission of Emma in the list proved that all too well.

"What if she really forgot?" A voice inside him, the one that always took her side, said. "After all, Emma has no connection to the case. There's no reason to protect her."

Garini shook his head and filled a glass with water. No, she had no apparent reason to protect Emma. But how much did he really know about Carlina? So what if every instinct inside him insisted he could trust her. Could he rely on his instincts or was he confused by hormones, a male urge to find a female? He loved the way her green eyes slanted like a cat's, reflected her every mood, shone with enthusiasm or flared in anger.

Cool it, Garini. He gulped down the icy water and could feel how it traced its cold way down his throat.

Maybe he should text a message, ask if she was all right. He checked his watch. Three AM. *Don't. She'll be fast asleep now. She won't reply, and you'll spend the rest of the night hunched over your phone.*

He sighed and returned to the bedroom. Time to listen to some music, to take his mind off things. The sound of a saxophone always managed to lift his mood, sweep away everything dark. Antonia Hart, maybe. Or Sam Levine. Music had never failed him.

Yet.

III

When he saw her standing behind the counter at Temptation, laughing at something Ricciarda had said, a weight fell from his shoulders. She was fine. *Thank God.*

He opened the glass door and smiled at them both. "Buongiorno."

Carlina's face closed. Her eyes darted away from him.

Damn it, she couldn't be nervous of him. "How are you?" He had to hear from herself that everything was fine. Never again did he want to spend a night like the last.

"I'm fine."

A standard reply. "Really?" His eyes focused on her, taking in every detail. "I mean it. Are you all right?"

She blushed, but her gaze met his this time. "Yes."

"Good."

He turned to Ricciarda. "I need to take your statement, but I would prefer to do it where we can't be disturbed. Is that all right?"

Ricciarda nodded, her face calm. "Of course." She addressed Carlina. "We'll be at La Piccola Trattoria, if you need me."

"Sure." Carlina nodded.

Ricciarda got her dark coat and put it on. It made her look like a sleek Madonna, with a dark hood to cover her head. She lead the way to the small restaurant across the street.

The Trattoria smelled of fresh bread and coffee. Garini's stomach grumbled. He had not taken the time for breakfast this morning.

As they took their places in a quiet corner, the waiter hustled up to them and wiped the wooden table with a moist cloth. It left shiny stripes on the surface. "Buongiorno, Ricciarda." The waiter smiled. He was in his twenties and could hardly take his eyes off her. "You are early today. Will you have the usual?" A curious glance went to the Commissario, but he didn't ask.

Garini wondered if he was considered too old to be a rival.

"Yes." Ricciarda smiled.

"How about you, Signor?"

"I'll have a pannini and an espresso, please." Garini took out his tape recorder and switched it on, so his question would also be recorded. "May I tape our conversation?"

"Certainly."

Again, her calm face surrounded by the dark hair reminded him of the Madonna. She was beautiful in a serene way.

"What do you wish to know?" Her voice was low. It sounded like cream chocolate.

"Please tell me about your day yesterday."

"Carlina and I started an hour early because we still wanted to put up the special nylon decorations."

"What time was that?"

"Around nine." Ricciarda said. "When we had done the decoration, Carlina went to the back of the store to unpack some more boxes, and I--"

"What did you talk about?"

"What?" Her blue eyes opened wide. "I can't recall. Let me see . . . " She turned a strand of her glossy black hair around her index finger. "Yes. We talked about copate biscuits, and we made a bet."

"A bet?"

"Yes. How many pairs of nylons we would sell."

The waiter brought them the espresso, a latte macchiato, and the pannini.

"I see. What happened next?" Garini bit into his pannini. It was still warm, and the cheese was full of flavor, just the way he liked it.

She didn't have to think about this one. "While Carlina was at the back, a customer came into the store and bought some bras and slips for his girlfriend. Later, I learned it was Trevor Accanto."

"When later?" He didn't take his glance off her. She seemed controlled and in charge. Not at ease, but many people became nervous when questioned by the police.

"I knew who he was when he said I should send the shopping bags to the Garibaldi Hotel because Carlina had told me about him before."

"What did she say?"

Ricciarda smiled. "She said he was charming and handsome and not to be trusted."

"So you were curious to get to know him?"

She shrugged. "I know many men who are charming and handsome and not to be trusted."

I bet you do. "And what did you think when you got to know him?"

Ricciarda sipped her latte macchiato. "That Carlina had been right."

"So you liked him?"

Ricciarda hesitated. "I was once hurt by a charming man." Her voice sounded rough. "That's why I don't allow myself the luxury to like them anymore." Her blue eyes met his a bit defiant.

"I see." Stefano took a mouthful of hot espresso. "Did he say anything else to you? Where he would go, what he would do?"

"I think he wanted to go running along the Arno. He was wearing running shoes."

"Did he talk to Carlina?"

"A bit. She said he should be careful."

Damn. "Careful of what?" His voice had sharpened.

"Careful with her cousin, with Annalisa. They were lovers, and Carlina didn't think it would last."

"Would you say it was a warning from Carlina?" *Say no.*

Ricciarda shrugged. "I can't tell; I wasn't close enough to understand every word. I only heard him say he had everything under control."

Famous last words. Garini decided to switch the topic. "Do you know the Basilica di Santa Trìnita?"

"Of course." Ricciarda smiled as if she remembered a lover. "I'm an active member there, and I often go to pray."

"So you know Padre Balli?"

"Yes." Her smile deepened. "He's a wonderful man."

"Did you by any chance go to church to pray on the day Trevor Accanto was strangled?"

Her face reddened. "No. And I think it's a disgrace to kill someone inside a church. Padre Balli must have been so upset. I feel very sorry for him."

"Have you seen Padre Balli since?"

For an instant, her lower lip trembled. "No. I'm not sure if I'll go back. I have the feeling that my church has been desecrated. It makes me feel so . . . so uprooted."

Garini didn't say anything. His mother had been a devoted Catholic, chastising herself for everything she did, be it wrong or not. A church would never feel like home to him, but he knew how she felt, having seen his mother's eyes when attending the service. "Please continue to tell me about your day." He took another bite of his pannini.

"We had no customers at all. It was disheartening. Finally, Carlina said she wanted lunch, so she left."

"When was that?"

"I can't recall." Again, she turned a strand of her hair between her fingers. "We don't keep exact hours, it always depends on the customers. I think it was at one."

"At one?" He frowned. Carlina had said twelve. *Has she lied again?*

Ricciarda shrugged. "Maybe it was earlier." She pushed back her hair. "In fact, I think it may have been earlier. I really can't recall."

"When did you go?"

"As soon as she came back. It was still dead, no customers at all, so Carlina said I could stay away a bit longer."

"So how long were you gone from the store?"

Ricciarda took a deep breath. "Half an hour at most. I didn't want to leave Carlina too long, as I had a feeling that she was taking it badly. But you can ask the waiter here. I always come here for lunch."

"I will." He said it with a sinking feeling. It was all too vague. He wanted to cross off suspects from his list, but instead, he was walking in a fog that was getting denser by the minute. Most of all, he wanted to cross off Carlina, not to prove to himself that she hadn't done it, but to make sure that nobody else would be able to point a finger at her. Damn it all. He had to show results, and soon, or Cervi would needle him with nasty comments.

He sent Ricciarda back to Temptation and summoned the waiter to the table. "Could you take a minute and answer some questions?" He showed his police identification.

The young man's eyes widened. "Golly." He slid onto the seat vacated by his idol. "Is Ricciarda in trouble?" He cast a haunted look at the restaurant. "I can't stay long, you understand, but if you need something from me, of course I'll tell you anything you need to know."

Garini could tell that he already saw himself in the role of savior, protecting Ricciarda. She had not talked to him on the way out, but maybe she had briefed him before. He had better make it clear this was a serious business. "We're checking the whereabouts of people connected with a murder that happened yesterday."

The waiter nodded with enthusiasm. "The rich American who was strangled at the Basilica di Santa Trìnita. I heard about it." He leaned forward. "What do you need to know?"

"First of all, can I record our conversation?"

"Yes, of course." He didn't hesitate.

Garini pressed the recording button. "Please give me your name and address."

"I'm Enrique Passo, and I live on Via Faenza, 13." His gaze was clear and direct.

No fear there. Time to make sure he got the right idea. "Before you reply, please be aware that this is a murder investigation, a serious breach of law. Choose your words with care and remember that you might be asked to swear to your statement in court. This is not the time to say what you think happened or what you believe or can't believe. I want the facts, and nothing else. Is that clear?"

The young man nodded, his face serious. He had lost his buoyancy, which was exactly what Garini wanted.

"Please tell me about yesterday from eleven thirty to two thirty."

The waiter frowned and pushed a hand through his brown hair. "It was quiet at first, very quiet. Usually, it's teeming just a few days before Christmas, but yesterday was odd."

That chimes in with Carlina's statement. "Yes?"

"So we only had the usual customers, old Signor Pepoli," he nodded toward the corner at his left where a white-haired man was reading the newspaper. "He comes every morning at ten and leaves at twelve."

"Who else?"

"Signora Barberini, she comes at eleven and drinks one espresso every day. Then two tourists I didn't know."

"Did you know the American?"

"No." Enrique shook his head with regret.

"Who else?"

"Ricciarda came for lunch, as always."

"When was that?"

He didn't hesitate. "She came at five minutes past one and stayed until one thirty-five."

"How come you can tell it to the minute?"

Enrique flushed to the roots of his hair. "I just know."

"Hmm."

"Was Signor Pepoli still there?"

"Oh, no, as I said, he always leaves at twelve. Ricciarda came later."

"Every day or was this an exception?"

"It's not always regular, it depends on how many customers they have." A smile made him look younger. "But I expected her earlier yesterday, as they had no customers at all."

"How do you know that?"

"I can see the shop window if I look into that mirror over there." Enrique pointed at the wall.

Garini got up and checked the mirror. It offered a great view of the door to Temptation. "Interesting." He returned to the table and waited for Enrique who had jumped up and served a customer in the break.

"Has this mirror always been there?"

"Well . . . " Enrique again turned bright-red. "Em. We recently put it there because it reflects the light much better."

I bet. "So did you happen to see Ricciarda come out of the store?"

"Listen, Commissario," Enrique pulled at the sleeves of his shirt as if it had suddenly gotten too small. "I'll be honest with you. She's a great woman," he said it with a kind of awe that showed how hopeless his case was, "and I can't help being in love with her. But I'm not harassing her or anything."

"I didn't accuse you of that." Garini's voice was calm.

Enrique eyed him. "No?"

"No." Garini smiled. "So please answer my question."

"What question? Oh." Enrique swallowed. "Yes, I did see her coming out. Her boss went first to have lunch, which is unusual. Usually, she lets Ricciarda go first. They never close during lunch-time, you know."

"Did you see when her boss went for lunch?" Really, this waiter proved to be a gold-mine. He could get quite used to him.

Enrique shrugged. "Around twelve, I believe."

Clearly, Carlina wasn't the object of his desire. But at least it fit with Carlina's statement.

"So Ricciarda left the store at one and came directly here?"

"Five minutes past." Obviously, the wait had been endless. "Yes, she came directly here, and she also returned directly to the store."

"Was she in any way different?"

He frowned. "No. She was calm, as always. Maybe quieter than usual, even. She's like a saint, you know, always friendly."

Gag. "Quite." Garini leaned forward. "And you are quite sure that Ricciarda didn't ask you to confirm these times? It sounds a bit too perfect, you know."

Enrique blanched. "She didn't. I tell you. I wouldn't want to hurt her, not for a minute."

"If you are covering for her, you would do her the worst possible service."

The young waiter sat up straight. "I only said the truth! I can't help it that I notice the time when she's here. It's . . . it's just the way it is. You can't blame her for that."

Indeed I can't, and somehow, you're more convincing than you know. Garini changed track. "Did you see an American in sports clothes going into the store? Middle-aged, slim, tall, black hair?"

Enrique shook his head. "I can't recall someone like that at all, but then, I don't see everybody." A lopsided smile. "When I know that Ricciarda is unlikely to come out, I stop checking the mirror. When was it?"

"Between nine and ten in the morning."

"Oh, no." Enrique lifted both hands. "We only open at ten, so I wouldn't have seen him anyway. Besides, in the morning, I'm often clearing up and can't keep an eye on the door of Temptation."

Garini switched off the recorder. "Thanks. I might come back later to check some details."

"Sure." Enrique jumped up. "Anytime." He hurried to serve his customers while Garini stared at his back with a frown. This young man was a bit too convenient. But then, if Ricciarda had needed an alibi, she would not have constructed one that was so obvious. Somehow, Enrique didn't look like a good actor.

Friendly, yes.

Open, yes.

Devious? Not at all.

He did not believe for one minute that someone as intelligent as Ricciarda would place herself in the hands of someone who might turn out to be a liability. Unless . . . He went up to Enrique and stopped him before he could get within hearing distance of the next table. "One more word, Signor Passo."

"Yes?"

"Be a bit careful in the next weeks."

Enrique's mouth went slack. "What? Do you think I'm in danger?"

"I didn't say that." Garini looked him straight in the eye. "Just avoid dangerous situations, will you?"

The waiter swallowed. "Yes."

When Garini left the café, his cell phone rang. With one hand, he pulled it out and answered it while using his other hand to pull the collar of his leather jacket closer around his neck. The wind had a sharp edge to it today.

"Hello, this is Piedro speaking."

"Piedro. What happened?" His assistant rarely ever went to the trouble of calling him.

"We just got a report about Signor Accanto's uncle."

"Good." Garini sensed his mood perking up. The uncle would help him to get a better picture of Trevor Accanto, to show another side he had not yet been able to investigate - about his family, about a person who had been with him over a longer period of time, as opposed to the ever changing women at his side. "What does it say?"

"He doesn't exist."

"What?" Garini felt his hope dropping to the floor with a thud.

"The report says they hunted for relations of Signor Accanto high and low, but they did not discover a single trace. He had a mother whose birthday was January 3rd and it seems he often came to see her when she had still been alive."

"Damn. When did she die?"

"Seven years ago. She was eighty-nine."

Garini's mood sank. It seemed Trevor had preferred all his relations to be short-lived or superficial. A sad life, when you thought about it.

"Commissario?" Piedro sounded insecure, as always.

"Yes?"

"Do you want to know anything else?"

Garini curbed his impatience. "Does the report mention anything else? If yes, then I'd like to know about it."

"Oh." Piedro sank into ruminative silence. "No, I don't think the report said much else."

Garini decided to read it himself as soon as possible, just to be on the safe side.

"Oh, yes," Piedro suddenly added with a voice as if he had discovered a new painting of Leonardo da Vinci in a hidden attic. "Now I know. His mother's neighbors remembered him."

"Yes?"

"They said he was very charming."

Garini closed his eyes in exasperation. *Tell me something new.*

"And that he loved the Christmas season in Italy."

"Hmm."

"Because it was so . . . so natural, and less artificial than in the States."

So that solved the question why Trevor Accanto preferred to come to Florence in winter. It sounded like a weak reason, but who was he to judge the idiosyncrasies of an American millionaire? Even so, it did not get him one iota closer to his murderer. "Is this all the report said? Nothing else at all?" Garini asked again.

"That's all."

Chapter 8

"Where are you?" The message blinked on her cell phone, innocent, innocuous, and yet, it released a storm of emotions inside Carlina. All day long, she had felt down, and even the meeting with the other Christmas Fair participants hadn't helped to release the feeling that she was walking under a dark cloud. All through dinner, she had sat like a statue, listening to her vivacious hostess Sabrina, the wife of the mayor, with only half an ear. She had lost Garini, and the void inside her ached.

But now, he had sent a message, and if felt as if it pulsed right through her veins. It wasn't exactly a lover-like message, and maybe he just needed to talk to her about the case, but at least he got in touch.

She frowned. It wasn't like her to be so desperate. When had she become dependent on Garini's approval? Drat the man.

She pushed back her chair and made sure everybody around her was busy with the conversations going on. They were discussing the last organizational things about the fair. Good. Carlina's fingers slid over the display. "At a restaurant close to Palazzo Pitti. Dinner with Mayor's wife."

His answer came a heartbeat later. "Impressive." She could almost hear the irony in his voice. "State banquet?"

"Prep dinner for the Florence Christmas Fair." Would he remember she had told him about it?

"Can I accompany you home?"

Carlina blinked. Did he know she had left the Vespa at home, planning to take a taxi later on, knowing she would drink too much wine? He didn't miss much. "Yep. Half an hour?"

"OK."

It was hardly a lover-like exchange, so why did she suddenly feel as if the room had turned brighter? She looked at her friend Rosanna across the table, discussing ways to decorate her flower booth with an interior designer she had not known some weeks previously. Even if the fair should prove to be a disaster from a sales point of view, it had brought them all forward, had created connections that would prove valuable, and had made each of them stronger.

Someone placed a hand on her shoulder. Even before she turned, Carlina knew it was Sabrina. Her perfume was unmistakable, French, expensive, lingering on long after she had gone. "Are you enjoying yourself?" Sabrina's voice was deep and resonant, almost like a man's.

"Very much." Carlina smiled at her. "I was just thinking that you helped us tremendously by bringing us all together. The men all have their clubs, their connections of old. We women need to learn how to network."

Sabrina nodded. "Thank you. That's exactly why I set up this fair." She looked around the table, her dark eyes shining. They made an interesting contrast to her short, light hair.

Carlina wished she could move with as much self-assurance as the wife of the mayor but maybe it was something that came with more experience. She estimated Sabrina to be somewhere in her fifties, though it was hard to guess because she was such an attractive women and seemed much younger.

A satisfied smile spread across Sabrina's face as she saw the animated people around her. "It's good to know that you can make a difference if you apply yourself to it."

Carlina glanced at her with curiosity. She didn't know Sabrina well, but the way she had focused on this project and had managed to bring it all together filled her with respect. "Somehow, I don't think it's the first thing you've applied yourself to." She smiled. "You seem an old hand at it."

Sabrina nodded. "Thank you. I have to tell you that I'm very impressed by your lace collection. I plan to be one of your biggest customers."

Something warm pooled inside Carlina. "How nice, thank you." The words sounded inadequate compared to her feelings. She had worked so hard, and to meet someone who appreciated it made such a difference. However, Sabrina's next words jolted her out of her happiness.

"I've heard you know the investigating officer of the Santa Trìnita murder." Sabrina moved her hand and watched the light sparkle on the flashy ring she always wore.

Carlina's mouth dropped open. "Who said that?"

Sabrina smiled. "My husband told me."

"Oh." *And just how does he come to know that?* She didn't dare to ask.

Sabrina pulled up a chair and sat next to Carlina. "He got a report from the police and told me about it."

"I didn't think I would figure in a police report." *What did it say?*

Sabrina rubbed her nose. "Maybe I shouldn't have told you. I think it's confidential. But Temptation is mentioned as one of the last places where--," she paused and swallowed, "where the victim was seen alive."

"Yes. Unfortunately."

"So you knew him?"

"Trevor?" Carlina smiled a bit. "Yes, I knew him."

"What was he like?"

I wonder why you want to know. Is it natural curiosity or is there anything else behind it? " He was charming. Good-looking. Very self-confident." Her words sounded reticent. *Just where is this conversation going?*

"I see." Sabrina looked at the wall opposite as if it had some interesting feature only she could see. "And do they already know who killed him?"

"Not that I know of. But I'm not in the confidence of the police." Carlina covered her cell phone with her hand. If Stefano should send another message now, it would say she had just gotten a message from "Aaawful Commissario". Garini had once made her program his name in a way that would make it come up first, so she could call him in a second if she needed him.

Sabrina laughed, a silver laugh that sounded light and fresh. "Of course they don't share news with civilians, I know that. I just wondered if maybe you noticed what they focus on, you know, what questions they ask. You might have realized that when the police interviewed you." She started to turn her shining ring on her hand. "I'm an avid reader of mysteries, and when Fabrizio told me about it, I wondered if you could tell me some details." She gave Carlina a charming smile. "You'll think my interest is completely gruesome."

"That's fine." Carlina couldn't help herself, she had to smile back. "I'm also curious myself. But so far, it doesn't look as if they've made much progress." The minute the words left her mouth, she felt disloyal to Garini. "Though they're hunting high and low."

"This Commissario, the one who's responsible for the case, is he good?"

"Very." Carlina nodded.

"Really?" Sabrina bent forward. "How do you know?"

Carlina swallowed. "We're . . . friends."

One finely arched eyebrow went up. "Friends?"

Carlina held her gaze. "Yes."

"I see." Sabrina dropped her gaze and turned her ring once again. "And do you think he will manage to solve this case?"

"I should think so. He's very intelligent." She looked at Sabrina. Something in her face made her add, "And incorruptible."

"That's great." It sounded like a mechanical reply. Sabrina looked over the table."Oh, that's Barbara, giving me a sign. I have to go." She jumped up.

Carlina followed her. "I've got to go, too. Thank you for organizing the fair." She bent forward and air-kissed Sabrina's cheeks. "Buona notte. I'll see you at the fair."

When Carlina came out of the building, the wind attacked her like a living thing. It jumped into her face and pulled at her hair, howling with anger. Carlina shivered and snuggled deeper into her coat. What a night. At least it had stopped raining.

A shadow detached from the building opposite the street and went up to her. "You'd better take this." Garini held out a thick scarf.

"Is that yours?" Her heart started to beat faster. *This is not a date. It's part of a police investigation, so stop behaving like a drooling sixteen-year-old.*

"Yes, it's my scarf, but I brought it for you."

Carlina laughed, pretending to herself and to him that the words didn't touch something deep inside her. "Thanks, but we won't be out long, so I don't think I'll need it."

In the uncertain light of the street-lamp, she couldn't make out the expression on his face.

"I thought I'd walk you home." The wind tore at his hair.

"You're kidding."

He looked at her in that inimitable way he had, without moving a muscle, without giving her the slightest chance to guess what he was thinking. "Would you hate it?"

The wind whipped up her hair and twirled it around her face. She looked at him, and suddenly, she knew that she would walk anywhere with him, gale or no gale. "I . . . ." She swallowed. "No."

He lifted the scarf as if he had done it a thousand times already, brushed back her hair, bound the scarf loosely around her head, so it covered her ears, then looped it around her neck. The howling diminished. What a difference it made if your head was covered. Or maybe the wind had stopped altogether. She couldn't tell.

"Better?" His voice was soft, his face close to hers.

His hands bound the scarf beneath her chin, and for an instant, she could smell leather and soap, before the wind blew his scent away.

She cleared her throat. "Yes. Thank you." *Now. Tell him now.* "Stefano, I--" She lost her nerve. It sounded too stupid.

"Tell me." His voice was quiet. He stood in front of her, his hands in his pockets now, as if he had all the time in the world.

"I didn't lie to you." Her throat felt raw. "I know it sounds stupid, and I know you won't believe me, but I forgot about Emma. I really did."

He didn't say anything. His gaze never left her face.

"It would make me miserable to lie to you." She bit her lips. "Believe it or not." The last came out too defiant, as if she was a teenager, unsure of her position in the world. She stared at her shoes, waiting for him to start questioning her, to probe deeper into her thoughts, into her family.

"I believe you."

Her head came up. Hope foamed through her as if it had shot through a geyser. "You do?"

"I do." He took her arm and turned her downhill, toward the city.

She fell in step with him. "Why?"

He glanced at her. "Why do I believe you?"

"Yes."

He pushed a hand through his hair. "I don't know." Another glance. "I shouldn't." He shrugged.

"Why not?"

"Because you're a suspect in a murder case. Because you had opportunity, motive, means. Because I know how fiercely protective you are of your family. Because of a thousand reasons."

His steps lengthened, and Carlina hurried to keep up with him. "But still you do believe me?"

"Yes." He didn't elaborate. He didn't sound as if it made him happy. He said it as if it was his karma, something inevitable, something out of his control, something you had to accept, even if it made no sense.

"I'm glad."

They had come into the light of another street-lamp. He turned his head. A small smile sat in one corner of his mouth. "Well, that's at least one of us."

She could have taken offense, but she knew why he said it. He was a man who didn't leave things to chance, a man who worked with instinct and hunches, but who never solely relied on them. A man who decided with care, who looked at things from all angles. And now, all of a sudden, he had come upon a blind spot within himself. He had come up to something he could not control, a conviction stronger than reason.

Yes, Carlina understood, and she knew what it meant to him to admit to this blind spot. She returned his smile, a bit lopsided, a bit ironic, but with deep understanding.

His smile deepened. He bent forward.

Carlina's heart-beat accelerated until she could feel it beating inside her throat. She leaned toward him.

A car turned into the street and revved up the motor behind them.

His head came up with a sharp move. One quick step, and he had placed himself between the houses and herself, so she was protected from the side of the street.

The moment of intimacy was gone.

The car passed by without slowing down.

He slipped his arm around her shoulders and resumed walking, his face closed.

Carlina caught her breath. She loved the way he pulled her to his side. It felt so safe, so secure. She had never noticed how well they fit together. Well, she had never had a chance. It was the first time he had placed his arm around her. "What was that all about?"

"Hmm?" He turned his head and looked at her as if she had spoken in another language.

"Were you afraid of that car?"

"Sort of."

She frowned. "Why?"

"A bad dream." His face remained immobile.

"A bad dream?" Her eyebrows climbed up. "What about?"

He gave her an enigmatic glance. "I dreamed you were kidnapped on the street."

A mixture of fear and exhilaration shot through Carlina. He had dreamed about her. But kidnapping? "Any particular reason why you dreamed of kidnapping?"

"None." He shrugged. "But I was glad to see you safe this morning at Temptation."

The fear left, and a deep happiness took its place. She gave him a small smile, then looked ahead. They had reached the end of the street and turned to the left, toward the Arno river. Carlina noticed he had matched his steps to hers. The wind pulled at her coat, but she felt warm, walking with Garini. Maybe talking right now wasn't necessary. Maybe she should just enjoy the moment, accept happiness even if it came with an unexpected surrounding. She didn't place her arm around his hip, instead, she kept both hands deep inside the pockets of her coat, but she also made sure she never moved away from him, giving him no reason to let go of her.

They walked downhill, the city center illuminated in front of them, glowing yellow in the light, like a town asleep, quiet and spun deep inside its dreams.

"So why did you want to walk me home?" she asked. "It's not exactly the right weather for walking."

"I wanted to talk to you."

"You could have done that in the car."

"The car pool was booked out tonight, and it would have been too quick." He sounded relaxed, sure of himself.

"Too quick for what?"

He smiled. "Too quick for everything." With his free hand, he touched the scarf above her forehead. "Warm enough?"

"Yes, thank you. And you?"

"Fine." Their steps echoed through the quiet night, but for once, it didn't sound menacing. They walked down a street with crooked houses. Many windows had Christmas decorations, their lights shining into the darkness.

Carlina smiled. *I'm exactly where I want to be.* She held onto that thought and wondered if she should insist on talking, insist on finding out whatever he wasn't telling her. *No. Don't destroy the moment. Go with the flow.*

They walked on in silence. Once, she slipped on the cobblestone pavement, but he held her and made sure she didn't fall. It felt good to be with him, good to have no distraction, good not to be hurried into anything. The hazy air twirled around them like an enchanted veil, hiding them from the real world. *Why can't life always be like this?*

As they crossed the foaming Arno river, Carlina broke the silence. "For someone who wants to talk, you're awfully quiet."

He laughed. It was a low laugh, and she could feel it more than she heard it. "I don't feel like talking anymore."

She smiled. "My very thought."

The words disappeared between them without leaving a mark. She was content to be silent.

When they stopped in front of her door, she looked up at him. "Thank you."

"Good night, Carlina." He pulled her closer.

She lifted her face to him and closed her eyes.

Something shoved into her back and propelled her forward, against Stefano's chest. "Carlina!" Her mother shot through the front door. "I'm glad you're home! I was worried."

Carlina suppressed a sigh and turned around. She didn't dare to look at Garini. "I'm over thirty, Mama, and it's not even midnight. Where's the problem?"

"The cards show me an impending tragedy!" Her mother lifted both hands. She had put on two identical bracelets with a multitude of golden trinkets that rattled against each other. A shudder ran through her body. "It's dreadful out here. Come in."

She opened the door and pulled them inside.

Carlina looked at Garini. His face wore a bemused expression, as if he was watching a rare species in the middle of mating season.

"Come in, come in." Fabbiola pulled them upstairs to her

apartment. "The cards are still on the table. I'll show you what I saw, and you will understand--"

She flung open the door to her apartment and rushed inside, her dress billowing behind her.

Garini held the door open for Carlina.

"I'm sorry," she said under her breath as she went past him.

"I wouldn't miss this for the world." His voice sounded amused. "I feel sure the future holds more than I can ever imagine."

She rolled her eyes and followed her mother into the living room.

It smelled of incense, something intense, Indian maybe. Carlina went to the window and opened it wide.

"Close the window!" Fabbiola waved both hands until her bracelets rattled like castanets. "The cards will blow away." She picked up her favorite cushion and held it over the cards like a shield.

Carlina sighed and closed the window half-way, then turned around.

Her mother threw the cushion aside and bent over the low wooden table where all her cards lay, spread out in an intricate pattern.

She needs to re-do her roots. Carlina averted her gaze from her mother's bent head and looked at Garini. He was watching her mother with a patient expression, both hands in his pockets, rocking back on his heels. *I wonder what he thinks.*

He looked up at that instant and gave her one of his rare smiles.

She could feel her face going hot. *I bet my ears are turning bright-red.*

Fabbiola frowned and shook her head. "There," she said with all the panache of a sorcerer who had conjured up his first white rabbit. She made a wide move with her right arm. "Look at this."

"I can't read the cards," Carlina said. "And I don't believe in them anyway."

Her mother pointed at something in the middle. "The black knight. The black knight means death." She picked up another card to the right. "And this!" She waved it in the air. "Children." The way she said it, she might just as well have said, "Cholera and pest".

Carlina rolled her eyes. "So what's bad about children?"

"They're danger." Her mother's voice turned sepulchral. "Great danger." She lifted her head and fixed Carlina with a stare. "Beware of children."

Carlina started to laugh. "I will take care that no children will attack me. Anything else, Mama? Should I be careful of . . . broccoli, maybe?"

"Broccoli? Why do you mention broccoli?" Her mother's eyes widened.

Carlina shrugged. "It's harmless. As harmless as children. That's why I thought of broccoli. I could also have said cauliflower. Or brussel sprouts."

Stefano's mouth twisted.

Fabbiola bent over the cards again. "It's funny that you mention it. I had one card here, one I couldn't quite interpret. The color green. Do you think . . . broccoli?" The next words got lost in a murmur.

Carlina checked Stefano's face.

His eyebrows had climbed up so high, they almost disappeared in his hairline.

Carlina decided it was time to call it a night. She took a step forward. "Thank you for warning me, Mama. Now I think we'd better--"

"Not only you." Her mother didn't look up. "Him, too."

"You mean Stefano?"

"Yes. There's danger. For both of you. Danger from the young."

"We'll keep it in mind." Stefano turned to the door. "Good night, Mrs. Ashley-Mantoni."

"Buona notte, Mama." Carlina gave her mother a quick peck on the cheek. "Don't worry. We'll heed your warning."

Her mother looked up and gave her a sudden smile. "Good. You do that. Good night."

She waved at them and turned back to her cards. The last they heard from her was a murmur. "Zucchini?"

As they left the apartment, Carlina said under her voice. "Don't worry, it's only a phase."

"Good God," Garini pushed a hand through his hair. "Don't tell me she has started on phases just like her father?"

Carlina suppressed a smile. "I'm not sure. But this is pretty harmless, compared to some of the phases granddad went through."

"So far," he said. "I shudder to think what might come next." But he was smiling as he said it. He lifted one hand and touched her cheek, but before he could do anything else, a voice floated up from below.

"Is that you, Carlina?" Emma poked her head over the staircase one floor down and craned it around to look up.

"Yes." Carlina suppressed a sigh. *Note to self: Never try to kiss someone with family in the vicinity of ten kilometers.*

They went downstairs.

Emma frowned at them. "What did you discuss with Fabbiola?"

"Oh," Carlina waved a hand. "This and that. Vegetables."

"Vegetables?" Emma's eyes threatened to fall out of her head.

"Yes, broccoli." Carlina lifted one eyebrow. "Anything else you need to know?"

Emma sighed. "No. I just wondered when I heard your voices." She turned to Garini. "Do you need to see the nylons again?"

"No, thanks. Once was enough."

"Oh. Then what are you doing here?" Her limpid gaze took him in.

Carlina cringed. *Emma, please!* "Stefano accompanied me home after the Florence Christmas Fair Meeting." She gave her cousin a menacing stare.

"Ah, I see." Emma seemed to lose all interest in Stefano and took her cousin by the arm. "Carlina, you need to come and see what I bought today. I really--"

"I was just going to say good-bye to Stefano." Carlina hung back and clenched her teeth.

"Well, you can do so now, can't you?" Emma opened the door of her apartment and went inside. "It won't take a minute, and then you can see what I bought. I'll be back in a minute."

"Neatly dismissed." His voice was ironic. "Does she dislike me so much?"

"I don't know." Carlina was puzzled. "I didn't think she did."

"Never mind." Stefano smiled. "Good night, Carlina."

"I'm sorry." She felt miserable.

"I'll see you soon." He took her hand and lifted it briefly to his lips, then turned and went down the steps.

"Carlina? Why are you standing on the landing like a sheep in a thunderstorm? Come in; it's damn cold on the staircase."

Carlina went into her cousin's apartment and closed the door behind her with care. "Can you tell me why you made a point of interrupting my date?"

Emma rummaged through a glossy shopping bag and didn't look up. "Was that a date? Sorry, I thought he was just investigating that murder again."

"He wasn't." Carlina made sure her voice showed how annoyed she felt. "And you knew that very well. So what's up?"

Emma didn't reply. Her shiny hair had fallen forward and covered her face, and she was still busy pulling things out of the shopping bag and pushing them back in again.

Carlina went to her cousin and took her by the shoulders. "Stop that; I know it was only an excuse to get Stefano out of the way. What's going on here?"

Emma looked up and sighed. Her soft mouth pulled down at the corners. "I just don't like him."

Carlina narrowed her eyes. "I think you're hiding something. You're afraid of him."

Emma colored. "Absolutely not. I just don't like his manners. He's so . . . abrupt."

Carlina had to smile. Lucio, Emma's husband, and Stefano were as different as sugar and salt, but was that enough to make Emma feel antagonistic to that extent? So far, she had egged on Carlina, had encouraged her to get into a new relationship with every unsuitable man she could drag to the surface. "He isn't a soft-voiced Casanova, if that's what you mean." Though giving her a hand-kiss had blown her away. It was an unusual gesture, outmoded, and yet, he had carried it off with ease and charm. She suppressed the need to lift her hand to her cheek.

Emma frowned. "Why are you grinning like a kid in front of the Christmas tree?"

Carlina wiped the smile from her face. "So you don't want to tell me?"

"I have nothing to tell." Emma closed her mouth with a snap. "But I give you a warning . . . make sure you keep your distance from that guy. You can't trust him."

Carlina lifted her eyebrows. "Noted." Her voice dripped

irony. She turned to the door. "Do you wish to add anything to that warning? Aren't you forgetting something?"

"What?" Emma stemmed her hands on her hips and glared at her cousin.

"Children." Carlina opened the front door. "Don't forget they are extremely dangerous." She shook her head. "Oh, these dangerous children. Vicious, I can tell you." She slipped through the door. "Not to forget broccoli. Nasty stuff, that."

Just before she closed the door with a soft click behind her, she caught a last glimpse of her cousin, who stared at her, mouth slack, eyes almost popping out of her head.

Chapter 9

"American tourist strangled with unbreakable nylons!"

The sunny morning eclipsed. Carlina froze in mid-movement and stared at the small booth on the corner of the street, where the newspaper hung, its headline screaming at passers-by. Not one newspaper, oh, no, dozens in crooked rows, hung like washing on a line. And every single one showed her frowning face, a blurred snapshot, with the distinctive Temptation logo in the background. *They must have taken it yesterday when I left the store.* She had never even noticed a photographer on the street. "She sold the murder weapon." It said in black capitals below her picture.

"Madonna." Carlina forced herself to walk to the tiny newspaper booth in spite of her weak knees. "I'd like one of the Quotidiano, please." She pointed at the blurred picture of her face.

The old man plucked the Quotidiano from its position and handed it to her without looking up. Then he stretched out his other hand. The fingertips were blue from the cold. "One Euro thirty."

As she took the paper, she met his gaze.

His eyes widened. "It's you." He swallowed so hard, his Adam's apple visibly jumped up and down. His hand started to tremble. "It's you!"

She tried a smile, but could feel it coming out as a frozen grimace. "I'm afraid so."

Every wrinkle on the old man's face stretched into a false smile. "Don't do anything to me."

"Of course not." Carlina sounded more exasperated than soothing. "I didn't kill him." She dropped the coins into his hand, but it was shaking so hard that a twenty cent piece dropped to the ground, behind the newspapers stacked in front of the salesman.

The old man didn't seem to notice. His pale eyes remained fixed on her face, and he backed off one step. "Go away."

Carlina bit her lip. She nodded and whipped around, clutching the newspaper like a lifeline.

At Temptation, she spread the paper onto the sales counter and read the whole lurid story. "A new lead has come up in the murder of the rich American Trevor V. Accanto. Until yesterday, we only knew that he had been strangled inside the Basilica di Santa Trìnita on December 18, but now our latest inside information reveals that the killer had a warped sense of humor: The American, who took a different lover in Florence on every Christmas vacation, was strangled with a pair of unbreakable nylons - one entanglement too much! The owner of the exclusive lingerie store Temptation, Carlina Ashley (see our picture to the right), sold the unusual murder weapon. She knew the victim but claims to have had no knowledge of the murder at the Basilica Santa Trìnita. The Italian police are closely cooperating with Switzerland, France, and the US in this murder as experts are investigating an international angle. Will the nylon-murderer continue, looking for unfaithful men all over Florence? Has she already picked out the next victim? Has your wife bought unbreakable nylons from Temptation on Via de' Tornabuoni? If yes, you'd better avoid dark places! Stay tuned . . . we'll keep you updated!"

Carlina's hand covered her mouth with her hand, her eyes wide. This was worse than she'd thought.

She lifted her head and stared unseeing at two teenage girls who were leaning against the shop window of Temptation, shadowing their faces right and left with their hands, peering inside. The second Carlina moved, they screamed and ran away. *Oh, my God.*

Her cell phone rang.

She checked the display and pounced on it like a cat. "Have you seen the Quotidiano?"

"This minute." Garini's voice was grim.

"What should I do?" Her voice rose to a hysterical pitch.

"I assume you're not willing to close the shop, are you?" His voice remained calm.

Carlina reared back. "Of course not! It's suicide to close a retail store three days before Christmas!"

"I didn't expect any other answer." He sounded resigned. "But you are aware that thousands of curious people will flock to your store and maybe even a nut-case or two?"

Carlina swallowed heard. "I guess. But I can't close anyway."

Silence.

She could not even hear him breathe.

Ricciarda came through the door, looking wind-blown and lovely. She smiled at Carlina and went to the back to hang up her coat.

Carlina forced herself to return the smile, then concentrated again on the phone. "Do you have any idea who leaked the information to the press, Stefano?"

"I do." He was quiet for a minute, then added. "Listen, I'll send you Piedro for the day."

"Piedro? Isn't that your assistant, the one who's a little slow?"

He made a sound in his throat. "A little slow is the understatement of the year. Compared to him, a snail moves with lighting speed. He's the worst assistant I've ever had."

"Oh."

"I want him to stand in front of your window and check the people going in and out. I'll also tell him to keep an eye on everything that goes on inside the store. If you feel in any way threatened, just give him a sign, will you? I'm sorry I can't send anybody else."

"But he'll freeze to death, standing all day outside Temptation!"

"If he does, I hope it'll hurt." Stefano's voice remained calm. "He's the one who's responsible for all the crap in the Quotidiano."

Carlina gasped. "Piedro did that? But how? Why?"

"Apparently, he met an old school friend yesterday; they had a bit of a good time, and in all innocence, or so he claims, he told him about the case. The good friend forgot to mention that he worked for the Quotidiano, though Piedro could have made some connection when he murmured something about being a free-lance journalist."

"Gosh." Carlina pushed the newspaper toward Ricciarda who had come back from the storage area. "Read this," she whispered and turned her back to her assistant, looking out of the window. Two men in business suits hurried past. One looked up at the name above the door, then dug the other in the ribs and pointed at the advertising sign for the nylons. "Mai più smagliature! No more runs!" Grinning, they both moved on.

Something inside Carlina twisted. She remembered her pride when the logo of Temptation had been etched into the glass above the door, picturing it as a synonym for beauty and luxury. Now it was a synonym for murder.

"Carlina?" Garini's voice sounded concerned. "Are you all right?"

"Yeah." Carlina pressed her lips together. "Did Piedro tell you all this voluntarily?" If he had done that, he was more courageous than she had ever suspected.

"Let say I extracted it bit by bit."

"I see." Carlina watched a woman stopping in front of the window. With her head hunched between her shoulders to protect herself from the cold, the woman looked at the advertising for nylons and narrowed her eyes, then shook her head and moved on.

Carlina pressed her lips together. "You can send Piedro over right now. The second a madman tries to kill me, I'll push him forward, so he can take my place."

She hung up and turned around.

Ricciarda looked up from the paper, her eyes huge. "Wow. What an accumulation of filth."

"Yes." Carlina clenched her teeth. "And what rotten timing. Everybody with nothing to do will flock to Temptation today. To make it look as if they are serious buyers, they'll try on everything in sight or pretend to need extensive advice, when all they want to do is ogle me and the store."

Ricciarda frowned. "It's unfair."

"Yes." Carlina lifted both shoulders. "We should convert Temptation to a souvenir-shop and sell buttons with a great slogan. Something like 'I was in the store where they sell unbreakable nylons as a murder weapon'. Then we could sell them for five Euros a piece." She snorted. "I bet I'd be a millionaire tonight."

Ricciarda gave her an encouraging smile. "I'm sure it won't be as bad as that."

"Let's hope not. I--" Carlina broke off and stared into space. "But what am I saying? Of course!"

Ricciarda blinked. "You'll make the buttons?"

"Not the buttons!" Carlina grinned. "But we can take the Temptation cups instead. Do you remember them?"

"The espresso cups with the golden Temptation logo? I thought you'd reserved them as gifts for good customers?"

"Yes." Carlina already reached for the telephone and started to dial. "But I had to order much more than I wanted in order to get the customized version. They're at my apartment, and thankfully, they're packed in small boxes, so they're not too heavy. I'll call Uncle Teo to bring them. We can build them into the decoration, and we'll sell them for fifteen Euros per piece." She started to chant, speaking like a vegetable seller at the market. "Come here, Signore, Signori, we have the perfect souvenir from the murderous store in old-town Florence." She stuck the phone between her shoulder and her ear while at the same time clearing some space on the sales counter for the cups. "Uncle Teo? It's Carlina. I need a favor from you - I wanted to ask if you could bring me the boxes with espresso cups from my apartment. You helped me to carry them upstairs some weeks ago, do you remember?"

"I'm so sorry, Carlina, but I don't have time today." Uncle Teo panted as if he had been running.

In the background, Carlina could hear a familiar sounding ping. She frowned. She knew that sound. What was it? "Where are you, Uncle Teo?"

"Oh, I'm on my way to see a friend."

Now she knew. The ping was the sound the bus made if you pulled the cable overhead to make it stop. "You're going by bus?" Carlina couldn't stop herself from sounding incredulous. Uncle Teo hated public transport.

"Em. " Uncle Teo cleared his throat. "I really have to go now, Carlina. I'm sorry I can't help today. Some other time, all right?"

"I . . ."

He hung up before she could finish the sentence.

"Wow." Carlina shook her head. "How odd." Now that she came to think of it, Uncle Teo had seemed very busy yesterday, and there was an air of suppressed excitement about him, as if he knew a secret. She frowned. Maybe he was planning a special Christmas surprise? *Heaven forbid.*

"We could ask Annalisa to bring the cups." Ricciarda had

overheard the exchange.

"Good idea." Carlina looked at her watch. "Where is she anyway? We said she should be here by nine thirty." She punched in Annalisa's cell phone number and waited until she heard a sleepy reply. "Good morning, sunshine," she said. "This is your employer speaking. You were supposed to be at work a quarter of an hour ago."

"Gosh, Carlina, don't be so unfeeling." Annalisa spoke low, her words slurred together. "I had an awful night and simply didn't feel like getting up early."

Anger shot up like a geyser inside Carlina. "I know a perfect recipe to get over this kind of problem, Annalisa. Get your butt out of bed and start to work. There's nothing like a bit of diversion to get over your troubles."

Ricciarda gave her a startled glance.

Carlina stopped herself short. She didn't often lose her tempter like that, but her nerves felt like chewed strings.

"How dare you speak to me like that?" Annalisa's shriek came through the phone loud and clear. "After all I've been through!"

Carlina took a deep breath. "I apologize. I'm a bit stressed out myself."

"How you can be stressed out when you've no idea what I've been going through and--"

"Annalisa." Carlina concentrated on making her voice sound calm and in control. "I need your help. Right now."

"What?" Her cousin was wide awake now. "Has anything happened?"

"Not really. It's just that the whole town will walk by Temptation today to check out what I look like because a dirty newspaper featured me as the most-likely murderer of Trevor." To her horror, her voice broke.

"What?" Annalisa seemed flabbergasted.

"That's why I need the espresso cups with the Temptation logo from my apartment." Carlina hastily continued. "I plan to sell them to every sensation-hungry person who dares to show his nose in my store."

"You want to cash in on Trevor's murder?" Annalisa's voice dropped to a whisper. "How mean is that? How can you only think of money when the most wonderful man on earth is dead?"

Carlina closed her eyes. The thought of selling the espresso cups had helped her to bear the thought of getting through the day. So maybe it was callous, but her behavior wasn't worse than that of the people she expected, and if they blocked up her store, she would lose more turnover than she could ever make with the stupid cups. Didn't Annalisa get that? "Whatever you say, Annalisa." A sudden tiredness swamped her. "You do whatever it takes to make you happy. I wish you good luck." She hung up, swallowed a lump in her throat, and turned to Ricciarda. "Am I callous if I sell the cups?"

Ricciarda shrugged. "You don't force anybody to buy them. The customers make up their minds what they want. I don't see anything wrong with that."

"Thanks." Carlina took a deep breath. "You know, we still have one box of the cups in the storage room. Let's get them out and decorate them."

They had just finished placing the espresso cups in a long row in the window with a sign "Souvenir from Temptation - 5 Euros", when a car stopped in front of the store.

Annalisa and Benedetta got out and started to unload several boxes, then Benedetta drove off again. Annalisa carried the boxes into the store and gave Carlina a sheepish look. "I apologize. Mama said I was out of line. She overheard our conversation."

Carlina gave her a tentative smile. "All right. Let's not fight. The world is difficult enough as it is."

II

Garini leaned against the light-yellow stone wall of a bank and sighed while going through his notes. He had talked to a million shop assistants - or so it felt - and everywhere, he had heard the same story - Annalisa had spent fabulous sums in cash after complicated and tedious discussions what would fit best to her style and her outfit. If she had wanted to leave a red trail all over town, she could hardly have done better.

Still, it didn't take long to strangle someone inside a church. It was a matter of two minutes, maybe five. As his luck would have it, Annalisa had been in between shops at the crucial time.

Damn. He would have liked to cross her off his list of suspects-
at least it would have made his life with Carlina a lot more
relaxed.

He pushed the notes back into his leather jacket and turned
toward the Arno river. Now to another point on his list, one he
had been postponing because it seemed like a waste of time - he
still had to talk to the waiter who may have overheard Carlina's
and Annalisa's conversation the night before Trevor's murder.
Not that it would get him anywhere, but he had to prove that he
had not overlooked anything in connection with Carlina. His
boss Cervi would be only too happy if he found a chance to stick
his finger into a hole.

With an inner shrug, he walked the short distance to Gino's
restaurant, went through the door, and looked around. The air
hung heavy and stale, and the feeble winter light hardly
penetrated through the small windows. His steps echoed in the
room as he went past deserted tables and upended chairs.
"Hello?" His voice sounded hollow.

"Yes, yes, I'm coming." A rotund man with dark curls hurried
from the back and fixed him with small eyes. "We're not open."

"Are you the owner of this restaurant?"

The man frowned. "Yes. I'm Gino Benvenuto. What do you
want?"

Garini suppressed a smile. For a man whose name translated
as "Welcome", and a restaurant owner at that, the name sat like
an ill-fitting coat on this broad man's back.

Garini pulled out his identification. "I'm Stefano Garini from
the homicide department. I need to talk to the waiter who served
at the tables two nights ago."

Signor Benvenuto stiffened. "Did he get into trouble?"

"No." Garini already felt sorry for the waiter. Signor
Benvenuto didn't come across like a boss who listened before he
punished. "I just need to verify the movements of two ladies."
He took a picture from his wallet. It showed Carlina and her
cousin Emma at Emma's wedding day and had been taken last
autumn. Stefano still had it from the last investigation that
involved Carlina's family, and he had tried to pretend to himself
that he had only forgotten to take it from his wallet. At least it
came in useful now.

He showed the picture to the restaurant owner. "Do you

recognize these ladies?"

Signor Benvenuto looked at the picture and pointed a stubby finger at Carlina. "She was here." His voice was gruff. "Eyes like a cat. I remember her."

"Was she in the company of the woman next to her?"

"Nah." Benvenuto shook his curly head. "She was with a redhead."

Garini fished out another picture printed from the Internet before he came out on his quest. "This one?"

Benvenuto threw a look at Annalisa's picture and nodded. "Yep. That's her."

"Can you remember how long they stayed?"

"They came around nine. Silvio will know."

"Silvio?"

"My waiter." Benvenuto frowned and looked at his gold wrist watch. "He'll be here in five minutes. If he's not late again, that is."

I hope he won't be late. Not so much for my sake as for his. Garini nodded.

Benvenuto turned his back on him. "You can wait here. I have work to do." He disappeared into the back without offering Garini a seat.

Garini took one of the upended chairs and placed it on the wooden floor, then settled on it to wait. Mr. Benvenuto gave him a bad feeling. He wasn't cool and arrogant like the habitués of crime, nor nervous like the innocent. He was dark and deep and certainly had something somewhere that he didn't want to share with the police. Well, for the moment, he wasn't interested, unless it somehow involved Trevor Accanto.

Garini moved his toes inside his shoes. It was getting colder every day, and the chilly draft around his legs didn't make things better. If only Annalisa hadn't started that love affair, then he would have had enough time to let his fragile relationship with Carlina grow into something stronger. Now, they were on opposing sides once again. He shook his head. What rotten luck. He rubbed his hands and turned up the collar of his leather jacket.

Fifteen cold minutes later, the door flew open and a cold gust of wind blew in a disheveled, young man. He stopped in front of Garini, much like a playful Saint Bernard dog, huge, hairy, and harmless. "Buona sera, Signor." He glanced at the empty room, and his face took on a puzzled expression.

He has better manners than his boss. "Buona sera." Garini got up. "I'm Stefano Garini from the homicide department, and--"

The young man took one step back, his brown eyes wide. "Did he kill someone?"

Garini never took his gaze off the waiter. "Who do you mean?"

"Signor Benventuo! Did he?"

"Not that I know of." Garini took out the two pictures. "I'm here because I need you to confirm something."

"Me? Really?"

Again, Silvio's expression reminded Garini of a Saint Bernard dog; he could almost see his tongue hanging out in eager and friendly anticipation. "Do you recognize these women?" He showed him the picture of Emma and Carlina.

The young man took it, and an expression of ridiculous dismay crossed his face. "So she really did it?" His voice sank to a whisper. "She looked so friendly."

"What do you mean?" A cold hand grabbed Stefano's stomach.

Silvio pointed with a trembling finger at Carlina. "She said she would kill him!"

"Can you repeat the conversation?" Garini's voice was sharp.

Silvio frowned and looked into space, then shook his head. "No. It was a busy evening, you know, and I was running to and fro all the time. I just remember that I came up to her table, and that she said she would rather kill him herself. I remember because it startled me. She had seemed so friendly earlier."

Garini's mouth felt dry.

Silvio pointed at Emma. "But that one wasn't with her."

"Was it this one?" Garini showed him Annalisa's picture.

"Yes! That's her!" Silvio nodded until his brown hair fell forward and hid his eyes. "Great hair. I like red-haired women." He gave Garini a shy smile. "She was really sad, and the other," he pointed at Carlina, "was angry at her." He looked as if he could relate to being surrounded by angry people.

"Can you recall anything else?"

Silvio shrugged. "The one with red hair only had a salad, and the other had gnocchi. It was our special on Tuesday night."

"Anything else?"

"I'm afraid not." Silvio looked at Garini with wide open eyes. "I say, is it true? Did she really kill the man she was talking about?"

"No." The answer came straight from his gut, clear, unequivocal. Garini cut himself short. *You're in too deep, my boy.* He nodded in the direction of the kitchen. "Do you need me to confirm to your boss that you're not guilty of anything?"

The brown eyes looked grateful. "Oh, would you do that?"

"Sure." *I know what it means to have an unfair boss.*

An hour later, Garini stretched in his office chair by lifting both arms high above his head. He sighed and looked with a despondent feeling at the screen on his computer. How he hated the bureaucratic side of his job. All the forms to fill in; all the explanations. Writing a report was bad enough, but at least it helped to clear his head. Government forms, however, could only be considered a punishment for unknown sins in past lives. Unknown, but terrible.

His phone rang. Garini pounced on it and accepted the call with relief. Any interruption would do. "Pronto!"

"Stefano, this is Peter." His friend sounded excited. "Can you come to the Garibaldi Hotel right now?"

"Right now?" Garini glanced at his watch. It was three o'clock in the afternoon, and he had to hand in the forms by six.

"I'd rather show you than tell you on the phone," Peter said. "I think it's important."

"I'll be with you in five minutes." Garini placed the receiver back where it belonged, went to the window, and looked out. A fine rain covered the dark cobblestones on the street with a filmy mist. He grabbed his heavy leather jacket and hurried from the police station.

When he entered the spacious lobby of the Garibaldi Hotel, the shining light made him feel welcome. It smelled of cinnamon and reminded him of Christmas. He still had to buy a gift for his father and sister and maybe . . . he hesitated. He wanted to give something to Carlina, but he couldn't think of anything that would suit.

Peter came forward to meet him, an air of suppressed excitement around him. "Thank you for coming." He took

Stefano by the arm and led him to the stairs at the side of the hall. "You've got to see this to believe it."

"I'm bursting with curiosity." Garini's voice was dry.

Peter gave him a glance and grinned. "I can't say it shows. You're pretty good at hiding your feelings." He led the way to the next floor, then opened the door to the Boccaccio suite and stepped aside to let his friend pass by. "Did I tell you that Mr. Accanto always insisted on having this suite?"

"You did."

"I'd have sworn I knew every single nook in this house, but this one surprised me." He pointed at the heavy bed which now stood on the other side.

"You've rearranged the room?" Garini went forward.

"Yes. It was Anne's idea. She said it would create more distance from the murder." Peter shrugged. "Don't ask me to explain that one. Women, you know."

Garini nodded. "I understand."

"You do?" Peter looked surprised. "I thought you--" He stopped mid-sentence. "Sorry. I didn't mean to imply . . . "

Garini gave him one of his rare smiles. "You didn't. Even though I'm not married, I do occasionally deal with women, you know."

Peter narrowed his eyes. "Stefano. Don't tell me you--?"

"What?"

"You've found someone?"

Garini's smile deepened in spite of himself. "Not really."

"But maybe?"

Garini inclined his head. "Maybe." He turned back to the room. "Now tell me what happened."

"Well, when Anne had talked me around the whole thing, she said she wanted to show me what it could look like, so we came up here. She wanted to shift the bed to the position where you can see it now, so, though I didn't agree, I finally gave in and helped her to push it over."

Stefano eyed the heavy wooden bed with the lush curtains. "Looks a bit heavy for two."

"The legs are hollow," Peter said. "I knew that. What I didn't know," he bent down and pressed the inside of the leg nearest the wall, "is that there's a small door here, so you have a perfect hiding place."

Garini knelt down and eyed the bedpost with its hidden cache. "Interesting." His fingers probed the oblong opening. "So you discovered it by accident?"

"Yes." Peter nodded. "When we moved the bed, I hit my toe on the bed post. The little door opened, and a small notebook fell out." He pulled it from his jacket. It wasn't much bigger than the palm of a hand, bound in black leather, with a fragile looking elastic ribbon holding the covers together.

Garini lifted his eyebrows.

"You won't believe this," Peter said. "I know he was a Ladies Man, but I'd never have guessed THAT."

His friend accepted the notebook without a word. On the fly leaf, a decisive hand had written the name Trevor V. Accanto in black ink.

"That's his signature," Peter said. "Turn the page."

Garini obeyed. A faded picture showed a tall woman with an extraordinary face. It wasn't mere beauty; she had a certain quality, a grace and reassurance that shone from the picture as if she had suddenly entered the room in person. The man who had his arm around her shoulders, a much younger Trevor, looked at her with a smile in his eyes that didn't need any explanation. The long black hair of the woman fell to her shoulders, and from the cut of her blouse, it became clear that the picture dated back some twenty or twenty-five years. Garini looked up. "Do you know her?"

Peter shook his head. "No. But she reminds me of a picture in a children's book I once had - Snow White." He nodded at the book. "You'd better go on."

The next picture showed the same man, the same look in his eyes . . . but another woman. She had blond hair, swept up into a chignon. Her eyes laughed into the camera with a mixture of mischief and fun. "Unknown woman number two – Laughing Eyes." Garini said and turned the next page. When his gaze fell onto the third picture, he froze. "Madonna." His voice was a whisper.

Peter came closer and looked over Garini's shoulder. "This one isn't quite as good-looking as the others, I must say." He looked at his friend. "Don't tell me you've recognized her?"

"I have." Garini's voice was grim. "She's the wife of my boss. Marcella Cervi. Twenty-five years younger, twenty-five kilos lighter. Damn."

"Bad luck." Peter made a face as if he had bitten into a lemon. "Do you have to show this book to your boss?"

"At some point, I guess. But not yet." He looked at his friend. "You know, I'm almost afraid to go on. Will this gallery continue for twenty years? How many suspects will I end up with?"

"Don't worry." Peter shook his head. "Mr. Accanto didn't return to Florence for fifteen years or even more. I believe he once told me he was too busy tripling his fortune during those years."

"I wish he had continued with that admirable project." Garini turned the next page.

A stunning Japanese woman smiled at them, with features chiseled clear and sweet and eyebrows as perfect as the waning moon. The man next to her had aged without losing his attractiveness, and their warm clothes were modern. Behind them, the statue of David stood in the weak winter light.

"Do you recognize her?" Peter asked.

Garini frowned. "I've seen her before; I'm sure of that, but I can't place her."

"It's Akemi Hateyama, the famous violinist," Peter said. "I've got a CD from her at home."

"Does she live in Florence?"

Peter shook his head. "I don't think so. Her father was Italian, but I believe she now lives in Tokyo. That picture was taken five years ago, by the way. I remember her, even though she didn't sign the guest book."

"Well, at least we know two names already. That's a start." Garini turned the next page, his mind still grappling with the concept of telling his boss that his wife Marcella had been the lover of a rich American some twenty-five years ago. If he was not mistaken, they had been married longer than that. *Damn.*

His gaze alighted on the next picture. Garini froze. A sudden urge to double up in pain gripped him, as if someone had boxed him straight into the solar plexus, but he stood transfixed.

"Stefano?" Peter shot a sharp glance at the picture, then at his friend. "What's the matter?"

Garini didn't reply. He stared at the picture without blinking.

This time, the attractive American was flanked by two women. On his right, a slim and sportive looking lady with a long pony-tail had her face half turned away from the camera, but still, she exuded vitality and health like an advertisement for a fitness club. Stefano hardly noticed her. The lady on Accanto's left hand side held his gaze riveted. She smiled at him from the picture with her cat-like eyes, eyes he knew so well. Her brown curls were ruffled by the wind. *Carlina.*

Peter turned on his heels and went to the wall where a wooden panel with intricate carvings hid a cupboard. He slid the panel aside, took out a small bottle of whiskey, two glasses, and filled both. "Take this." He pressed one glass into Garini's hand.

Stefano accepted it without looking up from the picture and tossed it down. The smoky taste filled his mouth. He felt the fiery drink going down inside him, settling him somewhat. "Thanks." It sounded rough.

"Carlina Ashley, the owner of Temptation." Peter's voice was sober. "So she's the one." It wasn't a question.

Stefano blinked. "What do you mean?"

"She's the special one; the one you mentioned earlier."

Stefano gave him a contorted smile. "Does it show that much?"

"Well, for a man who never shows his emotions, that was a pretty spectacular show." Peter smiled. "I don't blame you. If I had found Anne's picture in there . . ." He shuddered. "You needn't worry, though. She doesn't fit the rule. Her hair isn't long enough."

Stefano leafed back. Peter was right. All the other ladies had long and luxurious hair, way beyond shoulder-length, quite unlike Carlina's bouncy curls. His heart lightened, but aloud, he said, "She told me he was very charming."

"He was." Peter's voice was dry. "That doesn't mean she slept with him."

"No." Stefano took a deep breath. "Why didn't you think it was the other, that sporting goddess?"

"When you gripped the book harder, your thumb covered half her face, but you didn't seem to notice."

"You know, if old Garibaldi should ever kick you from the management of this hotel, come to me. I can use you on the force."

Peter grinned. "Will do."

Garini shook his head to clear it and turned back to the

notebook. "After this shock, things can't get much worse." He turned the next page and gasped. "Oh, no. Madonna, no."

"What?" Peter looked over his shoulder. "Who is it? Do you know her?"

"Indeed I do." Garini's voice sounded grimmer than ever. "It's Emma, Carlina's cousin. She married an extremely jealous man some months ago."

"If it doesn't have any bearing on the case, you don't need to tell him."

"You don't know that family." Garini still stared at Emma, who gave him a tantalizing smile from the crook of Accanto's arm. "Carlina is so protective of them, it's ridiculous. And the whole town is littered with Mantonis, so I'm bound to fall over them whenever I'm on a case."

"Makes me feel glad Anne doesn't have any family left."

"It has its advantages," Garini pushed a hand through his hair. "Now only her mother is missing to make this charade complete."

"Is the mother gorgeous, too?"

"The mother is unusual, to put it in a kind way. To put it in a blunt way, she's completely batty."

"Oh." Peter gave him a glance that spoke volumes.

With a feeling of dread, Stefano turned the next page, but this time, the woman looking back at him was a stranger. Relief flooded him. She reminded him of the Mona Lisa, with her sad eyes and a little smile that didn't give much away. "Know this one?" he asked.

"Not her name," Peter shook his head "though I do recall her face. Very quiet, she was. He usually liked more exuberant women; I remember thinking so at the time."

"Did you ever talk to her?"

"No." Peter shook his head. "We could ask some of our staff if they remember her, but I shouldn't think so." He shrugged. "We have so many people coming and going and as I said, she was so quiet that she didn't leave much of an impression unless you took the time to look at her, then you noticed her beauty."

"I see." Garini turned the last page and looked at a woman with glossy brown hair.

"This is the Frenchwoman," Peter said. "I told you about her. Suzanne something from Paris. She made a scene. I've never seen anything like it." He shook his head. "It was dreadful."

"If you should happen to find her address or anything else about her, get in touch immediately."

"I will." Peter straightened and crossed his arms in front of his chest. "That's it. The other pages are all empty."

"Thank God." Garini sighed. "It has almost given me a heart-attack as it is." He leafed through the empty pages. "No doubt Annalisa would have been the next in this unusual gallery."

"Annalisa?"

"The gorgeous redhead Mr. Accanto frequented this year. Another of Carlina's cousins."

"Ugh." Peter grimaced. "Bad luck." Then he gave his friend a glance and hesitated.

Garini frowned. "What?"

"I just wondered . . ."

"Well?"

"Will you show this book to Carlina Ashley?"

Garini took a deep breath. "Yes, I will. She knew him and might recognize some of the women for me. Besides, she can help me tackle Emma."

"Won't she object to do that?"

"You don't know her." Stefano looked at his friend. "She'll insist on holding her hand, making me feel like a damn inquisitor."

Chapter 10

"Ciao." Carlina's voice came softly through the phone, almost drowned by the sound of voices in the background.

"It's me, Stefano." Why did he have such a ridiculous feeling of happiness every time he talked to her? He cleared his throat. "Where are you? It sounds as if you're surrounded by a bus-load of people."

"I am, actually." Carlina chuckled. "Piedro has done me a good turn after all, though it didn't look like it this morning. People are almost trampling each other to death here, and I'm the queen of espresso cups today."

"Espresso cups?"

"Yeah. They have the Temptation logo, and though I had planned them to be a gift, I spontaneously decided to sell them this morning."

He grinned. "Good for you."

"Piedro is standing in front of the door, as you instructed," she continued. "I've told him to take a break at lunch-time, which he accepted, but he's back now."

"Good." He clenched his teeth. Piedro's indiscreet behavior had jeopardized her. He would not forgive this for a long time.

The babble of voices in the background seemed to swell. "Listen, I have to go. It's a bit crazy here."

"I have to talk to you in connection with the case, Carlina. Can we meet somewhere without your family interrupting?" He heard her swallow and held his breath. Would she clam up and refuse to see him?

"Sure," she said. "When?"

Relief flooded him. "Tonight, if you can make it?"

"I can."

He loved that about her. She didn't play hard to get. She either had time or she hadn't. As simple as that. "Thank you." He hoped she would hear the sincerity in his voice.

"Should I come to your office?" she asked. "It's about the only place in the world where I don't expect a family member to crop up without prior notice."

The idea of asking her into his dusty office filled him with dismay. He didn't want to alienate her altogether. "It's not an attractive place." His voice was rueful.

She laughed. "You're right."

Hearing her laugh made him feel better.

"I remember one very uncomfortable session," she added.

"So do I." Garini smiled. "There's one other place where your family doesn't go. Would you be willing to have dinner with me at my place?" He stopped himself short. He had not planned to say this, but now the words were out, and he could not take them back. Didn't want to, but still, he wasn't used to hearing himself say unexpected stuff.

"I didn't know you can cook." She sounded surprised.

"I can't." He suppressed a feeling of panic. "It'll be only omelet."

"I like only omelet."

He heard the smile in her voice, and something inside him skipped. "At eight thirty?"

"I'll be there. Do I need to bring anything?"

"Nothing but yourself."

He hurried home via the small supermarket around the corner, bought eggs and herbs, fresh bread, and a bottle of wine. Then he tidied the apartment, laid the table, and opened the bottle of Chianti. He felt a thrill of excitement and happiness humming inside him. "You're a fool, Stefano," he said to himself. "By the time she'll have seen the picture of Emma, she'll be ready to kick you around the place." But when he opened the door to her, her cat-like eyes smiled at him as if they had never been at odds. He cleared his throat. "Come in."

Carlina looked around the small kitchen, remembering the last time she'd been here. It hadn't changed. The small table at the side was set for two. No candles, no napkins. The whole setting was practical, reduced to the basic needs, without any unnecessary frills or adornments. Just like Garini, in fact. She stole a look at him. His light eyes that never seemed to miss anything were concentrated on getting her a drink. In the beginning, she had felt intimidated by him. Now, it was different. She knew and accepted his unemotional facade and the way he pounced on things like a tiger. But somehow, she wasn't on the opposing side anymore. Without noticing it, she had slipped right next to him, in spite of the facts, which, again, put them at odds. How strange.

He filled two heavy glasses with Chianti and passed her one.

"Grazie." Carlina inhaled the fragrance of the rich wine. "Hmm."

He lifted his glass and looked into her eyes.

She couldn't read his gaze. Was it tenderness? Regret? Her heart gave a nervous flutter.

"I'm not sure what we should drink to," he said.

"That we'll soon find the murderer?" She used the word "we" on purpose, and by the way his lips twitched, she knew he had noticed.

"That, and that we'll still be friends afterwards."

Carlina swallowed. That didn't sound good. What on earth had he discovered? She took a small sip. "It's a nice wine," she said.

"I haven't forgotten that you were once engaged to a man who owned a famous vineyard."

"Oh." She had forgotten it. "That should have put me off the wine, but fortunately, it didn't."

"Carlina." He leaned against the stove and looked at the glass of wine in his hand, turning it in circles. "Do you think we could have dinner together without talking about the murder case?"

"Of course." The clenched muscles in her stomach relaxed. The confrontation would not come right away. First, the thin ribbon of friendship that linked them had a chance to become stronger. She was all for it.

"Thank you." He placed his glass on the table and took some eggs from the fridge. "Can you crack the eggs for our omelet?"

"Yep. I'm great at breaking things." She took the eggs from him.

Their hands touched, and for a fleeting moment, their gaze locked.

Carlina could feel her face going hot and turned away with a quick move.

As they prepared dinner, Carlina told him her lazy vacation by the beach last November and the day tours she had taken. She did not tell him how often she had thought of him.

He described the beauty of the snowy Alps and how much he liked to go skiing. He said that he liked to see his sister for five days a year, but never more, as they would then inevitably start to fight. His sister would stay with her in-laws in Switzerland over Christmas. He did not mention having felt lonely, but he asked her how she planned to spend Christmas.

Carlina explained that in her family, it was the custom to give each other self-made gifts only. Her aunt Benedetta had found an easy way out by producing the most delicious chocolate truffles in different variations every year. Emma made tiny balls of soap with rose leaves and other herbs. Her mother usually crocheted something dreadful, like covers for toilet rolls. "The best idea is Uncle Teo's." Carlina grinned. "He learned years ago how to fold five-Euro-bills into tiny frogs that jump if you press your finger onto one end. It's a sort of Origami technique, I believe. So we all get frogs for Christmas."

"You're kidding."

"Nope."

He shook his head. "And what do you do?"

"It throws me into a panic every year," Carlina said. "But for once, I'm well prepared. I've designed a collection of lace underwear in collaboration with the Florentine company Bartosti, and my first collection will be sold at the Florence Christmas Fair." She tried not to sound too proud. "So all the female members of the family will get new underwear this year. Even if I didn't make the lace myself, I figured it would still qualify as self-made, as it's my own collection."

He nodded. "What about Uncle Teo and Ernesto?"

Carlina grinned. "No lacy underwear for the men. Instead, I visited a wine cave this summer where you can fill the bottles yourself. I figured that would qualify as self-made."

"That sounds much better than crocheting."

"Doesn't it?" Carlina grinned. "Though now that I come to think of it, it's possible that my mother is doing something different this year. I've not seen her crocheting at all."

"Is that a good sign?" Garini asked.

"I don't think so." Carlina frowned. "At least, with

crocheting, we know what's going to happen, and we can bury the result somewhere."

The omelet was a success. Light and fluffy, with oregano and "Herbes de Provence" and a bit of milk, it tasted like a happy summer day. The fresh bread was soft and sweet and had a thick crust. They dipped it into salted olive oil.

"There's something immensely satisfying about good bread, isn't there?" Carlina inhaled the fresh fragrance of the bread. "It makes me happy."

He gave her one of his rare smiles. "Cut yourself another slice."

"Thanks." Carlina savored another slice, then leaned back and stretched. "This was lovely, thank you so much."

"It's nothing compared to your aunt Benedetta's cooking."

"It was simple and good. Just my kind of food." She smiled at him.

"Thanks. "Stefano got up. "Would you like a cup of coffee?"

"Very much so."

He went to the cupboard and took out a jar. As he spooned ground coffee into the battered filter of the coffee machine, he said, "I tried to get out of this case."

Her happiness fell away like a warm coat sliding from her shoulders. "Yes?"

"My boss didn't want to hear of it. He ordered me to continue."

Phew. She made sure her relief didn't show, as she didn't want to alienate him again. "I see."

"Today, I have received a piece of evidence that pulled the case wide open. I have half a dozen new suspects."

Good. Then you won't focus on Annalisa. Carlina didn't voice her thoughts but concentrated instead on composing her face into an impassive mask.

He gave her an enigmatic glance. "And no, that doesn't mean I'll forget all about Annalisa."

"Damn!" Carlina jumped up. "I thought I'd made sure my thoughts don't show."

His mouth twitched.

He was laughing at her! She crossed her arms in front of her chest. "It's unfair. You can read my every thought."

Stefano switched on the coffee machine and turned to her.

"It's fate." His smile faded. "Carlina."

"Yes?"

"Before we talk about the case, I want you to understand three things."

Her own smile fled. "Yes?"

His light eyes focused on her with the intensity of a sunbeam. "First, I do not for one second believe that you killed Trevor Accanto."

"Good." She swallowed. "I didn't, by the way."

"Second, I can't say the same thing about the rest of your family."

"But--"

He held up his hand. "Third, if I want to investigate this case in the correct manner, then I have to keep an open mind on everything and everybody. This includes everything, even evidence that points your way."

"I understand." Her voice sounded flat. "I'm a suspect."

"Yes." It sounded tired. "But you're also--" he hesitated.

"Yes?"

"You're also . . . you." He took a deep breath. "Anyway, as I told you, a new bit of evidence has come up, and I've decided to show it to you, to discuss possibilities."

Carlina narrowed her eyes. "Why are you doing that?"

"Because you might be able to help me."

She nodded. "All right. What do you want me to do?"

"I want you to look at some pictures and tell me if you recognize these women." He left the kitchen and came back a minute later with a black notebook in the palm of his hand. "Be careful. It's the original. I made a copy, but the colors don't show well, that's why I brought it."

Carlina accepted the book, sank back onto her chair, and opened it with care.

He pulled up his chair and settled next to her, his body turned so he could see both her and the book at one glance.

She could feel his presence beside her, could even get a whiff of that typical Garini smell, a mixture of leather and soap. *I won't be able to concentrate.* She focused on the book and leafed through the first two pages. "What is this?"

"It's a gallery of Trevor Accanto's conquests."

Her chin dropped. "You're kidding." She shook her head and

looked at the book with her nose wrinkled in disgust. "How . . . demeaning."

"Care to explain?" His gaze never left her face.

"I knew he had a different lover every year, but I liked him nevertheless. However, to imagine that he put them up in a gallery like some sort of weird hunting trophy . . . that's," she shrugged. "I don't know, sick, somehow."

"I agree."

Carlina turned back to the book which now lay closed in her hand. "And you say you know some of these women?"

"Yes." His voice was sober. "And so do you."

Their gaze met.

"Shocking?" she asked.

"I'm afraid so."

Carlina took a deep breath. "All right." She opened the book by touching it with her thumb and her index finger only, as if it contained some highly infectious bacteria.

"So that's the first one." Carlina studied the picture. "It was taken quite some time ago, wasn't it?"

"Twenty to twenty-five years ago, I'd say."

"Hmm." Carlina stared at the woman. "What amazing black hair. I have a feeling I've seen her before, but very faint, as if I'd known her superficially. But I can't place her." She looked up. "Do you know her?"

"No. I've dubbed her Snow White." He shrugged. "I have to keep them all apart somehow."

She nodded. "I see. It fits." She turned to the next page. "Wow. She has amazing eyes."

"I call her Laughing Eyes."

"Sounds quite fanciful." She grinned. "I'd have expected you to give them numbers."

Garini's mouth twisted. "Numbers don't conjure up pictures in your mind. I need to place them quickly."

She nodded and looked at the picture again, then wrinkled her forehead in thought. "I have the same feeling with her. Somehow, she seems familiar." She looked up. "Do you think it's wishful thinking?"

"I think it's quite natural. You've lived all your life in Florence, and you've probably seen most of the female population in your store at some point or other."

She smiled. "That's true. But I haven't lived all my life in Florence. We only came back from the US when I was thirteen."

"I know." He sounded unperturbed.

He remembers everything. Carlina returned to the little book and studied the next picture. Then she looked up. "It's not wishful thinking. This one, here," she pointed at the picture, "I don't know her at all."

"I do." Garini's mouth tightened. "She's likely to cost me my job."

"What? Why?" She stared at him.

"She's the wife of my boss."

Carlina covered her mouth with one hand, her eyes wide. "Oh, no. Does he know?"

"Not yet." Garini looked grim. "I'll tell him as late as possible. I've even been tempted to remove the picture." He shrugged. "My assistant Piedro, the one who stood watch at your door all day long. He's Cervi's son."

"Ugh."

"Exactly." Garini's voice was dry. "I've left the copy at the office, but I locked it into the safe."

"Good." Carlina turned the next page.

"We're now jumping ahead a few years," Garini said. "This one was taken only five years ago."

"I know her." Carlina nodded. "She's a famous musician. A violinist, isn't she?"

"Yes. Her name is Akemi Hateyama. I've already asked Piedro to find out where she was at the time of the murder. If we're lucky, she spent the whole day with friends in Tokyo, so we can cross her off the list."

Carlina turned the next page and gasped. "Ileana! I'd forgotten her."

"Ileana?"

"Yes, Ileana Marani. We went to school together. She always was a stunner." Carlina frowned as she looked at the picture. "You know, I resent being in there, among all those other women. It makes me feel . . . dirty." She frowned. "I guess he couldn't get any other picture with her. She hates cameras, always turned away. I believe I still have a class picture of our graduation where she only shows her back." She shook her head. "I can't even recall when this picture was taken."

He didn't reply.

She looked up and found his gaze on her with an expression she couldn't read. "What?"

He took her hand and lifted it to his lips. "Thank you."

Her throat turned dry, and her heart-beat accelerated. She could feel the warmth of his fingers around hers, and it stirred something deep inside her. "What for?" It sounded like a croak.

"For reacting as you did." He released her hand.

The warm feeling didn't go away. "Oh." *I want you to touch me.* The thought darted through her brain and left her breathless.

"Does Ileana still live in Florence?" He focused on the task at hand as if he kissed hands all the time. His face showed no emotion.

"Oh, no." Carlina shook her head and forced other thoughts away. "She moved to Rome several years ago."

"Does she sometimes return, for Christmas, to see her family?"

Carlina shrugged. "I don't know. I've never seen her."

"I'll find out. Now that I have her name, it'll be easy." He pulled out a small notebook and wrote down Ileana's name. "Can you tell me something else about her?"

"She was great at sports," Carlina said. "Clever, too. We all thought she would go very far." She smiled. "I think she has, actually. She now works for the government, if I'm not mistaken."

"Great." Garini frowned, his voice dry.

"Why does that sound so ironic?"

"Government means politics, and dealing with them is a bit like holding a firecracker in your hand. It's likely to jump into your face."

Carlina nodded and turned the next page. Her hand stilled in mid-movement. Her breath caught. For an instant, nothing but the sound of the fridge humming in the quiet kitchen filled the room, then she found her voice. "I don't believe for one second that this is Emma." She lifted the book to study the picture in every detail."It must be a fake!"

He didn't say anything.

"Don't tell me it's true!" Carlina stared at Garini. "It can't be Emma! I don't believe this!" She looked up and stared at him with wide eyes.

His face turned more wooden than usual.

She swallowed and took a deep breath. "So it IS her."

"I'm afraid so."

Carlina shook her head. "When was this taken? She wasn't two-timing Lucio, was she? He's so jealous; he'll throw a fit."

"We know he had the Japanese girl-friend exactly five years ago, and it looks as if the album continues with one picture per year. If that is the right assumption, it was exactly three years ago."

"Three years ago." Carlina did a quick calculation in her head. "I believe she wasn't going out with Lucio then . . . " she frowned. "I'm not sure, though. I can't recall when she started to date him; I'll have to ask her." She turned on him with wide eyes. "Don't tell Lucio anything. Promise me that."

He held her gaze. "I can't promise anything."

She could feel her face going red with anger. "But don't you see that this might destroy her marriage? She was only married some months ago!"

"I'll not talk to Lucio if I can avoid it. But I need to talk to her."

"Of course!" She shot him a quick glance. "Stefano . . . can I be with you?"

He made a strangled sound in his throat. "I knew you would ask that."

"Well, of course!" She squared her shoulders. "Emma will need me."

"If you promise to stay in the background and not to answer for her or to influence what she says, then you can stay. But no hidden messages. Is that clear?" His face looked stern.

"Perfectly clear, Commissario." She said it in an exaggerated way, as if making fun of him, but she meant it. He could still be rather frightening if he looked like that.

"Why don't you ask her to come to Temptation tomorrow?" Stefano said. "We could go to the café across the street. It shouldn't take more than half an hour."

"All right." Carlina nodded. "I can ask her to have lunch with me."

"But remember, not a word about this."

Carlina swallowed. "I feel like I'm trapping her."

"You're not. I can also accompany you home right now and

ask Emma to talk to me right away."

"Madonna, no! Lucio will have a fit if he ever learns about this." She made a weak move with her hand toward the notebook.

"So you'll arrange the meeting and won't say a word?"

She took a deep breath. "I will."

He bent forward. "I'm not sure if you're aware that this is absolutely irregular. I have no guarantee that you won't go and tell Emma everything. Then you have the whole night to concoct a perfect alibi."

"I gave you my word." Her voice was small.

His light eyes fixed hers. "That's why I'm going along with this crazy scheme."

Their eyes met. She could hear herself breathe, could hear her jeans rustling as she made a small move. He trusted her. She had a feeling he didn't do that very often.

He nodded at the notebook. "Continue, please."

She turned the next page. When she glanced at the face of the woman in the picture, instant recognition pulsed through her. She jumped up. "I know her!"

He gave her a sharp glance. "You do?"

"Yes! Yes!" Carlina's voice was high and loud. "She's the one. She killed Trevor! I'm sure of it!" The case was solved. Relief made her feel light and happy.

He reached out his hand and pulled her back onto her chair. "Calm down. Why on earth do you think she's the murderer?"

Carlina turned to him, her cheeks hot. "Because she's the unknown woman who bought the pair of tights this morning! The one who paid cash."

His eyes narrowed. "Are you sure?"

"Positive." She beamed at him. "Isn't it perfect? We have it all! A motive - she was Trevor's lover. The weapon - she bought the nylons a few hours before. The place - she was on the spot. Temptation is just around the corner from the Basilica."

He shook his head. "It sounds a bit too perfect to be true."

"Hey, this is no mystery book!" Carlina grinned. "I think it's great. Now you can stop suspecting my family."

Stefano frowned. "If we find her - and that's a big if, mind you - then it's still possible that she has an unbreakable alibi for the time of the murder."

Carlina waved the unbreakable alibi away. "It'll be fake, and we'll crack it."

"Yeah, sure." He looked at her picture. "I have to find out her name."

"What is your nickname for this one?"

"Mona Lisa."

"Right." Carlina nodded. "Mona Lisa did it."

"I admit everything points in her direction, but I can't drop all the other leads, Carlina."

"Oh, I know." Her good mood didn't abate. "But it'll be routine more than anything else."

"Hmm." He looked back at the book. "There's one last picture you haven't seen."

Carlina turned the page.

"Do you know her?"

Carlina shook her head. "No."

"She's French, from Paris, and her first name is Suzanne."

"I remember that Trevor talked about her last year." Carlina looked at the picture again. "But I never met her."

"Did he say anything that might give us a clue about her last name?"

"No. He only said general things, that she had light-brown hair and clear skin. I remember that."

"She seems to be the only one who couldn't cope with being dropped. She returned to Florence last January."

Carlina frowned. "What did she do?"

"She went to the management of the Garibaldi Hotel and made a scene, trying to get his address, but of course they didn't disclose it."

"Wow." She made a face. "I have to say it's a bit much to change your lover every year and to return to the same hotel. Trevor made himself a sitting target."

"It worked for a long time." His voice was dry.

"Yes. Maybe the women felt too embarrassed to come back. Or maybe they knew it was hopeless?"

Stefano shrugged. "I still find the whole concept hard to believe. He must have been very full of himself."

She put her head to the side, considering. "Yes, he was conceited. But he got away with it because of his charm."

"Annalisa would not have accepted it."

Carlina shuddered. "Oh, no. It would have been dreadful."

"How is she coping now?"

Carlina looked at him. Was this a private question or did it belong to the investigation? She decided it didn't matter. She would say what she thought. "She's very upset. I think it helps her to work at the store."

Stefano reared back. "She does WHAT?"

Carlina lifted her eyebrows. "She helps at the store. The Christmas season is one thing, being featured in the newspaper is another. They almost trampled us to death today." She grinned. "At least most of them felt they had to buy something, even if it was only an espresso cup."

Stefano got up, put his hands into the pockets of his jeans and took a swift turn around the kitchen. "I don't like it."

She stiffened. "What do you mean?"

He turned and looked at her. "Annalisa is one of the top suspects. She had a motive; she had a pair of the unbreakable nylons; they have disappeared without a trace, and she has no alibi for the relevant time. I don't like her being close to you all day long. I don't trust her."

"She had no motive at all!" Carlina jumped to her feet. "I keep telling you, she wanted him alive! She wanted to marry Trevor."

He didn't budge. "What if they met, Annalisa proposed to him, and he said in unmistakable terms that he would never consider marrying her?"

Carlina rolled her eyes. "Then she would have pouted and would have made a plan to seduce him into changing his mind. She would not have strangled him!"

"Still." Stefano shook his head. "I don't like it. She's the most self-centered person I've ever met."

Carlina crossed her arms in front of her chest. "I do not need to be protected from my family, Stefano!"

He pressed his lips together. "Fine."

Carlina grabbed her handbag and pointed at the little book on the table. "I really don't know why you harp on about Annalisa. The suspects in there should keep you busy for weeks. Start with Mona Lisa." She went to the door. "I have to go."

He followed her. "Carlina."

"What?" When he said her name like that, her knees turned

soft like Tiramisu. He stood right beside her, so close, she could get a whiff of his scent. *How can I feel so attracted to him even while he makes me angry?*

"Be careful."

"I always am."

He stood in the small entry hall of his apartment long after she had hurried down the stairs. *I shouldn't have said that.* He shrugged and returned to the kitchen. *It's not like me to treat her so wrong - I should have known that any reference to her family would raise her hackles.* But to keep Annalisa at Temptation all day long, and to say at the same time that she was always careful! He shook his head. Carlina was never careful. She took sudden notions into her head and stuck to them, no matter what facts came up.

With a grim mouth, he picked up the book. *I'll make a list. It'll help me to clear my head.* He sat down at the table, took a sheet of paper and started to write. Then he rearranged the lines so that he first listed the women with access to the unbreakable nylons. If only that one pair of nylons hadn't been stolen. Theoretically, every single suspect could have been the thief. Well, maybe not. The morning of Trevor's murder had been quiet, and Carlina would have recognized the face if that person had been inside the store, even if the theft had not been discovered. He hesitated, then decided that Carlina might not have recognized the older pictures, but would definitely have recognized the women of the last five years, so it was safe to cross them out.

Unless several people had worked together. He shook his head, dismayed by the wide range of possibilities that thought conjured up. For the beginning, he would start with the assumption that the murder had been done by one person only, and that it had been unplanned. If that didn't bring any results, he could still rearrange the facts later.

When he leaned back half an hour later, he felt better, even though he winced every time he looked at the first name. He had put it there on purpose, to prove to himself how open-minded he was, but his fingers itched to cross it out with a big stroke.

Suspect / Access to Nylons / unclear Alibi

Carlina Ashley / YES / YES

Annalisa Santorini / YES / YES
Ricciarda Fazzolari / YES / NO
Emma Trentini / YES / ?
"Mona Lisa" / YES / ?
X (the thief who had stolen a pair of nylons) / YES / ?
Leopold Morin / NO / YES
Gertrude Asseli / NO / YES
"Snow White" / NO / ?
"Laughing Eyes" / NO / ?
Marcella Cervi / NO / ?
Akemi Hateyama / NO / ?
Ileana Marani / NO / ?
Suzanne X / NO / ?

For Carlina, the case was already solved. She knew how many people had access to the nylons, and of the six possibilities, four belonged to her family. He knew her well enough to count Ricciarda as family though technically, she was only her employee - but that didn't stop Carline's fierce loyalty. That left him with Mona Lisa and X. *Just great.*

He stretched and got up. Tomorrow, he would arrange for Mona Lisa's photo to appear in all newspapers. Then he would interview Emma. He also had to show the pictures to Ricciarda, to confirm Carlina's statement. As to X, he could only hope for luck.

Garini opened his laptop and wrote an e-mail to Piedro, telling him to find out the whereabouts of Akemi Hateyama and Ileana Marani on December 18. For Piedro's mother, Marcella Cervi, he had to find a different solution. He shuddered as he considered the possible implications. He had to tread with care.

Chapter 11

Her honey-colored hair had been swept up into a chignon. Her cheeks were red from the biting wind outside, and her dark eyes looked . . . crazy. Carlina's subconscious noted these facts even before she noted the small gun in the lady's hand.

Disjointed thoughts zigzagged through her brain. Ricciarda had just left Temptation to buy new window cleaning spray and disinfectant. She would not be back for another twenty minutes. Her phone was inside her handbag, out of reach behind the counter. Stefano was nowhere close.

"Close the door by key." The tall lady made a move with her gun. She spoke with a French accent.

Something hot coursed through Carlina. She knew this lady. She had seen her picture. It was Suzanne, Trevor's lover of last year. The one who had made a scene at the Garibaldi Hotel. Her mouth went dry, and her knees started to feel like mush.

"Hurry."

Carlina cleared her throat. "The key is in my handbag."

Suzanne came a step closer. "Get it. I am right beside you. I will watch while you take out the keys, and if you make one false move, I will shoot you. Is that clear?"

"Perfectly clear." Carlina's voice came out as a croak. She went behind the counter, moving with deliberation and care to avoid a hasty reaction by Suzanne. Her fingers touched the smooth surface of the cell phone as she felt for her keys, but she didn't dare to press a button.

Suzanne was right beside her, looking over her shoulder. She smelled of perfume and something else, something that made Carlina's pulse jump up another notch in fear. Suzanne was sweating.

"Hurry." Her voice was low and threatening.

Carlina pulled out the key, went to the door, and locked it.

Then she turned around. "Done."

"Good." Suzanne made another move with her gun. "Now we go to the back, where no one can see us."

A sickening feeling swept over Carlina. "The storage room is in the back."

"Lead the way."

If only she would stop waving that gun about. What if it went off? Suzanne seemed a bit too nervous to be in control. Carlina inched past her and swept the curtain aside. The motion detector clicked on several bright spotlights in the ceiling. The familiar smell of dust and new clothes welcomed her. Her sanctuary. Her business. Invaded by a crazy woman. Madonna. She cleared her throat again. "There's not much room in here."

"Never mind." Suzanne closed the curtain behind them without taking her gaze off Carlina. "Now talk."

"What?"

"Talk to me about Trevor. The newspaper says you saw him last."

"I didn't."

"Don't lie to me." The gun made an erratic move. "Tell me!"

Humor her! Carlina forced herself to sound calm. "He came early in the morning, around nine o'clock."

Again, the gun waved, and the large eyes narrowed in suspicion. "You're lying. The shop doesn't open until ten."

Carlina's cell phone started to ring.

"Ignore that and answer my question."

Carlina pulled herself together with an effort. "We opened early because of a special promotion. He had planned to go running."

Something twisted in Suzanna's face. "Go on."

"He stopped by and bought a few things."

Suzanne bent forward. The mouth of the gun hovered an inch before Carlina's stomach.

Sweat ran down between Carlina's shoulder blades. She clenched her teeth.

"Was she with him?"

"Who?"

"The current lover." Hate flamed out of Suzanne's eyes.

"No." It came out as a croak.

"Who is she?"

"I don't know." Carlina didn't hesitate but she could feel her face going hot.

"Don't lie to me!" Suzanne's face contorted. "She killed him. I know that. She will pay for it."

"The police are still investigating." Carlina tried to make her voice firm. "They will find the murderer."

"The police are useless." Suzanne lifted the gun and pressed the nozzle against Carlina's chest.

Carlina inched back until she could feel the wooden edges of the shelf pressing against her shoulders.

"I know you are related to her."

A drop of sweat rolled down Carlina's brow. "Related to whom?"

"The current lover."

Carlina opened her mouth and closed it again. She was a rotten liar. *Distract her! Attack is the best form of defense.* "The police are looking for you." She heard herself say.

Suzanne froze. "For me?"

"Yes. They know you made a scene at the Garibaldi Hotel a year ago. You left your address. If I was you, I would get the hell out of here." She balled her fists. Would Suzanne believe her?

Suzanne stared at her. "You mean I'm a suspect? They think I killed Trevor?"

"Yes." Carlina held her gaze.

Suzanne collapsed in laughter.

Carlina stared at her in dismay.

The gun now pointed at her feet. Suzanne doubled over, her voice rising in hysterical gusts of laughter - or was it sobs?

Quick like a flash, Carlina folded her hands as if in prayer, raised them and brought them with a thud down on Susanne's hand.

The gun fell with a crash to the floor and slithered toward the curtain.

Suzanne shrieked something in French.

Carlina threw herself with her full length on the floor and grabbed the gun.

Suzanne landed on top of her.

The breath rushed out of Carlina's body. It felt as if every bone had been broken by the impact. "Get off!"

Suzanne grabbed her hair with both hands and pulled at it.

Carlina gasped in pain, but she didn't let go of the gun. Instead, she tried to twist around, so she could train the pistol onto Suzanne, but now Suzanne grabbed her hands, still pinning her down with her weight. Her long fingernails left marks on Carlina's hands. "Give me the gun!"

Someone pounded on the glass door of Temptation.

Suzanne flinched. For the fraction of a second, she loosened her grip.

Carlina bucked like a horse and pulled the gun underneath her.

Suzanne slid aside.

The pounding on the door became louder. "Open up!"

Carlina twisted aside, ducked away and rose to her knees in one fluid move. Her foot got entangled in the curtain, but she kicked herself free and trained a wobbling hand on Suzanne. The gun glistened in the spotlights. It felt slippery in her sweaty hands, and her breath came out in harsh gusts. "Don't move."

Suzanne stared at her, her chest heaving. "It's not loaded."

Carlina's throat turned dry. She took a step back until the curtain stretched around her, then slid aside. She was now standing outside the tiny storage area. "Don't move," she repeated.

Suzanne jumped to her feet and lurched forward. "Stop me, if you dare."

Carlina held the gun in the general direction of Susanne's legs and pulled the trigger, her face distorted by fear.

A deafening sound filled the little store room. The glass door and all the windows rattled. Dust billowed up, and the lower end of a shelf collapsed.

Suzanne fell to the floor, clutching her leg. Something red squirted out between her fingers. "You shot me! How dare you!"

The floor seemed to move below Carlina's feet. She stared at the blood, a pounding in her ears.

The front door of Temptation burst open.

Carlina looked over her shoulder.

Garini, Ricciarda, the waiter from across the street, and Carlina's mother rushed in.

Carlina's eyes focused on Stefano. "I shot her," she said. Little bright shooting stars curved through her vision, and she had the odd feeling that the light was dimming. She felt dizzy.

Stefano gave her one look, then knelt by the prostrate woman at his feet. He fished out a pair of handcuffs and clicked them on with surprising speed.

"What do you think you're doing?" Suzanne tried to pull away her hands, but it was too late. "It wasn't me! She shot me!" She clenched her hands and made a move with her head at Carlina. "Don't you see the gun? I'm the victim here! I demand to see a lawyer! Now!"

"I knew it." The stars on Fabbiola's wide skirt glistened as she glided toward them, the cushion as always firmly tucked underneath her arm. "The stars were telling me so. A shooting, and danger." She looked around her, a puzzled frown on her face. "But where are the children?"

Carlina blinked.

Fabbiola wiped the children away. "Anyway, I am here, my child. I will protect you."

She grabbed the cushion with one hand so it wouldn't fall to the floor, then opened her arms wide as if to enfold Carlina into a bear's hug, but somehow, Garini managed to come between them. "Let me take that gun first." He held out his hand.

Carlina handed it over, feeling too stunned to say anything.

His light eyes scanned her face. "That's a new shade of green," he said.

Carlina managed a wobbly smile. "Do you like it?"

"I prefer the other one." His voice was ironic.

She wasn't fooled. She had seen the concern deep below the surface. The ground beneath her stopped shaking. "Will you arrest me?"

"Arrest you?" Fabbiola's voice filled the little store with indignation. "Have you gone out of your mind? He has to deal with me first! No one is going to arrest my child while I am beside her. No one, I say!" She placed her hands akimbo on her hips and pushed a belligerent face toward Garini.

"As it happens, I don't plan to arrest anyone just now, Mrs. Mantoni-Ashley." Garini took out his cell phone and punched in a quick number. "I'll call the doctor for this lady first, and then we'll document what happened."

"If you don't wish to arrest me, then take off the manacles!" Suzanne gave him a dark look. "You have no right to withhold me. No right at all."

He gave her a reassuring nod, turned his back on her, and started to talk into his phone.

Ricciarda stood on the edge of the scene, her face white. "Are you all right, Carlina?"

"Yes." Carlina swallowed. "How did you manage to find help so quickly?"

Ricciarda took a deep breath. "When I came back and found the door closed, I knew something odd was going on. Then I saw the curtain of the storeroom move. I . . . I don't know why, but it scared me." She took a deep breath. "I ran to get Enrique's advice, and we called the police. Signor Garini came only two minutes later." She sounded impressed.

"And I," Fabbiola drew herself up and squeezed the cushion she held between her hands. "I knew you were in danger. The cards told me, and I knew I had to come."

"Thank you, Mama." Carlina also smiled at Ricciarda and Enrique. "Thank you very much for acting without hesitating. How did you manage to get through the door?"

"The Commissario did it. He had a special tool."

"I can't believe you're talking about doors," Suzanne still held her leg though it had stopped bleeding. "I am the one who got shot here, but you put ME in manacles and discuss doors. You're not normal."

Carlina looked at her. The crazy gaze had gone. A petulant woman was left, a woman of great beauty but ravaged by emotions. "Why did you come?" she asked.

"I wanted to know about Trevor." She started to sob. "I can't believe he's dead. He was so full of life."

Carlina's face softened. She took out a tissue and passed it to Suzanne.

Garini turned around and assessed the situation with one glance. "The doctor will be here in a few minutes." He took out a tape recorder. "I'd like to tape your statement."

Suzanne shook her head. "I won't say anything. I want a lawyer."

Garini didn't hesitate. "I'll arrange one for you." He made a short call, then turned to Carlina. "Can you tell me what happened?"

She nodded and glanced at the tape recorder. It blinked with a red light, showing it was running. "My name is Caroline

Arabella Ashley," she said.

"I know your name." His face was impassive. "You can skip that part."

The way he said it warmed something inside her. An almost forgotten verse from the bible popped into her mind. "I know your name; you are mine." When had she last heard that? At her first communion? Carlina smiled and focused on her story with an effort. "This morning, Ricciarda went out to buy some cleaning stuff. As soon as she had left, Suzanne came in."

"When was that?"

Carlina shook her head. "I really can't recall. Quite soon after we had opened."

Ricciarda cut in. "It was a quarter past ten."

Carlina nodded. "Suzanne threatened me with the gun. She forced me to close the door of Temptation. Then she made me go into the storeroom."

Her mother hissed in her breath.

Stefano's face remained impassive. "Go on."

"She thought I had been the last to see Trevor alive. She wanted to hear all about it. Then she asked me about Trevor's last lover. She wanted to find her and take her revenge on her because she was convinced that she had killed Trevor."

"Annalisa?" Fabbiola took a step forward. "How dare she insinuate that my dear niece would so such a thing?"

Carlina winced.

"I knew you lied to me." Suzanne fixed Carlina with a dark stare. "You slimy, little--"

"That's enough," Garini cut in. "Please continue, Carlina."

"I . . . I wanted to distract her, so I told her that the police were looking for her already and suspected her of being the murderer. I told her to run."

Enrique whistled. "Quick thinking."

"You took an appalling risk." Stefano's voice was grim.

"I don't understand." Fabbiola looked at her daughter. "How come you know her? She's French, isn't she?" It sounded as if no self-respecting Italian would ever know a French citizen.

"It may have been a risk, but it worked." Carlina looked at Garini. "She doubled over laughing."

"Laughing?" Fabbiola echoed in disbelief.

"Laughing." Ricciarda stared at Suzanne as if she she had

grown another arm.

"That's when I jumped at her to get the gun."

Garini closed his eyes for an instant.

"Wow." Enrique clapped his hands. "I'm impressed."

"There was a . . . a struggle." Carlina looked at the marks on her hand. "But I managed to get the gun in the end. That's when she said it wasn't loaded. She came toward me, to get it, and that's when I . . . when I shot her." She bit her lips. "It was self-defense."

Garini looked at her with an expression she had never seen before.

"It's all lies!" Suzanne said with a hiss. "I was in her store to buy a new bra. And suddenly, she starts to scream at me. She locks the door, and I'm so scared, I take out my gun, and then she fights me for it, and attacks me. I'm going to sue her!"

"You!" Fabbiola planted her feet wide apart, an inch from Suzanne's hip on the floor, and hitched the cushion underneath her arm higher. "Don't you dare to repeat this filth ever again. My daughter would never attack anybody. Never!"

Garini switched off the tape recorder. "Not unless she feels it's necessary," he said so low only Carlina could hear.

"You can check my police records," Suzanne said. "There is nothing against me. Nothing at all. You will find that I, Suzanne Morin, have led a blameless life."

Garini whipped around and stared at her. "What did you say your name was?"

Suzanne drew herself up. "I'm Suzanne Morin. If you took off these absolutely unnecessary manacles, I could show you my . . . " she hesitated and added in French, ". . . my carte d'identité."

At this instant, a thin man with a black bag hurried through the door. He looked around, nodded at Garini, and dropped to his knees beside Suzanne.

"Who is this man?" Fabbiola's voice quivered with outrage.

"The doctor." Garini didn't take his eyes of Carlina.

"Why is he treating a criminal who tried to kill my daughter? I have no patience with such luxury." She gave a sniff full of contempt. "It is only a scratch anyway."

Garini's lips twisted. "Dottore?" he asked. "What do you say?"

"The lady is right." The doctor was already busy binding up the wound. "The bullet only grazed her leg. It'll soon be a distant memory."

Carlina felt a wave of relief, coupled with fatigue, sweeping over her. She swayed and grabbed the sales counter to steady herself.

Suzanne folded her arms in front of her chest. "A scratch! It's not a scratch! She marked me for life!" She pointed at Carlina. "This woman tried to kill me, and you all pretend it was me! You're all in cahoots with each other! It's the Mafia. This is only a farce." Her voice got louder every second. "I need an attorney. A French attorney! I insist!"

Piedro burst through the door, his gelled hair standing up in spikes. "Here I am, Commissario," he informed his boss with a grand air, as if they had been waiting for him for ages. His gaze fell onto the attractive woman on the floor, and his eyes widened. "Golly."

Garini nodded at his subordinate, then addressed Suzanne. "This is my assistant Piedro Cervi. A police car is waiting for you outside, to take you to the police station, where you can wait for the attorney of your choice. You can then prepare your line of defense with him. My assistant Piedro Cervi will then take your statement, and I'll join you later."

Piedro visibly grew. He squared his shoulders and helped Suzanne up from the floor. Together with Garini, he escorted her to the waiting police car.

His departure broke up the group that had watched everything as if in trance.

Enrique gave Ricciarda's raven beauty another wistful glance, then waved and said he had to return to the Café.

"I'm glad she has gone." Fabbiola shook her head. "She made me nervous, that one."

Ricciarda took a deep breath. "Boy, do I agree. This was an exciting morning."

Garini came back with long steps. "Where is Annalisa?"

Carlina's eyes widened. "Do you think she's in danger?"

"No." His voice was curt. "But she needs to take your place at Temptation."

"My place? At Temptation? Why, in God's name? Yesterday, you almost tore me to shreds for allowing her to work here, and today, you ask me where she is." All at once, things seemed too big to take in. She blinked.

He looked at her and narrowed his eyes. "Today, things are different." He grabbed her arm and led her back to the store room where he took one of the foldable chairs from the wall. "Sit down and call her. She has to come here. I need you with me."

Carlina felt too rattled to resist. She dialed Annalisa's number, cut short her apologies for not having appeared at work in time, and asked her to come to Temptation to help immediately without divulging any background information.

Annalisa promised to come within the next fifteen minutes.

Fabbiola suddenly remembered that she urgently needed to buy Padano Grano cheese for lunch by order of her sister Benedetta and rushed from the store with an airy wave of the cushion.

The doorbell rang, and a pair of giggling girls walked in. Ricciarda went to the front of the store to deal with them.

Carlina leaned her head against the shelf behind her, closed her eyes, and took a deep breath.

"Don't you ever do this to me again." Stefano's voice was low, but it had a harsh edge.

Her eyes flew open. "What do you mean?"

"Getting yourself almost killed." He bent forward and took her chin in his hands. His light eyes bore into hers. "I've never been so scared in my life."

His fingers felt warm and firm, and the expression on his usually so imperturbable face warmed her deep inside. "I didn't do it on purpose, Garini."

"I know." He shook his head as if he still couldn't believe it.

"Where are you taking me now?"

"Home." His mouth was grim. "Your home, that is."

"That's not necessary. Give me another five minutes, and I'll be fine again."

"It's very necessary. I told your great-uncle that he could help me by shadowing Leopold Morin."

"Who?" Carlina looked puzzled.

"The French tourist who fainted on top of Trevor Accanto."

She got there with lightning speed. "Morin?" Her hand crept to her cheek in dismay. "You mean they're related?"

"It's possible. What if they got divorced because Suzanne

couldn't get over Trevor and Leopold Morin decided to take his revenge? Alternatively, she could be his sister, and he feels that Trevor had to be punished for making a wreck out of her."

Carlina's head whirled. "It's all a bit much for one morning. But I've never heard of a murderer who faints on top of his victim."

His mouth twisted. "You don't know Leopold Morin. He's a persnickety man. I wouldn't put it past him to do the deed and then faint in horror."

"What about the nylons? How did he get them?"

Garini shook his head. "I don't know. We'll figure it out later. But first, I need to warn your Uncle Teo and take him off the case."

"So that's why he was so busy these last days and looked like Santa Claus with a secret." Carlina got up. "I thought he had figured out a new way to fold money for the Christmas gifts."

"Into kangaroos?" he asked.

Carlina gave him a sharp glance. "Are you making fun of my family?"

He gave her one of his rare smiles. "I'd never dare."

But when they walked into Benedetta's kitchen, the one place where they could be sure to find all the family information they needed, any lingering trace of amusement dropped from his face. "What on earth--?"

Leopold Morin was sitting at Benedetta's kitchen table, right next to Uncle Teo.

They looked up at the same time, tears running down both their faces.

"Why are you crying?" Carlina darted forward. Something sharp pricked her eyes. She blinked and recognized the mountain of brown, paper-thin peels in front of the two men and the glistening pieces of white onion in the bowl between them.

"They're cutting onions together." Garini's mouth was grim. "What a charming family picture." His voice was acid.

Uncle Teo ducked his head.

Benedetta peered around the door of a cupboard where she had rummaged around. "Ah, the Commissario, and Carlina! Are you staying for lunch? Do you know Leo?" She waved at the two men. "He's French, but his Italian is beautiful." She kissed her fingertips. "So impressive."

Carlina's gaze darted from one to the other.

Leopold Morin was shifting on his chair like a five-year-old with a bad conscience.

Uncle Teo wiped away his tears, winked at Carlina, and got up. "Listen, Commissario, I need to talk to you."

He took Stefano by the arm and pulled him out of the room.

Benedetta lifted her eyebrows and looked at Carlina. "What's going on?"

"Nothing." Carlina followed the men and closed the door behind her.

"He was lonely," Uncle Teo was in the middle of a voluble explanation, both hands twirling in front of his chest. "And me, I know what it's like to be lonely. So we sort of . . . talked."

"I told you to keep your distance, Signor Mantoni!" Garini's voice was glacial.

"Well, yes, I know." Uncle Teo moved his head from side to side as if considering the idea. "And I admit that the first contact wasn't voluntary. I . . . well, I bumped into him."

Stefano didn't say anything, but his silence was intimidating enough. It swirled around him like a black cloud.

"And we . . . we started to talk, and then I realized what a nice man he was." Uncle Teo beamed at him.

Garini pressed his lips together.

"You can trust me, Commissario." Uncle Teo nodded to himself. "I've been around for almost eight decades, and I know people. Leo would never hurt a fly. Never."

Stefano's face didn't twitch a muscle. "Your harmless Leo was found on top of the victim in a dead faint."

"Yes, he told me so." Uncle Teo wrinkled his nose. "A bit disgusting, especially for him. He easily finds things disgusting, you know, and--"

Garini interrupted him, "And this morning, a Suzanne Morin threatened Carlina with a gun at Temptation."

Uncle Teo turned his head in surprise and peered at Carlina. "Oh, my. Are you all right, Carlina?"

"Yes, I am, Uncle Teo," Carlina came closer. "But I really think you should have obeyed the Commissario. It could be dangerous, you know."

"Nonsense." Uncle Teo drew himself up, and before they could stop him, he turned on his heels, burst through the door into the kitchen and launched himself at his new friend. "I say, Leo, is it possible that you are related to a Suzanne Morin?"

The sharp vegetable knife dropped with a clatter onto the shiny tiles on the floor. Leopold Morin turned as white as the onions in the bowl next to him and fainted.

Benedetta jumped forward and caught his slight frame before he could drop to the floor. "Have you gone out of your mind, Uncle Teo?"

Garini suppressed an oath. Two long steps brought him next to the Frenchman. "We need to lie him down somewhere."

"In my room." Benedetta lead the way.

Garini carried the lifeless Leopold and laid him down on Benedetta's bed. Then he looked around. The whole room was painted in lilac with only the ceiling left in white. Lilac curtains filtered the weak winter-light, and even the bedspread had a deep purple hue.

Benedetta held a peeled onion beneath Leo's nose.

His eyelashes fluttered, then opened. "Where am I?"

"In my bedroom." Benedetta sat on the bed and started to rub Leopold's hands.

An expression of panic came into Leo's eyes.

"I'm here, too." Uncle Teo bent forward. "And so is the Commissario."

"The Commissario." Leo repeated. His eyes opened until the whites showed all around.

"You don't need to be afraid," Uncle Teo sat on the other side of the bed. "The Commissario is almost a member of the family. He looks fierce, but underneath, he's not that bad."

Carlina choked.

Garini took out a small notebook. "I need to take your statement as soon as possible, Mr. Morin."

Leopold Morin sighed and closed his eyes again.

"He needs more time," Benedetta gave the Commissario a dark look. "He has only just come back from a deep faint."

"I don't have much time, Signora." Garini returned the look with an impassive face.

"It's all right." Leopold lifted his hand. "I will tell you everything."

"I'd like to tape your statement if I may." Garini pulled the small tape recorder from the pocket of his leather jacket. "And I should tell you that you have the right to ask for the presence of a lawyer."

"I don't need a lawyer, and yes, you can tape everything I say." Leopold started to talk without opening his eyes.

For once, the whole Mantoni family kept quiet, and only the cultivated voice with the slight French accent filled the purple shadows of the room.

"I got married to Suzanne eight years ago. I always knew she didn't love me as much as I loved her, but that didn't matter to me. I also knew she married me after a big disappointment, but I didn't care. We were happy, or so I thought."

Leopold took a deep breath. The tight control of his emotions was only visible in the stiff way he held his hands flat on the lilac cover, at the sides of his body. "Last year, we decided to go to Florence for the Christmas holidays. I spent the morning in the Biblioteca Medicea Laurenziana. It's my favorite library. When I came back to our hotel room, I found a letter. Suzanne had left me . . . for a man she had only met that very morning. She said it had been a "coup de foudre", love at first glance. She said he was the one man she had been waiting for all her life. She asked me to forgive her."

No one moved. The quiet voice held them enthralled.

"I know it sounds unbelievable, but it happened like that. I tried to find her." The voice grew tight with the memory. "She had turned off her phone. I didn't find a trace. I thought they had left Florence. Finally, I decided to go back home. I waited for Suzanne to come back. I waited for weeks."

Carlina swallowed. She had a lump in her throat.

"Then, one day in January, Suzanne was back at her work. She looked like a different woman, crazy, worn-out, a decade older. I tried to make her talk to me. She said he had dropped her. He had dropped my Suzanne. He had destroyed her." His thin shoulders shook. "She didn't want to come back to me. She said she wasn't worth it."

He fell silent.

"Please go on, Signor Morin." Garini's voice held a gentle note.

Leopold opened his eyes and looked at him. "I found out his name. I found out that he came back to Florence every year. And every year, he had a new lover. I decided to go and see him. I wanted to see the man who had destroyed my Suzanne."

Benedetta caught her breath so loud, they could all hear it.

"And I did." Morin sat up. "He was attractive, yes, but I could not see the reason why women loved him so much. I followed him wherever he went. I tried to understand. It became . . . an obsession."

"Did you ever talk to him?" Garini asked.

"Yes." The thin face looked tired. "I once asked him the way to the library. He knew it. He was a well-educated man." He fell silent and looked at his hands.

"What happened next?" Uncle Teo's voice sounded rough.

Garini gave him a warning glance.

"I found out that he often went to church. He never stayed long. Five minutes, sometimes less. He didn't go to confession; he just prayed." Leopold closed his eyes for a brief moment. "That morning, I didn't feel like following him into the building. I knew he would come out soon, and it . . . it perturbed me to see him pray. It seemed a sacrilege. I couldn't bear it. So I went to the café across the street and ordered a coffee. It was such a cold day. I never stopped looking at the doors, though."

"Did you see anybody come in or go out? Anybody you knew?" Garini bent forward.

Leopold didn't hesitate. "No. I saw some women, but with their thick coats and scarves, they all looked alike. I wasn't paying attention to the women anyway; I only wanted to follow him when he came out again." He shrugged. "But he didn't come."

Benedetta's eyes grew rounder every second.

"I finally decided to find out what had become of him. As far as I knew, there was no other exit to the church, but maybe I wasn't well informed. I went inside. It was icy and dark. I walked slowly, as if in admiration of the building. Like a normal tourist." He gave a little nod. The pink skin on his scalp showed through the short-cropped hair. "I didn't see anybody. I thought I had missed him, but to make sure, I went to the front." He shrugged. "He always used to pray in the front. The back seat wasn't the right place for him." He swallowed so hard, his Adam's apple moved visibly. "I stumbled over him. I knew immediately it was him. I can't tell you why. That's the last I remember until . . . "

"Until?" Benedetta bent forward.

"Until that dreadful Swiss woman tried mouth-to-mouth resuscitation on me." His thin lips twisted at the memory, and a bit of color came back into his pale cheeks.

Garini stared at him without twitching a muscle. "What about your wife?"

Lines of sadness appeared next to Leopold's mouth. "She cut off contact and filed for a divorce. I haven't seen her since August."

Carlina and Garini exchanged a glance.

Then Garini bent forward. "Are you willing to swear that you haven't seen her since August?"

He looked surprised. "I swear."

"Have you been in touch with her in any other way? The phone? E-Mail? Letters?"

"No. Nothing at all." Leopold shook his head in slow motion. "She said it was too painful for her."

Garini leaned back. "Your wife, Signor Morin, threatened Carlina Ashley," he made a move with his hand and indicated Carlina, "today with a gun."

Leopold gasped and jumped from the bed. "Suzanne is in Florence? Why?" He swayed and grabbed the bedpost to steady himself.

"Because she wanted to know about the current lover of Trevor," Carlina said. "She is convinced that this year's lover killed him. Now she wants to take her revenge on her."

Benedetta gave a little cry. "But that's Annalisa."

Leopold looked confused. "Who's Annalisa?"

"My daughter!" Benedetta looked at the onion she still held in her hand as if surprised to find it there and threw it aside. "I have to go to her!" She turned toward the door.

"Suzanne is now at the police station." Garini's quiet voice stopped her. "Annalisa is in no danger whatsoever."

"But what if they let this Suzanne go?" Benedetta crossed her arms in front of her chest. "She will come here, and she will want to hurt Annalisa!"

"They have strict orders not to let her go until I'm back."

"Madonna!" A voice came from the door. "What are you all doing in Mama's bed-room?"

"Emma!" Bendetta hurried to her eldest daughter. "Annalisa

is in danger!"

Emma laughed. "You must have misunderstood something, Mama. Usually, it's Annalisa who presents a danger for others."

Benedetta stamped her foot. "How dare you say such a thing about your sister, Emma?"

Emma shrugged. "I know her." Then she looked at the assembly with surprise written large in her brilliant eyes. "You still haven't explained while you're all standing around the bed?" She craned her neck. "Has anything special happened?"

Garini gave her a measuring glance. "I'll explain everything to you in a minute, in Carlina's apartment. Would you go upstairs? Maybe Carlina can go with you?"

Carlina nodded and took her cousin by the arm, but when Garini started to speak again, she stopped at the door.

Garini slipped the recording machine back into his pocket and turned to Leopold. "I would advise you, Signor Morin, to stay with your friends." He gave Uncle Teo a glance. "You will not help anybody if you rush to the police station now."

Leopold wrung his hands. "Suzanne! Is she . . . is she all right?"

Garini shook his head. "Physically, she only has a scratch that will soon heal, but I'm afraid she's not quite . . . "

"What?"

" . . . of sound mind."

Leopold started to tremble.

"A psychologist will talk to her, but it would surprise me if she should be left alone after this."

"Left alone? You mean she'll become institutionalized?"

"I don't know." Garini gave him a long look. "I'm inclined to believe your story, Signor Morin. If it is true, you should know one thing: It is not your fault."

The Frenchman looked at him, his skin stretched tight over his face. "I wasn't enough for her."

"That's her mistake, not yours." Garini said. "For the time being, stay here. Please."

Uncle Teo nodded and placed a hand on Leopold's shoulder. "Let's get you something to drink, and then we'll eat lunch. Benedetta is a wonderful cook, and you'll feel better after you've eaten something."

Emma looked at her cousin. "Talking about lunch - weren't

we supposed to meet at Temptation today?"

"Plans changed." Carlina drew her through the door. "Come upstairs, and I'll explain everything."

Two minutes later, when Garini closed the door to Carlina's department behind him, fear flared up in Emma's eyes. "What is this?" She turned on her cousin like a swift falcon. "A cross-examination?"

Carlina looked at the floor. "Garini needs to talk to you, and I thought you might want to have me close. But I can leave, if you'd rather not have me here." She turned toward the door.

"Stop." Emma held out her hand. "You can stay." With a sudden turn of temper, she dropped onto Carlina's comfortable sofa and stretched out her long legs. "So, what's the deal, Commissario?" She gave him a look underneath her long lashes. "I hope it's nothing too dreadful." Her watchful eyes belied the playful tone.

He took a piece of folded paper from his jacket and handed it to her. "It's this." His gaze stayed on her face.

"The incriminating document." Emma's voice mocked while unfolding it. "Hand it over to the criminal, and she'll--" she choked and stared at the picture, then jumped up. "This is a Photoshop-job!"

"I'm afraid not." He stood like a tree, not an emotion visible.

Carlina watched her cousin with a worried frown.

"Where did you find this?" Emma held the paper away as if it was contagious.

"In Trevor Accanto's papers. We know you had an affair with him three years ago."

Emma threw a scared glance at Carlina.

Carlina looked at her, helpless. She opened her mouth, but a glance from Stefano made her close it again.

Suddenly, the air seemed to be sucked out of Emma, and with a small moan, she dropped the paper and covered her face with her hands. "Don't tell Lucio." The words were a whisper.

He picked up the document and stored it away in his pocket. "I won't unless it's absolutely necessary."

Emma lifted her pale face to him. "Lucio won't understand."

"Could you tell us about it?"

Emma shuddered. "I will, but only if you don't switch on that infernal tape recorder. And you're not taking any notes, either!"

"In that case, you might have to repeat the information officially later." Garini didn't budge an inch.

Emma shrugged. "I don't care. Do you want to hear my story or not?"

"I do."

Carlina couldn't stand it anymore. She sat next to her cousin and took her hand.

Emma gave her a small smile, then turned to Stefano with an impatient move. "Oh, sit down, Garini. I don't want you to tower over me while I spill my guts."

Stefano sat on the chair with the leopard print cover and bent forward. "Please start."

"I met him at the mercato on the Piazza Lorenzo Ghiberti, a week before Christmas. Mama had sent me to buy some olives. You know, Carlina, Mama insists that Giulio's olives are the best because of his oak casks. As usual, Giulio asked me to test different olives, and suddenly, Trevor was standing next to me. We tested the olives together and compared them. It was fun. His Italian was perfect, and he was so . . . charming."

Carlina nodded. She knew exactly what Emma was talking about.

"The rest you can imagine. He told me from the start it was only a Christmas fling. That's what he called it." Emma's smile was wry. "I didn't believe him, but I kept him a secret from my family." She took a deep breath. "Four weeks later, he left. His phone didn't work anymore, and I never had his address in the US."

"Did you try to find him?" Garini asked.

"No." Emma lifted her head. "I have my pride. Besides, I realized I had made a fool of myself. I don't like that feeling. Lucio deserves better." She pressed her lips together. "Is that enough?"

"Not quite." Garini shook his head. "Can you tell us anything else about him, about his character?"

"He was generous," Emma said without hesitating. "He was great fun, but he had those fixed rules, and if you tried to get too close, he would clam up." She frowned. "He hated the idea of being tied down."

"I can imagine." Garini's voice was dry.

"I got the impression that he once had a nasty experience, and that was why he made sure he played the game by his own rules."

"Can you be a bit more specific?"

"No." Emma shook her head and stared into space. "Oh, and he was a devout Catholic. He went to church at least once a week, and he sometimes stopped to pray, on a whim."

Garini lifted his eyebrows. "A philandering Catholic?"

Emma shrugged. "It takes all sorts."

"Did you ever see him again?"

Emma nodded as if she didn't want to remember. "Once, last year. He was at a concert, together with another woman. I pretended I had not seen him."

"What did you feel when you saw him?"

Emma gave him a look that spoke volumes. "Do you really need to know?"

"Yes." He held her gaze.

"I was embarrassed." She balled her right fist. "I had just become engaged to Lucio, and I didn't want to remember how stupid I had been."

Carlina felt sick. How Emma must have suffered . . . and she had never even known it.

Garini nodded. "What did you think when you heard that he was Annalisa's lover?"

"I couldn't believe it. Of course I knew that Annalisa had a new love interest, but I had no idea that it was Trevor until Mama mentioned his name in passing. I dropped my fork on the floor and hid under the table to get my face under control." Emma lifted her slim hand and pushed back her hair. "Next I heard he had been killed. I couldn't believe that, either. He had been so full of life." She took a deep breath. "Then again, he had it coming."

"Did you suspect Annalisa?"

Carlina winced.

"Not for a minute." Emma didn't hesitate.

His light eyes narrowed. "Is that the famous Mantoni loyalty or are you speaking the truth?"

"It's the truth." Emma spat out the words. "Annalisa would never have killed him. She wanted to marry him. Delusional, of course, but I couldn't very well tell her that she could stop dreaming that particular dream."

Garini pulled out a piece of paper he had prepared earlier. It showed all the unidentified women from Trevor Accanto's notebook next to each other - with Trevor's side cut off, and not in the order of their appearance inside the notebook. "Please look at these pictures and tell me if you know any of these women."

Emma pursed her lips and rolled her eyes, but held out her hand with a bored motion. "Let me see." She glanced at the pictures without interest. "I've never seen any of them." Then she pointed at the blouse of snow-white. "What an awful top. This one could have done with professional help to get her outfit organized."

Garini ignored her remark. "Are you quite sure you don't recognize anyone?"

"Yes, I am. I already told you!" Emma glared at him.

"However, a few moments ago, you said you had met Trevor with another woman at a concert last year."

Emma gave him an irritated glance. "So what?"

Carlina flinched. She knew Emma's aggressiveness came from feeling cornered. Would Garini understand? His face didn't give anything away. *I hope Emma speaks the truth in spite of her fears.*

Garini looked unmoved, as if he didn't recognize aggressiveness even if it bit him. "Are you willing to swear that you have never seen any of these women? Try to picture them with another outfit, their hair done up, maybe?"

Emma bent over the paper again with an exaggerated sigh, made a show of examining each face, held up the paper against the light, put it down again, and finally said. "No. I don't know a single face."

Carlina swallowed. Usually, Trevor had stuck to one woman per vacation. If that had been the case, Suzanne Morin would have been the woman with him during the concert one year ago, but Emma had not shown the slightest sign of recognizing her.

"Listen, Commissario," Emma pressed her lips together. "At the concert, I only saw her for a fleeting moment. The light wasn't strong, and I admit I focused more on Trevor than on her at the time, so it's no wonder if I don't recognize her, even if she should be part of this odd gallery." She made a contemptuous move with her hand toward the paper. "Where does it come from anyway?"

He fixed her with one of his immobile stares. "I can't tell you."

Carlina closed her eyes. She knew he said it to protect her; after all, she had been part of the odd gallery, but she also knew how Emma would react to that statement.

Emma jumped up, her eyes flaring. "Fine. Do you need to know anything else, Commissario?"

"Not at the moment." Garini got up too.

"Good." Emma took two swift steps toward the door. "Because I am extremely fed up with being interviewed." Her head held high, she walked out of the apartment like a queen.

Behind her, the door closed with a bang.

A wave of tiredness swept over Carlina.

Stefano turned to her with a sigh. "That wasn't easy. Thank you for sticking to the rules." He frowned. "You look pale. Do you need to eat something?"

With slow moves, she got up from the sofa. Her legs felt as if made of old rubber, mushy and brittle. "Actually, I think I need a hug." To her horror, her voice broke.

Without a word, he opened his arms.

She ran into them.

He crushed her to his chest and held her tight.

Her head fitted right next to his shoulder, and her nose was pressed against his neck. She inhaled his scent and closed her eyes. Tears pricked behind her lids, tears of relief, of happiness, of exhaustion. She could feel his lips against her hair, and for an instant, life was perfect.

She couldn't tell how long she was in his arms, not moving, not wanting to be anywhere else, ever, but finally, he lifted his head.

"Carlina?"

"Hmm?"

"You've had a big scare today, and I think you're in shock. I want you to stay at home for the rest of the day."

With regret she took a step back. "I can't, Stefano. It's only two days to Christmas. This is the most important time of the year. I can't put my feet on the sofa like any old Medici lady. I have a business to run."

He hesitated, then bowed his head. "All right."

Relief pulsed through her. He took her business seriously. He understood how important it was to her, even if it cost her something, even if she wasn't in the best of shape to cope with it. He took her seriously, treated her like an equal. She smiled.

He blinked. "What's that for?"

"What?"

"That thousand watt smile."

She could feel her face going hot. "I . . . it's because you don't treat me like a weak lady."

He shook his head. "You'd consider that an insult, hmm?"

"Yes."

He smiled. "I see. Would you accept it if I prepared something quick to eat while you stayed on the sofa? Once you've had lunch, I'll take you back to Temptation."

"Willingly." She dropped onto the sofa. Truth be told, she still felt rather wobbly.

He took her leopard spread and covered her with it, tucking in the ends around her.

It felt odd. She'd never seen Garini as a caretaker.

"Now rest."

She closed her eyes. "I doubt you'll find much to make lunch with."

"I'll manage."

She heard him walk to her kitchen. It was a tiny place, with the roof crooked above him, and she didn't think he would be able to find enough food, but he surprised her. Fifteen minutes later, he came back, carrying a tray with a large plate. On it, he had arranged some olives, toasted bread with butter and several slices of typical Florentine sausage, a bit of her favorite cheese - Marzolino di Lucardo - and for dessert, a bowl of yogurt with sugar, and a cup of coffee.

As they shared the meal, Carlina felt herself touching ground again. "I needed that," she said in surprise.

"I know." Stefano dropped a bit of cheese into his mouth and looked around him. "Why do you have so many things with a leopard design?"

She smiled. "Because I like it."

"I see."

"Don't you like it?"

He grinned. "No. It's too dramatic, too heavy for me." He looked at her. "It suits you, though."

"You mean I'm dramatic and heavy?"

"No." He took the empty tray and got up. "But you have many unexpected layers."

She pushed the leopard cover away. "I'll help you."

"Please don't." He went to the kitchen. "I'd rather you rested a bit longer."

"But I--"

He looked over his shoulder, and his eyes smiled into hers. "Humor me."

She dropped back. "Oh, all right." She listened to him clattering around in the kitchen. It felt good, as if they belonged together. "Stefano?"

"Yes?"

"Where are we now?"

"With the case, you mean?" He dropped something into the sink with a metallic sounding clang.

"Yes."

"I've reached a state of almost total confusion," he said. "There are way too many women about."

She laughed. "I bet it's a man after all."

"That's not very likely." Another clang accompanied the words. "But I'll keep an open mind. Do you have anyone special in mind?"

"Madonna, no." Carlina laughed. "I still put my money on Mona Lisa."

"We've put her picture into the newspapers today. I hope someone will recognize her." A cupboard door banged. "I also plan to show the pictures to Ricciarda this afternoon, when I drop you off. Maybe she'll know more about Mona Lisa."

"I doubt it." Carlina frowned. "If I remember correctly, Mona Lisa only talked to me on the morning of the murder." Then she shrugged. "But who knows, maybe Ricciarda can help anyway. Once you have Mona Lisa, you'll have your case solved, that much is sure."

"So you don't think it was Suzanne?"

Carlina hesitated. "I . . . no, I don't think so after all. She seemed completely around the bend, but her fixed idea was quite the opposite - she wanted revenge for the murder of Trevor. That doesn't tie in with the rest, does it?"

"Not really." He came out of the kitchen, drying his hands on a hand towel. "She will have to be treated, though, and it'll be a long time before she'll be out on the streets again."

"Poor Leopold."

He gave her a sardonic look, "I'm not worried about him. The Mantoni clan will keep him busy until his wounds are healed."

Carlina threw a cushion at his head.

He caught it and returned it to her. "Enough resting on the sofa, lady. You're fit to return to the world now."

Carlina laughed and got up. "You know one thing? I wonder where my mother is. She should have been here long ago, checking on me."

Stefano winked. "I asked Uncle Teo to keep her busy."

Chapter 12

"I'm so glad you're back, Commissario!" Piedro, who had been sitting with drooping shoulders on a chair, jumped up with alacrity.

"What a warm welcome." Garini took off his thick jacket and hung it onto the peg behind the door. "What happened?"

"That Frenchwoman, this . . . this Suzanne . . ." Piedro's voice petered out.

"Yes? What of her?"

"I think she's crazy." Piedro opened his eyes wide. "I mean . . ." He made a move with his hand. "Mental."

"I think you might be right."

"She seemed all nice and friendly until the lawyer started to talk about Trevor Accanto's murder, and then, she suddenly turned into a sort of . . ."

"Well?" Stefano lifted his eyebrows.

"A monster."

"Oh?"

"Yes!" Piedro took a deep breath. "She shouted and hissed and cried. It was real scary. They asked a psychologist to come, and he said she should go to a closed ward."

"Good." Stefano nodded. "For the moment, that's the best place for her to be."

Piedro looked at him with big eyes. "Is it true she attacked Carlina Ashley?"

"Yes."

"Wow. I mean, that must have made you angry."

"It did." For once, Piedro had hit the nail on the head. Stefano closed his mouth with a snap. Were his feelings that obvious? His challenging gaze dared his subordinate to go on.

Piedro swallowed and had sense enough to change the topic. "I have not yet received any confirmation on the Japanese woman and the one who now lives in Rome, but they promised to send me the reports tomorrow at the latest."

"Good." Stefano frowned. "Please check when Suzanne Morin entered the country."

Piedro nodded.

"You'd better make a note," Garini said.

"I can remember it." Piedro looked at the floor.

"Are you sure?"

"Yes."

"All right." Stefano didn't mention the previous times when Piedro had dropped several leads at once. Today, he had to remember only one thing.

"Em." Piedro shuffled his feet.

"Yes?"

"We got a report by special courier today, from America."

Stefano lifted his eyebrows. "Where is it?"

Piedro pointed at the in-tray on Stefano's desk. "I put it there."

Stefano reached for it. "Have you read it?"

"I tried to, but it's all in English."

When Stefano opened the cardboard folder, a hint of a sweet smell wafted up to his nose. American paper. *It smells different than ours*. He wondered why. Did they mix anything special into the pulp?

"Can I leave now, Commissario?" Piedro slid to the edge of his chair. "It's my mother's birthday tomorrow, and I still have to buy a gift for her."

"Her birthday, you say?" Garini looked up from the American report. This was the opportunity he had been waiting for. "I thought it was your parent's wedding anniversary, or did I get that wrong?"

"Oh, no." Piedro shook his head, not suspecting anything. "My parent's wedding anniversary is in May, not in December."

"It'll be twenty-six years the next May, won't it?"

Piedro looked surprised. "No. They've been married twenty-three years." He smiled. "I can remember because I'm twenty-two."

"I must have mixed up something." Garini returned the smile. "Yes, you can go." When the door had closed behind Piedro, he narrowed his eyes. Twenty-three years. If he was lucky, the affair had taken place before the Cervi marriage. That would help. Hopefully. He had to tackle Marcella Cervi later today, but first, he wanted to read what the US had to tell him. The first document was covered with a decisive handwriting in black ink. Trevor Accanto's will. *Finally.*

"I, Trevor Vincent Accanto, am of sound mind as I write this, my last will. At first, I played with the idea of giving each of the wonderful women who have shared my life a piece of my fortune, but I imagine that some of them might find it difficult to explain the sudden riches to their current partners, and also, it would be an effort to find them all again, when I have so successfully lost them in the past years."

Garini swallowed. Thank God the American hadn't gone through with that impulse. While it would have given him the name of every woman concerned, it would also have multiplied their motives for murder. He shuddered when he imagined Lucio learning about Emma's involvement with the rich American by way of an inheritance. What a mess this man had created. He turned back to the document. "So, instead I donate my whole fortune to a new-found institution that will support young women with children born out of wedlock. The Trevor V. Accanto foundation will be situated at my mansion in Boca Raton, Florida, and all the necessary details are already laid out in the corresponding Business Plan."

The document ended with the signature Garini had already seen on the fly-leaf of the notebook.

Young women with children born out of wedlock. Garini frowned. Could it be that Trevor Accanto had illegitimate children somewhere and knew about them? Apparently, he had not cared to help them directly and had preferred to found an institution. *Children* - Fabbiola's prophecy came out of nowhere into his mind. *Beware of children.* He shook himself. *What utter rubbish.*

The police at Boca Raton had included a summary about the life of Trevor Accanto that sounded like the eulogy at a funeral - an astute business man, not only fair but also generous, generally liked, a pillar of the Catholic community, president of the country club, owner of countless first-class properties . . . Garini felt slightly sick. He did not suspect the US police of being bribed, which only left one conclusion - the millionaire had come to Italy to sin in style while leading a blameless life at home.

He shrugged. Well, why not? If only he hadn't managed to get himself killed in Florence. Still . . . something irked him. Something about this man was not right - he was too glib, too superficial. On an impulse, he pulled his phone closer and asked to be connected to the contact name given on the American report. He was put through without a hitch and soon found himself talking to the man who had put all the data together, Sergeant Dan Matador. He explained his situation, looking for words more often than he wanted, regretting his impulse. *I should have looked up some words beforehand.* But Sergeant Matador seemed to be a patient man, and when he started to speak, Garini gave a silent prayer of thanks that he spoke slowly, with pauses in between that left enough time for taking a quick note.

"I see what you mean," the sergeant said when Garini had finished his explanation. "You're looking for a more personal connection - for friends."

"Exactly." Stefano was glad to have found someone who was quick on the uptake.

"Well, I noted the same thing. Mr. Accanto was well-known in the community, of course. He often donated money at sponsorship events, and I remember that he briefly spoke at the inauguration of Boca Raton Plaza."

"The Boca Raton Plaza?"

"A new shopping mall he purchased and re-vamped two years ago." Dan Matador paused and added. "But he didn't have friends."

"No?"

"No. I talked to the people he usually did business with, to his lawyer, his architect, his banker, the other members of the golf club. They were full of praise, but when I asked them if they would consider themselves to be close friends, they all said it had been a more superficial relationship."

"His housekeeper?"

"His housekeeper has been with him for twenty-seven years. She said he traveled a lot, always to Florence in winter, but that he remained by himself when he was at home."

"Didn't he entertain?"

"Oh, yes, he did entertain, but never less than twenty people at a time. He didn't have one or two special friends, nobody to share confidences with."

Garini chewed on that piece of information for a moment. *What a lonely life.* "What do you think he did if he wanted advice?"

"Then he got the best people in the industry, paid them handsomely, and remained in friendly contact forever."

"I meant personal advice."

Now it was the Sergeant's turn to be quiet. "I don't know."

"The report says he was never married. Did he have women friends?"

"No." The answer of the Sergeant was decisive. "Nothing like that."

"Family?"

"He mentioned an uncle in Florence."

Garini gave a snort. "This uncle was only an euphemism for an attractive woman - a different one each year."

"So I gathered from your initial contact request." Sergeant Matador sounded unconvinced. "But I find it hard to reconcile that with the man we knew."

"It seems he built up two separate worlds and never mixed them."

"Apparently."

Garini frowned. If Accanto had managed to build up two separate worlds, what had stopped him from building up a third or fourth one? The American's passport had shown stamps from all over the world, with the only repeated entry being Italian immigration. However, the US was a huge country. Maybe Accanto had built another world within the US. "You said he traveled a lot. Do you happen to know if he went to other places within the US again and again, just like he did with Florence?"

"We checked that," Sergeant Matador said in his slow way, "but we found nothing."

Discouragement hit Garini. He had clung to his hope that the roots for the murder were far away from Florence, far away from Carlina and her family . . . but every clue led him to nothing, leaving him with a mess much too close to home. Why couldn't the rich American have a disgruntled wife, an heir with expensive hobbies and a furious business partner, cheated by a huge amount of money? That would have been some help. Instead, he had behaved like a universally loved saint when at home.

"How about his financial situation? Where did he get his money from?"

"He was a very rich man - inherited the lot from his father when he was nineteen and continued to enlarge it with clever investments. He'd already retired years ago and lived on the interest. There's nothing wrong with his business. We looked into that very thoroughly, thinking he might have done himself in."

Garini blinked. "The idea of strangling yourself with a pair of nylons inside a church seems a bit far-fetched."

"We only learned about the details of his death later." The Sergeant sounded hurt.

"I see." Garini suppressed a sigh, thanked the Sergeant, and hung up. While his hand was still on the receiver, someone knocked on the door. A head with black spectacles and hair that looked like overcooked spaghetti poked around and blinked into the weak afternoon light as if he had just emerged from eternal darkness.

"Arturo. Come in." Garini waved at the computer expert of the police station. Maybe he had found something of better value on Trevor Accanto's laptop. One could always hope. "Did you manage to crack the password?"

"Yup." Arturo nodded. "'Twas easy."

Of course. Arturo found everything technical easy. Buying a loaf of ciabatta was a different matter. "What was it?"

"Carpe_Diem."

Seize the day. That fit. Trevor Vincent Accanto had understood the art of living in the present, with no thoughts about the past or the future. "Did it reveal anything else?"

"Music." Arturo didn't believe in wasting words.

"Music? What kind of songs?"

"Classics. And sweet stuff for ladies."

Garini eyed Arturo's blue jeans that looked as if he had last taken them off in July. He hoped Arturo would not come any closer. "Anything else?"

"Nah." Arturo shook his head. "Shame. Great hardware. Too good for a juke box."

"How about correspondence?" Garini felt desperate. Couldn't the victim have left any clue at all?

"Some e-mails. Mostly orders for music." Arturo shrugged. "Jewelry too. Expensive."

"But no other business correspondence?"

"Nah."

Of course not. That would have been too easy. "Thank you, Arturo." Garini waited until the door had closed, then got up and squared his shoulders. Now he had to tackle the next point on his agenda - the wife of his boss. Sometimes it was difficult to remember why on earth he had chosen this profession.

The temperature had dropped still further, and Garini pulled up the collar of his leather jacket as he got out of the car in front of Cervi's house. He clenched his teeth as he mounted the few steps toward the villa and pressed the bell with a ridiculous feeling of inevitability.

She opened the door herself. *Thank God.* "Good afternoon, Signora Cervi." Stefano forced himself to smile at the wife of his boss.

She had improbable blond hair, piled high on her head, a tanned face in the middle of winter, and glitzy earrings combined with a Chanel costume. The twenty-five kilos she had gained in the last years had shrouded her beauty in a more cuddly frame, but they didn't conceal how attractive she had been, even when she frowned. "Commissario Garini? Is anything the matter with my husband?" Her voice was the least attractive thing about her - it sounded high-pitched and squeaky.

"None at all." He shook his head. "I'd like to discuss a personal matter with you, if I may."

"Of course, though I can't for the life of me imagine what you'd like to say to me." She opened the door wide. It was decorated with a tasteful Christmas wreath and a tartan ribbon, looking very American and out of place.

He followed her into the villa. Marcella Cervi had been an heiress with excellent political connections. She spent her days on several committees and unofficially ran parts of the town. Garini had met her at several official meetings and soon realized that she was a dangerous woman, greedy and unhappy. Whenever possible, he gave her a wide berth, but he knew he had to interview her just like all the other women on his list if he didn't want to lose his self-respect. Still, he wished he was anywhere but in Cervi's opulent villa right now and only hoped that his boss wouldn't take it into his head to return home on this frosty winter afternoon.

She opened a door to a room too perfect to be decorated by anyone but an interior architect. A white carpet complemented the shiny wooden floor, white brocade curtains were held back with broad linen tassels, and the walls were painted in a soft muddy color that was probably called misty taupe in the designer's catalog. Elaborate stucco provided an adequate frame for the glistening chandelier, and the furniture - a sofa and two armchairs - were too pristine white to have ever been put to serious use. In the middle reigned a low table made of heavy glass. The only note that didn't fit was the smell of cold smoke.

Marcella Cervi draped herself on one of the large armchairs and pulled a cigarette from a golden case. "Do you want one?"

"No, thank you." Garini pulled the copy taken from Trevor Accanto's little book from his jacket but held it so she couldn't see the picture.

"I forgot, you're always uber-correct." She narrowed her eyes, lit the cigarette and pulled at it with a nervous move, then bent forward and placed the spent match with care onto a heavy glass ashtray.

"I'll be brief," he said.

"You always are." Her voice sounded tart.

He ignored her, though his heart-beat accelerated. *She'll make this difficult.* "You will have heard that the millionaire Trevor Accanto was strangled at the Basilica di Santa Trìnita four days ago."

She didn't reply.

He didn't take his gaze off her and thought he could see a cautious withdrawal, a watchfulness in her eyes. "When we got access to Signor Accanto's private documents, we found this." He passed her the picture. "It was part of a highly suggestive album, one that leads us to believe that the ladies shown were his lovers."

Marcella Cervi looked at the picture without moving. For an instant, her fingers clenched on the paper, then they relaxed again. She lifted her head. "What is your question, Commissario?"

"I'd like to know everything you can tell me about Signor Accanto."

She pulled at her cigarette again and gave a high-pitched laugh. "I suggest that you concern yourself more with the present than with the past. If I had had a grudge against Trevor, I would not have waited some twenty years before acting on it."

"When was this picture taken?"

She shrugged. "I don't recall exactly, it's all so long ago. Twenty-five years ago? Twenty-six? I don't know."

Garini didn't take his gaze off her. "I think you could remember very well if you wanted to."

She blew a ring of smoke into the air. "I assure you, dear Commissario, that I never remember unimportant things."

"Were you already married then, Signora Cervi?"

She bent forward, her dark eyes suddenly sparkling in anger. "So this is it? I admit I'm surprised. I'd never have taken you for the kind of man who goes for a bit of blackmail every now and then."

Stefano clenched his teeth. "I am investigating a murder, Signora Cervi, no more and no less. Your husband doesn't know that I'm here, and if the information I get from you has no connection to the murder, I will not tell him about it."

She leaned back and gave him a supercilious look. "What about your reports?"

Damn. With unerring instinct, she had placed her finger into the wound. As the wife of his boss, she knew that he was obliged to put every single bit of information, no matter how unimportant, into the reports. If he offered to leave out the information, he was making himself vulnerable, and she would use it to her advantage as soon as she was out of danger.

However, if he left it in, he also knew that Cervi would take it as a personal insult and would take it out on him. He couldn't win.

Stefano held her gaze. "My report will contain every word we have exchanged." He had by no means decided what he would do with the information he could get from her, but under no circumstances would he tell her so. What a difference to Carlina, Carlina who was straight-forward, honest, and never played games. Suddenly, he missed her with such intensity that it felt like a shot of pain going straight through him.

"Aha." She stubbed out her cigarette. "So I've not been mistaken in you. That's something, at least." She got up. "However, I see no need to give you any further information. My past has nothing whatsoever to do with the murder of Trevor Accanto. You have my word on that." She gave him a faint smile. "That should be enough."

Garini stretched out his legs, pretending to make himself comfortable. "Pray remain seated, Signora."

She met his cool gaze with a look of blazing temper. "What do you want? I'm not going to tell you anything."

He took out the pictures of Snow White and Laughing Eyes, with Trevor cut away. It cost him an effort to reveal their pictures to someone as uncooperative as Marcella Cervi, but she had been Trevor's lover a year or two after them, and she might remember their faces as they had been then, even if the women had changed drastically in the meantime.

"Could you look at these pictures and tell me if you recognize these women?"

As he had expected, her curiosity was stronger than her hostility.

She held out her hand.

He first gave her Snow White.

A quick shake of the head. "Never seen her."

Laughing Eyes.

Her eyes widened. She opened her mouth, then she closed it again. "Never seen her, either." She returned the pictures. "Is that enough or do you plan on remaining sitting here for the rest of the day?"

He got up without hurrying. "You have given me all the answers I need." *So she knows Laughing Eyes but wants to keep the secret.* He frowned. Why? It could be loyalty. Hard to imagine in a woman like Marcella Cervi. He could better imagine that she would hide her knowledge for other motives . . . power, for example - or maybe even blackmail. Yes, he could see Marcella Cervi using her knowledge to get an advantage she would otherwise not have had. If that was her plan, it was dangerous.

He turned at the door and fixed her with his most intimidating gaze. "I have to warn you, Signora Cervi, that this killer is ruthless."

She lifted a mocking eyebrow. "Aren't they all?"

"Possibly." His voice was dry. "If you should realize that you want to add something to your statement, get in touch with me immediately."

"I could also tell my husband." She gave him a saucy smile.

Heaven forbid. "Of course." He nodded and went down the stone steps leading from the villa. An icy wind blew straight between his neck and his collar, but he felt better outside, with a bigger distance from the wife of his boss. *Phew.* Now he had to look for a woman in competition with Marcella Cervi. Who could it be? An acclaimed beauty? Maybe even a previous lover of her husband. Stefano shuddered. He'd rather not investigate a case that had its roots deep in the Cervi family.

On an impulse, he took out his phone and called Carlina.

"Hello Commissario." Her voice was faintly mocking, but tender.

He could feel his mood lighten. "Hi."

"Is anything the matter?" Her voice sounded worried now.

Strange, how much he wanted to smooth that fear away. "No. Nothing more than you already know, that is."

"Good." A pause.

He could hear her taking a deep breath, as if steeling herself for something.

"So why are you calling?" she asked.

He hesitated, then said the first thing that came to his mind. "I wanted to hear your voice."

"Oh." She laughed.

It sounded as if it was a private laugh just for him, low and intimate, and it gave him goosebumps. "Are you all right? No after-effects from the shock this morning?"

"I'm fine." Her voice was calm. "The rest at lunch time helped a lot."

"Good."

"You sound strange," she suddenly said.

"Strange?"

"Yes. Preoccupied."

He gave a snort. "No wonder. I just interrogated the wife of my boss."

"I see." She sounded thoughtful. "Was she cooperative?"

"Not in the least." He felt better already, just talking to

Carlina. "In fact, I'm one hundred percent sure that she knows one of the other ladies, but she didn't tell me. I assume she is working to her own agenda."

"Scary."

"Hmm." He could get addicted to this. "So, what are you up to tonight?" he asked.

"We have a meeting with Sabrina."

"Sabrina?"

"She's the mayor's wife, the one who organizes the Florence Christmas fair."

"I remember. You also had a meeting with her the night I walked you home."

"Yes. By the way--" she broke off.

"Yes?"

"Oh, nothing."

Garini frowned. Was she hiding something? Something to do with the case? He opened his mouth to ask, but she beat him to it.

"We're all of us meeting at the historical palazzo where the Christmas fair will take place. It's called the Palazzo Davanzati. I'm sure you know it. We'll discuss how to set up the booths, and then, she'll invite us to her home for a drink." Carlina sighed. "It'll be a long night, but I think it'll be worth it. I have to make sure I find a chair somewhere. It would be too cruel if she invited us without sufficient chairs."

He smiled. "When is the fair going to take place?"

"Tomorrow."

Garini frowned. "Tomorrow, the twenty-third? Isn't that one of the biggest shopping days of the year? How will you manage?"

"The fair will only start at three in the afternoon and will continue until ten at night. I'll set up the booth early in the morning," Carlina sighed, "between six and nine, in fact. I've asked my mother to tend the booth between nine-thirty and three, because I plan to spend the morning at Temptation. I know that quite a few of the other store owners will do the same thing."

"Sounds exhausting." *I hope her mother won't let her down.*

"If you run a small business, you have to be flexible. Anyway, in the afternoon, I'll leave Annalisa and Marianna at Temptation and will return to the Christmas Fair together with

Ricciarda."

Garini frowned. "Who's Marianna?"

"You don't know her, but she's a part-time help. She often helps out when I'm on vacation or in other emergencies."

He grinned. How like her to call a vacation an emergency. "And on the twenty-fourth?"

"That'll be the last and most hectic day of the Christmas battle." Carlina sighed again, "and I'll probably fall asleep in the middle of midnight mass when it's all over." She laughed. "But I usually do that anyway."

"I'll see if I can drop by at the Fair tomorrow," he said.

"That would be nice. You can do some last minute Christmas shopping."

"Last minute is done on the twenty-fourth," he answered. "But maybe it's time for a more sedate lifestyle."

Chapter 13

Sabrina's steps sounded hollow on the polished parquet floor. The medieval room on the first floor had a high ceiling with small windows giving onto the street, but the early winter night had already closed in, blackening out the view of the honey-colored stone houses opposite.

Carlina followed Sabrina together with the other exhibitors. She studied a hand-written map and tried to find the right location for her booth.

"I had to promise the town that we would under no circumstances nail anything onto the wainscoting or damage the parquet floor." Sabrina said to the group. "That's why we developed the cardboard folding walls with the soft edges as a background for each booth."

Carlina smiled. She was delighted with the crinkled gold foil and the distinctive Temptation logo in the center of her folding wall. It made a great backdrop for the three mannequins she planned to show. Three hollow black cubes would serve as storage areas and sitting places at the same time. She had asked Sabrina for a position in a corner, so her customers would be able to try on her special lace underwear behind the folding wall without being seen.

Sabrina turned around and faced the group of fourteen women in front of her. "So if you plan to bring any additional furniture, make sure you glue felt underneath any sharp edges." She handed out large pieces of felt with an adhesive on their backs. "I've brought one for each for you, and you can cut it into the necessary size. If you need more, come back to me."

Carlina fingered the gray felt. It felt furry and a bit rough. How typical of Sabrina to prepare every detail.

"Also, we have to make sure not to place anything over these trapdoors." Sabrina pointed at several squares, placed in a long row, on the floor. "They might not be sturdy enough to bear the weight."

"Trapdoors?" Carlina asked. "What use did they have? There's no room beneath here, is there?"

"No." Sabrina shook her head. "Below this room is only the arch that is part of the main entrance. In medieval times, if your enemies tried to storm the house, you could open the trapdoors and pour liquid lead onto them. That proved to be quite an efficient way to stop them."

Carlina's friend Rosanna shivered. "Gosh, I would think so." She gave the trapdoor next to her a wide berth.

Carlina shook her head. "It's funny; I've lived in Florence so long, but there are still so many things I don't know."

"That's because you're not a tourist." Rosanna said. "When they come to Florence, they spend a full week looking into every crook and nanny, listening to the complete history, starting with Caesar's colony . . . and afterwards, they're experts."

Carlina smiled. "Well, as long as they manage to look into our stores as well, I'm fine with that."

They advanced together with the group. Sabrina explained that the bathrooms were on the same floor just around the corner, and that she would open the building at six o' clock the next morning, so they could start the setting-up of their booths. Several ladies groaned.

Sabrina smiled. "You can come later, if you wish, but I know that some of you have to be at your own stores later in the morning. As long as everything is done by three o'clock, you can start whenever you want. The Christmas fair will officially close at ten PM, and afterwards, we'll start the dismantling. We have to return this room to its original condition by midnight."

Carlina clenched her teeth. Maybe she had taken on too much. It was sheer lunacy to leave Temptation to Marianna and Annalisa, just one day before Christmas. But she felt she personally had to be at the Christmas fair to study the reactions to her new lace collection. If they resembled in any way Annalisa's feelings, the collection would be dead before it was born. She had decided to take Ricciarda with her because she knew that it would be impossible to deal with any crowds if she was on her own. Also, as soon as Temptation closed in the evening, Annalisa would join them at the fair, to help during the last hours and with the dismantling. At least, that was the plan. However, if they should only have a few customers, Carlina had already decided to send them home early.

She suppressed a sigh. Hopefully Annalisa would prove to be a help and not a hindrance. What if she had one of her fits in front of a customer?

She shook her head. *Nothing will happen. It's just another crazy Christmas.* Once the fair was over, she only had the 24th to survive, and on December 25th, she could collapse, sleep until eleven, and later sit down to the traditional family lunch that Benedetta would have prepared with as much love as usual. In between, she still had to wrap her gifts, but that was done in less than thirty minutes . . .

Sabrina clapped her hands. "I'd now like to invite you to a small drink at my home, to celebrate that we have survived the preparations. We'll drink to success, because tomorrow evening, we'll be too exhausted to do so. It's right behind the Uffizi Museum."

Laughter greeted her announcement.

When Carlina dismounted from her Vespa in front of Sabrina's house, she thought her joints would crack, being frozen by the sharp wind. It seemed to get colder every day. Maybe they would even have snow. She shivered and hunched deeper into her jacket. "As long as it doesn't snow tomorrow," she murmured. If it snowed, traffic in Florence would come to a total stand-still. The inhabitants would either refuse to set a foot outdoors or would drive as if their cars had developed into drunken centipedes, with legs slithering all over the place - with the exception of a few chosen lunatics who drove as if they had seven lives to lose.

She was grateful for the warmth of Sabrina's house when the door was opened to her. A glass of Prosecco, the festive Christmas-tree in a corner of the elegant living room, and the babble of excited voices lifted her mood. "I wanted to say thank you for inviting me to join the Christmas Fair," she said to Rosanna who was sitting next to her on a modern chaise longue. "I really appreciate it. I got to know so many interesting women."

Rosanna lifted her glass and clinked it with hers. "I'm glad you were able to join. Here's to our success tomorrow." Her pixie-like face shone.

They smiled at each other and drank.

Carlina placed her glass on a small side-table and turned to her friend. "I need to go to the bathroom. Do you happen to know where it is?"

"Yes." Rosanna pointed toward the back of the house. "You have to cross the music room, past the piano. Just go straight on. You can't miss it."

Carlina winced when she got up. Her feet were hurting her. After all these years, she should be used to standing all day long, but for some reason, it didn't get better. With mincing steps, she crossed the room and opened the door Rosanna had indicated. When she closed it again behind her, the babble of voices was cut off and sudden peace descended. Carlina took a deep breath and looked around. The piano room had an unusual shape, like an octagon, placed in a strategic position in the middle of the house. Several doors led from it.

It smelled of hyacinths. Carlina turned her head - now she could see them standing on a sideboard. Next to it two tall lamps threw muted pools of light against the stucco ceiling. Their light reflected on the shiny surface of the grand piano and the silver frames that decorated it. "What a serene room." She went past the piano, one hand trailing over the smooth surface.

By pure chance, her gaze came to rest on one of the silver-framed pictures, and when she recognized the faded picture, she froze in horror. She stopped in the middle of her move, her hand half stretched out toward the picture. *It can't be.* Carlina swallowed. Her heart beat hard against her chest, and her breath came out in sharp gusts.

She looked around her. She was still alone in the room, but the peace she had felt earlier had gone. Suddenly, the smell of hyacinths had become suffocating - and the silence a threat. She bent forward and narrowed her eyes. No doubt. The woman in the picture was Laughing Eyes, Trevor's second lover some twenty-five years ago. And now she knew why she had seemed so familiar. The different hair cut had misled her, and the changes that came with many years, but she should still have recognized the bone structure, and of course those unusual eyes. It was Sabrina.

A door clicked softly behind her.

Carlina whirled around.

"Ah, you're admiring the pictures," Sabrina came up to the piano, not a hair out of place.

Carlina's heart stopped for an instant. She cleared her throat. "Yes." Her voice sounded rough. "It's a lovely room." She made a wide gesture with her hand and turned away from the pictures. "Gorgeous flowers." *Anything to distract her.*

Sabrina gave her a sharp glance. "I see you've recognized that ancient picture." She shrugged. "I should have hidden it, but I had forgotten that it was on the piano until I caught you staring."

Oh, no. Disconcerted by the direct attack, Carlina took a step back and faked a smile. *Pretend you haven't heard her.* "I think I'll return to Rosanna. She'll be wondering what became of me."

"Not so fast." Sabrina's cool hand encircled Carlina's wrist. "I think we need to talk."

"I really have to go." Carlina took a step to the door and pulled her wrist away.

Sabrina let her arm go but blocked the way with her body. "You don't need to be afraid of me, Carlina." She smiled. "I won't hurt you."

Carlina shivered. She had never noticed how tall Sabrina was. Her slim figure might well stem from extensive sessions at the fitness studio, making her stronger than she looked, stronger than Carlina. She forced herself to meet Sabrina's gaze. "You don't have to explain anything to me." Her voice sounded way too squeaky, showing her fear louder than words.

"But I want to." Sabrina closed her lips until they were a tight line.

Carlina sent a silent message to Garini. If ESP worked, this was the moment to prove it. *I'm in danger.* She turned half away from Sabrina and used the move to slip her hand into the pocket of her trousers, assuming a relaxed stance. If she could call Garini without Sabrina noticing it, he might get here in time. He had once made her program his name so it came up on top, but she couldn't recall which button she had to press first. Her fingers slid over the tiny keys. Darn. She had no idea if she was reaching him or somebody else, somebody totally useless, like the answering machine at Temptation, or, even worse, her mother. To cover up her gestures, she shrugged and faked a smile. "Well, if you want to talk, go right ahead."

Sabrina picked up the picture and looked at it with a frown. "It was a long time ago."

Carlina measured the distance to the door. It was too far to escape. "Yes."

Sabrina looked up, her face distorted with hatred.

Carlina flinched.

"Marcella Cervi was here this afternoon. She saw a picture in the police files. A picture of me and Trevor. Marcella recognized me, but she didn't tell anybody - or so she said." Her shoulders shook. "I thought I was safe. Twenty-five years, and now this old story is blowing up into my face."

Carlina pressed a few more keys, praying silently. *I'm in danger.* "What story?"

"I had been married one year. Only one year, but Trevor blew me away." A wistful smile played around her lips and disappeared.

A sudden feeling of sadness swamped Carlina. *I've heard this before.*

Sabrina lifted her head. "Can you imagine that Marcella Cervi had the effrontery to blackmail me? She came to my house today and threatened to blab unless I helped to push her into the top position on certain committees." Her eyes blazed with anger.

Carlina took a shaky breath. *Is Marcella Cervi still alive?* "Really?" It sounded like a croak.

"That slimy, inefficient, fake--" Sabrina broke off, her chest heaving.

Carlina took another step back.

Sabrina narrowed her eyes and followed her. "Stay."

"I think you should talk to the police," Carlina swallowed hard. "They know what to do with blackmailers."

Sabrina laughed.

The mirthless sound chilled Carlina.

"Oh, I don't need the help of the police." Sabrina narrowed her large eyes. "I have my own way to deal with Marcella and her kind."

"Great." Carlina took another step toward the door. "I . . . I'm glad to hear that." *Why does nobody have to go to the bathroom? Have they all left?*

Sabrina's hand shot forward and grabbed her wrist again. "I don't want you to run to the Commissario now. Stay."

Carlina felt sick. *I'm in danger.* "Why did you kill Trevor?" The question came out of her mouth before she could stop herself.

Sabrina reared back. "Me?" She sounded flabbergasted. "I didn't kill Trevor."

Carlina's knees started to tremble. "You . . . you didn't kill Trevor?" Her head whirled.

"Of course not." Sabrina shook her head. "Oh, I knew he was in town every Christmas; I met him at a reception of the American consulate three years ago." Her mouth twisted. "He was with a girl young enough to be his daughter."

Either Sabrina was a very good actor or she wasn't lying. Carlina sank onto the piano bench. "But . . . if you didn't kill him . . . why did Marcella Cervi try to blackmail you?"

Sabrina threw back her head and laughed. "This Commissario of yours has to be a very unusual man if he accepts that you're having affairs right and left."

"Oh." Carlina blinked. "You mean Marcella threatened to tell your husband about that ancient affair with Trevor?"

"Of course." Sabrina frowned. "What on earth did you think?"

"I thought she threatened to tell the police that you were Laughing Eyes!"

"Who?"

Carlina dropped her head into her hand. "That's what the Commissario called you when he saw that picture of you and Trevor."

"So you have seen it?" Sandra's voice was hard. "Was that part of the normal police procedure or does it have something to do with your special relationship?"

Carlina straightened her back. "He officially asked me if I could identify you. Remember, I was one of the last people to see Trevor alive." She gave Sabrina a glance that spoke volumes. "I still don't get it. Why didn't you go to the police? Trevor had many lovers, and even if it places you into an inner circle, it doesn't automatically follow that you killed him."

Sabrina flattened her short skirt over her hips. "My husband is rather close to Cervi. Once it's part of a police record, it's a matter of time before my husband knows about it."

"I see." Carlina gathered her courage. "And what did you

mean when you said you knew how to deal with Marcella Cervi and her kind?"

Sabrina sat next to Carlina. "I happen to know a few things about Cervi that would not . . . let's say they would not foster his career."

Carlina caught her breath.

Sabrina gave her a lopsided smile. "That's the other side of the coin when it comes to my husband's friendship with Cervi." Her smile grew malicious. "Knowledge is power."

"Did you tell her so?"

"Not yet." Sabrina shook her head. "I wanted to get some more details. I told Marcella to come back to me tomorrow. I plan to check it out tonight, and tomorrow, well, tomorrow, I'll send her packing." A grin bared her teeth.

Carlina looked at her. She liked and admired Sabrina, and from all Garini had said, the Cervi couple didn't rate highly when it came to integrity. *I could tell her that Marcella has been Trevor's lover, too, a year later. Then she'd have a totally different standing.* She bit her lips. *You can't do that. Stefano entrusted that knowledge to you.*

"Why are you looking at me like this?"

Carlina averted her eyes. "I'm just trying to take it all in." The facts she had learned flashed at such astonishing speed through her mind that it felt as if she was looking at a turning kaleidoscope. It made her dizzy. Marcella Cervi, Sabrina, Emma, Annalisa, Suzanna . . . it was dreadful. "I don't get it," she said. "Here we have tons of women who should be willing to kill him, but instead, they mourn him as if he had been a saint."

A sad smile tugged at Sabrina's mouth. "He was a very special man."

Carlina turned to her. "Do you have any idea who killed him?"

Sabrina shrugged. "None."

"Nobody who was angry at him? Hated him?"

"Well . . . now that you say it . . ." Sabrina frowned. "There was one incident." She shook her head. "Funny, I'd almost forgotten it, but now that you asked if someone was angry . . ."

Carlina bent forward. "Yes?"

"I had been going out with Trevor for a week or so, when one night, a woman waited for me as I came home. She had long hair, and she held a baby in her arms. It was crying; I remember that."

"Yes?"

"She appeared next to me just as I reached my house. She scared me to death because she held out the baby to me and claimed I had stolen the father." Sabrina shook her head again. "I remember it was a windy night, and the wind whipped up her hair. She looked as if she was out of her mind. For an instant, I thought she would attack me."

"What did you do?"

"I was afraid my husband would hear her. So I pushed her aside and said I had stolen nobody's man as I didn't take any slaves. Any man at my side was there because of his own free will."

Carlina swallowed. "And then?"

"She repeated that I had stolen Trevor and said I would have to pay for it."

"Gosh."

Sabrina shook her head. "She was a lunatic, and stupid besides. I told her I would call the police if she didn't get out of my sight."

"So she left?"

"Yep." Sabrina nodded. "I was scared that she would go to my husband, but apparently, she didn't think of that. I've never heard or seen anything from her again."

Carlina nodded, deep in thought. Could this woman be the "mistake of the past" Trevor had once referred to? Was she the woman they had dubbed Snow White? She turned to Sabrina. "Listen, Sabrina, you have to tell the police."

Sabrina frowned. "Not now, surely?" She checked her diamond-studded watch. "It's almost midnight."

"Garini won't mind."

"But I mind!" Sabrina shook her head. "I've got the Christmas fair tomorrow, something I have prepared for months, and I won't spend the last hours of this night sitting at a cold police station."

"He could come here."

"No chance." Sabrina got up and shook her hair. "I have to see my guests out now. Tomorrow morning, I'll open the fair room at six o'clock. Your Commissario may talk to me after the fair. I just don't have time for murder right now."

Carlina got up and placed a restraining hand on Sabrina's arm. "It might be dangerous to delay this information. Stefano could be here in five minutes, and it wouldn't take long. Please. I'm uneasy about this."

Sabrina laughed. "Nothing happened to me in the last twenty-five years. I don't see the slightest reason why anything should happen now." She went to the door that led back to the living room. "And please don't run to him and tell him every word I said. Even if he should call at my house tonight, I will not answer." She opened the door and looked over her shoulder, meeting Carlina's gaze with a bit of steel in hers. "Besides, if that should happen, I might just mention to my husband that I'm not convinced about the quality of our police force. Have I made myself clear?"

Sabrina's words echoed through Carlina's mind as she returned home and prepared for bed. By now, she was exhausted. Her legs and arms felt as if they were filled with lead, heavy and unwieldy, not part of her at all. She brushed her teeth with slow movements and blinked at the mirror with red-rimmed eyes. Garini would be livid if she didn't tell him everything. On the other hand, he could not force Sabrina to talk in the middle of the night. It wasn't worth waking him. She checked her watch once again. Past midnight. Maybe he was still awake? In the end, she decided to compromise by sending him a message. If he was awake, he could still call her back. "Call me." These two words would be enough.

Feeling better already because of her decision, she took her phone from the pocket, but when she checked the display, her mood plummeted. It was dead. At some point during the evening, it had run out of power. *Damn.* No wonder her helpless pressing of several buttons hadn't conjured up Garini. For the first time, she regretted having canceled her land-line at her apartment.

Disgusted, she flung her phone into the charging station. No way could she run downstairs and call Garini in the middle of the night from another phone. If she did, she would have to stay up the rest of the night, explaining to her family what on earth was going on.

She would have to send that message first thing tomorrow morning. Her alarm was set for five thirty. Garini would hate her, but she couldn't help it.

Carlina dropped into her bed like a log. It creaked, and her heavy limbs seemed to melt into the mattress. Maybe she should try the ESP communication once again. Though if it hadn't worked in the piano room, where she had invested her whole being into trying to reach him, it would not work now, with her already in a semi-comatose condition. Maybe she had to ask her mother to give her a crash-course in supernatural communications. Carlina smiled with closed eyes and pulled the bed cover higher. She couldn't do anything right now. She had to sleep. It would be a hell of a day tomorrow - and she had to stop thinking of it. Now.

But sleep wouldn't come. Sabrina's words turned round and round in her head, and in the end, Carlina got up again with a sigh. She had to get it off her chest, or she'd never get a minute of sleep. She pulled her trusted fountain pen from her handbag, found an ancient notebook, and wrote down the conversation as she remembered it, word by word.

Chapter 14

She knew something was wrong the second she opened her eyes.

Something out of the ordinary had happened. Slowly, the knowledge filtered into her.

It was too quiet. She had woken without the sound of the radio that switched itself on when it was time to get up.

Carlina opened one eye and squinted at the illuminated display of her alarm clock. Six fifteen. She gasped and jumped out of bed. She was supposed to be at the Christmas Fair at six for the set-up - fifteen minutes ago!

Carlina flung on her clothes, rushed through the apartment, and gathered her stuff like a lunatic. Thank God she had everything packed. A big box contained the first samples of the new lace underwear, and she hoped she would manage to strap it onto the Vespa. More goods as well as the three mannequins and black boxes, which she had ordered especially for the fair, would arrive around six thirty - if the transporting company was on time. Carlina brushed her teeth, grabbed an apple as a substitute for breakfast, and hurried from the apartment.

Ten minutes later, she braked with squealing tires in front of the ancient palazzo Davanzati. A huddled group of woman stood at the entrance, rubbing their hands together and stomping their feet against the cold. It was still dark, and frost covered every surface with minuscule spikes, glittering yellow in the light of the street-lamps.

"What's the matter?" Carlina put her feet to the ground to steady the overcharged Vespa and took off her helmet. Whew, it was cold. "Why are you all standing here?"

Rosanna lifted both hands in a helpless gesture. She seemed smaller than ever, wrapped tight into a scraggly coat that looked as if it had belonged to an extra large sheep. "Sabrina is the only one who has the keys, but she hasn't turned up."

Sabrina. Liquid ice poured through Carlina. *I forgot to call Garini this morning.* "Have you tried to call her?" Her voice sounded sharp. *What if something happened to Sabrina?*

"We tried, but she doesn't answer her phone." Rosanna shook her head. "We'd hoped she would arrive any minute now. None of us has the number of the guy who's taking care of the building, so that's not an option, either."

I have to talk to Garini. Now. Carlina had slung her handbag diagonally across her chest during the ride, so it would be safe but still accessible. With one swift move, she pulled it over her head and opened it to take out her cell phone. Mid-move, she stopped. "Oh, no! I don't believe this!"

Rosanna stepped closer. "What's the matter? Why are you wailing like that?"

"I forgot my phone. I need to call Ga--" just in time, she remembered that Rosanna didn't know about her relationship with Garini. "I need to call someone."

Rosanna held out her own phone. "You can take mine."

Carlina bit her lips. "Thanks, but I don't know the number by heart." A sudden wave of fear engulfed her. What was going on? What had happened to Sabrina? This was her project, and she had worked for its success for months. Nothing but a catastrophe would stop her from coming. A heavy weight pressed down on Carlina.

Another woman came closer.

Carlina recognized her as the owner of a small store that sold typical Florentine needlework. Her name was Lisa. She sold the most attractive quilts Carlina had ever seen, thick and fluffy, and yet, with an unmistakable Italian design.

"Do you have any idea what we can do, Carlina?"

Carlina unstrapped the box from her Vespa. "Here. You take my samples. I'll drive to Sabrina's house. I'll be back as soon as I know more."

Rosanna accepted the box. "You do that. Good luck."

Carlina's heart hammered as she rushed to Sabrina's house on the outskirts of the old town. *I should have called Garini last night.* Her mouth felt dry. *Damn, damn, damn. He will be furious with me.* When she had to stop at a red light, she took a steadying breath and expelled it in a white cloud. *Sabrina just overslept, like I did. I'll ring the bell so hard I'll wake everybody in the house.*

But when she turned into the street of the mayor's house, shock made her wobble. It was blocked off with police tape. She skidded to a stop, just one inch from the tape. "Oh, God." In the distance, she could see people milling around the entrance of Sabrina's house, but it was too dark to make out any details. Her heart felt as if it would jump out of her throat any minute.

She jumped off the Vespa and ducked underneath the tape.

A uniformed policeman appeared out of nowhere and caught her by the elbow. "I'm sorry, but access is forbidden here." He was in his mid-twenties, his brown hair cut so short that his ears glowed red in the cold.

Carlina stared at him. "I need to talk to Sabrina Aventuri, the wife of the mayor!" She pointed at Sabrina's house. "It's urgent!"

He looked at her in silence, his face set. "I'm afraid that's not possible."

Carlina swallowed. "Is she--? What . . . .?"

"I'm not at liberty to give you any information."

Carlina drew herself up. "Are you familiar with Stefano Garini of the Homicide Department?" Her voice wobbled.

The young policeman narrowed his eyes. "And what if I am?"

"I need to talk to him. Can you connect me to him?"

"What do you mean?"

"Via the phone." Carlina almost stomped her feet. "I need to talk to him urgently."

"What's your name?"

"Carlina Ashley."

"Don't move." He went aside, took out a cell phone and started to murmur into it.

Carlina moved her hands inside the gloves. Her fingers were frozen, but at the same time, she could feel sweat rolling down between her shoulder blades. She was having a nightmare. Surely she would wake up any minute now?

A figure detached itself from the throng of people by Sabrina's house and hurried toward them.

Carlina took a shuddering breath. She would recognize him anywhere, even if she could see nothing but his outline. She ran toward him, and this time, the policeman didn't stop her.

"Garini!"

He caught her by the arms, his face grim. "What are you doing here, Carlina?" A blinking Christmas tree in a window to his right illuminated his face for an instant, giving each shadow a razor-sharp edge.

She quailed inwardly when she saw the fierce expression in his eyes. "I . . . I need to talk to Sabrina. She was supposed to be at the palazzo Davanzati at six this morning, to open the doors for the Christmas Fair, but she didn't turn up, and we can't start with the set-up. I came to find out where she is."

His eyes narrowed. "Who knew that she was supposed to be at the palazzo at six?"

Carlina shrugged. "Gosh, everyone. We had discussed it yesterday during the last meeting."

"When was that?"

"I left at midnight or so." Carlina met his gaze. "Stefano, what happened? Is she--?"

He put his arm around her shoulders and held her tight. "She was shot this morning in front of her house. The call reached us at a quarter past six."

Carlina swayed. "It's my fault." She covered her mouth with her gloved hand and retched.

"What?" Stefano released her and bent forward. "What are you saying?"

She twisted to face him. It took all her courage to continue. "I found out yesterday that she is Laughing Eyes."

His face stilled. He stared at her without moving, thunder in his eyes.

"I . . . I tried to call you immediately. At first, I thought she was the killer and feared she would harm me, but it turned out that she was only afraid of her husband learning about the affair." She swallowed. The way he looked at her reminded her of a hawk . . . and she was the mouse. She forced herself to go on. "When I came home, it was past midnight. I was bone tired. I wanted to send you a message, but my phone had run out of power. I didn't feel like going down to Mama to phone - it would have involved endless explanations. So I decided to call you this morning."

"You didn't." His voice was flat.

"I overslept and ran from the house in a panic. I forgot my

cell at home, and when I realized that, I was already at the palazzo. I wanted to call you from Rosanna's phone, but . . . you see, I don't know your number by heart."

He shook his head. "It's an improbable story, Carlina."

Her throat hurt. "I know."

His light eyes never wavered an instant from her face. "Is there anything else I should know urgently?"

Carlina wrecked her brain. He had asked her before, and she had failed him. "I . . . I don't think so, . . . oh!"

"What?"

"I just remembered that I wrote down the whole conversation with Sabrina yesterday." She glimpsed at him. "To avoid forgetting important things."

"Good." A glimmer of a smile played around his lips, showing the small scar in one corner. "Do you happen to have the report with you?"

"I . . . actually, I do. I stuffed it into my handbag yesterday night." She pulled out the notebook and handed it to him.

"Thank you." He glanced at the blinking Christmas tree to his right and shook his head. "I need to talk with you in more detail, but not here, not now. You're freezing."

Carlina stared at him. She felt all at sea, like a ship without a rudder, blocked, unable to choose a way to go. It was a strange feeling, unfamiliar and upsetting. "What should I do now?"

Stefano frowned. "You said that all the women are waiting in front of the palazzo to start the Christmas Fair?"

"Yes."

"You stay right here." He looked at her. "And I mean here. Sabrina is still in front of the house, and I doubt that you want to see that. I'll get the keys you need and will take you back to the palazzo."

Carlina took a trembling breath. "You mean we should continue with the fair?"

"Why not?" His light eyes were cool. "Didn't you tell me it was her dream to do this fair? She wouldn't have wanted to cancel it now, would she?"

Carlina swallowed. It seemed callous, but he was right. Besides, it would restore a sense of normality, would give her something to cling to until she had gotten over the shock.

"I'll be right back." He turned on his heels and strode back to

Sabrina's house.

Carlina stood frozen and stared at the blinking Christmas tree without seeing it.

Five minutes later, Garini bundled her into a police car and put the heating at full blast.

"Is it really okay to take time off from the case, just to bring me to the Fair?" Carlina shivered. How dreadful to speak of Sabrina as "a case".

Stefano gave her a glance. "I'm not taking time off. These people are the last to have seen her; they all know when she planned to leave her house, and she spent a lot of time with them. If I find any clue, I'm likely to find it there."

Carlina closed her eyes. Of course. How stupid to think he had offered to accompany her out of sheer chivalry.

"In this case, however," Garini kept his eyes on the road, and his tone was light and non-committal, "I was glad to have a justification to stay at your side."

A bit of warmth seeped into Carlina.

The crowd in front of the palazzo had gotten bigger, and they all surged forward as the police car stopped on the curb of the narrow road. At the side, Carlina could see her well-wrapped mannequins and several boxes. Obviously, the transport company had come and gone, and with the house still closed, they had dumped everything on the sidewalk.

Rosanna's pixie-like face appeared at the window. "Carlina! What happened? Did you have an accident?"

Carlina shook her head and got out.

Garini came around and stopped right behind her. He took her lightly by the elbow.

It felt good to have his solid presence so close. Carlina took a deep breath to steady herself.

"Are you all participants in the Christmas Fair?" Garini asked.

A murmur rose and several heads nodded.

"I'm afraid I have bad news."

Garini's voice sounded unemotional, as always, but Carlina knew he hid his true feelings. She also knew that he would watch the crowd for any unusual signs and would register anything out of the ordinary.

"Sabrina Aventuri was shot this morning in front of her

house."

Someone stifled a scream. Two women to Carlina's left clasped their hands in front of their mouths in an almost identical gesture, their eyes wide with shock, but most stood frozen, too stunned to move.

"That's . . . that's impossible." Rosanna's face had paled.

"I'm afraid it's the truth," Stefano said. "I'm Commissario Garini from the homicide department of Florence. We have already started to collect all facts pertaining to this case. I'm in charge, and I'm also acquainted with Carlina Ashley."

All eyes turned to Carlina.

She swallowed. Acquainted. What a neutral word. He could have said she was a friend. But then, maybe he had done it to protect her. If he presented himself as her friend, people could take it out on her when emotions bubbled out of control.

She cleared her throat. "We have discussed the situation, and I think that we should go through with the Fair. It was Sabrina's dream, and she worked very hard to realize this event. I believe she would have wanted us to continue."

A babble of voices filled the street.

Lisa, the Florentine quilter, crossed her arms in front of her chest. "I don't agree at all. It's disrespectful. We should celebrate a mass for her, not continue to sell as if nothing had happened."

Rosanna placed a hand on her arm. "I understand your feelings, but I really think Carlina is right. Sabrina would have preferred the Christmas Fair to a mass. Besides, we can still do that later."

Carlina saw a few heads nodding. "We can't force anybody to join, and I realize it's a shock - to all of us. Unfortunately, time is running out. Shall we take a vote?"

"Yes." Lisa nodded and turned to the group. "Who thinks we should continue?"

Almost all hands went up.

"All right. We'll go on, then." For some reason, the decision relieved Carlina. She took the key Garini held out to her. "I'll open the door now, so we can start with the set-up.

The next hours rushed past as if someone had set the time into fast-forward mode. Carlina worked with flying hands. She had to have everything in top condition by nine thirty, so she would arrive in time for the shop opening at Temptation. She planned to stay at Temptation as long as possible and to return to the Christmas Fair just in time for the official opening this afternoon. To cover the waiting time in between, she had asked her mother to mind the booth. Hopefully Fabbiola wouldn't be late. Her booth was placed close to one of the trapdoors, and every time she stepped onto it, she had a hollow feeling. She had to warn her mother not to place anything on top. They'd had enough catastrophes for one day.

From the corner of her eye, she watched Garini moving around, taking statements. He did not talk to her, but from time to time, their eyes met, and each time, she felt a mixture of elation and nervousness bubbling up inside her. She was happy to have him close. Somehow, it made her feel safer, but on the other hand, he distracted her more than should be legally allowed.

Across from her, Lisa set up her booth in a spectacular manner - she had organized a huge gilt bed that looked as if it had last housed Lorenzo the Magnificent and piled all her quilts on top. Carlina eyed it and gave a wistful smile. She'd love to drop onto that bed and sleep a few hours. But that wasn't on the cards - not yet - not for a long time.

Maybe she could lend a few of her own samples to Lisa, to decorate at her store. After all, a bed and underwear complemented each other perfectly well. The thought made her smile.

"That's a wonderful quilt," she called out to Lisa. "I love the cream, very classic." *It would also go with my leopard print cushions.*

"Thank you." Lisa winked. "We'll see what's left after the show, and maybe we can do a little barter bargain."

"Sounds like a deal." Carlina turned around to see another co-exhibitor standing in front of her with an anxious face. All the time, people came up and asked her questions. For some reason, they seemed to consider her as Sabrina's successor. Carlina tried to help as much as she could, but quite often, she simply didn't have an answer. Sabrina had pulled all the strings, and her loss made itself felt all the time. The general mood was subdued - usually, someone would have organized a ghetto blaster, and people would have shouted and laughed. Today, all sounds were muted.

At a quarter to ten, Carlina had instructed her mother what to do, took a rushed leave from Garini, and hurried over to Temptation. She did not have to walk very far, and the brisk walk in the cold air dispelled some of the exhaustion she already felt. The sky was laden with dark clouds, hanging low and threatening over Florence. *It will snow yet.* Usually, Carlina enjoyed being out during the day, even if it was just for a short time. She always felt like a girl skipping school lessons when she did that, but today, in spite of the sparkling Christmas decorations in the windows to her right and left, the dark clouds above Florence seemed to have seeped into her mood - and no wonder. She still couldn't believe that someone had shot Sabrina. Who could have done that? And why? Had it anything to do with Trevor's death or were the two murders unrelated? Carlina took a big step to avoid a dog pile and hurried on. One thing was clear - the murderer had come from an inner circle. Not many people knew that Sabrina had planned to leave her house before six this morning. Carlina shivered and lifted her shoulders. That didn't make things better. What did Garini think? She couldn't imagine that he would consider her to be a suspect, but if the two murders were related, she was too damn close. Who? Who could have killed them? Her mind was running in circles.

At Temptation, the pre-Christmas rush hit them like an avalanche. No sooner had they opened the door than customers streamed in . . . more men than usual, flustered and in need of being reassured that they were buying the right thing. It was so busy that Carlina didn't even find the time to inform her co-workers about Sabrina's death. In fact, she didn't want to. She dreaded the emotions, particularly Annalisa's reaction. She might end up in hysterics. So she held her mouth and pretended to herself that nothing but her work existed. Of course she had to inform Ricciarda before they went to the Christmas Fair, but that could wait.

By two o'clock, Carlina had the impression that the world was turning around her in circles. She listened to her customers as if on autopilot, gave advice, smiled, counted cash . . . and was miles away.

"The day is twice as long if you start working at six," she whispered to Ricciarda as she re-arranged the bras according to size on the hangers. "No matter what the mathematicians say."

"I didn't start at six," Ricciarda pushed a strand of hair from her brow, "but I feel worn out already."

For the first time that day, Carlina focused on her assistant. Ricciarda was pale, her face strained. *I should have noted earlier.* "Listen, we'll be working late tonight. Let's go to the café opposite and sit down for twenty minutes. We'll eat something and rest our feet."

"Will we have the time?" Ricciarda looked as if she wanted to agree but didn't dare to.

"We'll make time." Carlina informed Marianna and Annalisa that they were leaving early and grabbed her coat as well as her handbag.

Annalisa pulled a face, but Marianna waved at them with a cheerful grin. "Don't worry, we'll manage."

"Thank you so much. And don't forget to lock the security door tonight." Carlina pulled Ricciarda through the door before another customer could stop them.

The cold wind was invigorating after the over-heated atmosphere at the store. "I bet we'll have snow later on," Carlina said. "Doesn't it smell like it?"

Ricciarda lifted her nose into the wind like a dog and shook her head. "I don't smell anything. It's not very likely that we'll have snow, is it? The last time was three years ago, I think."

Carlina laughed. "Maybe I imagined it."

She waited until they had reached the coffee stage before she broke the news to Ricciarda.

Her assistant sat as if made of marble. "I . . . I don't believe this," she finally said. "How can Sabrina be dead?" With a tired gesture, she rubbed her face.

Carlina shook her head. "It's crazy. In fact, we can only hope that the Christmas Fair will be an immense success, so we won't have time for a single thought to spare. Otherwise, everyone will sit in her booth, sunk in brown studies." She shuddered. "You can't imagine how dreadful it was, setting up everything this morning, with that knowledge hanging over us."

"Gosh, I can imagine." Ricciarda was speaking without emotion, staring straight ahead.

Carlina took her by the arm. "You're in shock. Do you want to drink another espresso, maybe?"

Ricciarda shook her head and managed a wan smile. "No,

thank you."

"If only Garini finds the murderer soon. This second victim increased the pressure on him, you know."

"I can imagine." Ricciarda still spoke in that far-away voice.

Carlina decided to keep on talking until Ricciarda had found her footing again. "I'm sure it has something to do with that album. If only we could identify all the women and talk to them. Some of them seemed so familiar!"

"Really?" Ricciarda frowned.

At least it's a reaction. "Yes, but I can't make the connection. You didn't recognize anybody when Garini showed you the pictures, did you?"

Ricciarda shook her head. "I didn't."

Carlina gave her a sharp glance. Her assistant sounded more the thing now, and even a bit of color had returned to her face. *Good.* "We have to go." She put enough money on the table and gave Ricciarda an encouraging smile. "Just a few more hours, and we can put up our feet for hours." When they got up, Carlina's back hurt, and it took a conscious effort to put weight on her hurting feet, but in spite of her bodily and emotional exhaustion, a little tingle of excitement remained. *Will the new collection be a success?* She loved the lace-bras and panties, but her masterpiece was a dressing gown going down to mid-calf and ending in several triangular-shaped tails. It looked bohemian and sexy and utterly enchanting. She had tested the prototype at home, catching herself wondering if Garini would like it.

She caught her impression in the mirror of the café as they left - she was smiling. *What an odd mix a human being is - so many emotions so close to each other.*

The Christmas Fair had just opened its doors to the public, and they slipped in together with the first visitors. "Carlina!" Her mother rose from one of the black boxes and hurried to enfold her in a hug. To celebrate the occasion, she had put on a new pair of wide trousers in black, sprinkled with gold-dust. This she had combined with a golden jacket that looked fit for a TV-star. To top it off, she had put a golden ribbon into her henna-red hair, the ends trailing onto her shoulders. Even the cushion underneath her arm had a new cover, with golden stars, not silver ones.

From the corner of her eyes, Carlina saw Ricciarda staring

and couldn't suppress a chuckle.

"You look amazing, Mama." Carlina returned the hug. "Thank you for manning the fort. Did everything work out all right?"

"You haven't told me about the wife of the mayor!" Fabbiola stuck her hands on her hips. "She was shot in front of her own house this very morning and all you talk about is lacy underwear! I told you there was danger! Danger from children, danger from--"

Carlina closed her eyes for a brief moment. "Yes, danger from broccoli. But I haven't seen any children around, and if you're suggesting that Sabrina was shot by a child, I'd like to know where you got that idea from!"

Ricciarda grabbed a price-list, slipped into the background and made herself familiar with the booth and its contents.

Thank God. She's a true professional. Carlina focused again on her mother. "Listen, Mama, I think it's better if you don't spread rumors like that."

Her mother pressed her lips together and lifted her chin. "Everyone was a child once. You'll mark my words."

"Quite." Carlina took her by the arm and walked her to the side of the booth. "I don't think you've had time to check out the other booths. Why don't you do that now? I bet you'll find wonderful stuff. Sabrina--" she cut herself off and swallowed, then continued with an effort, "Sabrina had a gift for choosing the right combination of artists."

"Hrmpf." Fabbiola gave her a hurt glance, hitched her cushion higher underneath her arm, and waltzed off.

Phew. Carlina turned around. "So, what do you think?" She looked at Ricciarda who was sitting on one of the black cubes and studying the price-list. "Is the presentation okay?"

Ricciarda looked up and nodded. "It's great. I really love those black mannequins. They show off the lace to its best advantage."

"Thank you." Carlina collapsed onto the other black cube and looked around. She was satisfied with the result of her work, and for the first time that day, she had time to focus. So far, only a few customers had appeared. Soothing piano music from the loudspeakers mixed with the babble of voices. It smelled of oranges from Rosanna's booth, who had created Christmassy still lifes by combining oranges and flowers. They looked spectacular.

Garini doesn't seem to be here. She had looked out for him ever since they had entered the building, but apparently, he was gone. *I wonder what he's doing right now.*

Lisa gave her a friendly wave from across, and Carlina waved back.

"Shall we make another bet?" Ricciarda asked. "I'll stake a bag of Ricciarelli cookies, and I bet we'll sell at least fifteen of these dressing gowns."

Carlina shuddered at the memory of their last bet, but she tried to hide her revulsion. "They're very pricey," she said. "Ten would be a lot already."

"Deal." Ricciarda smiled. "I'd like to look around for a bit, if I may."

"Sure. So far, we're not being trampled to death." She broke off, shocked by her own words. *How often we use the words death and don't even mean it.*

Chapter 15

"Commissario!" Piedro hurried over the crooked stone pavement of the Piazza Mentana.

Garini turned around. He had hoped for five minutes by himself to get his thoughts into order while grabbing a bite to eat as a late substitute for lunch but Piedro looked as if he had big news. "Yes?"

Piedro panted from running. "We just got a call."

"Yes?" Garini decided to continue walking. If Piedro stuck to his usual reporting style, he would have ample time to finish his meal before he came to the vital part.

"It's about this Ake . . . Ake . . ."

Garini frowned. The stutter was new.

"The Japanese woman," Piedro said in desperation. "Can't remember her name."

"Ah." Garini opened the door of the small trattoria and motioned Piedro to go through. Christo would surely offer them a cheese sandwich even though it was late for having lunch.

"They say she had a concert on December 19 in Tokyo. Thousands of people heard her play."

"December 19? That's one day after the murder of Trevor." Garini did a quick calculation in his mind. What was the time difference to Japan? If Akemi Hateyama had taken a flight directly after the murder, could she have arrived in time for the concert, taking the time lag into account? He'd have to look it up - no use trusting Piedro with such a calculation. It would only occupy him for hours. He looked at his assistant. "Do you want to eat something?"

"Oh, yes."

Of course. They ordered cheese sandwiches and sat down in a quiet corner. Two minutes later, Christo slid the plates with the sandwiches in front of them.

Piedro drew himself up. "The report says that Ake . . . Ake, whatever, did the last rehearsal on December 18, and several people testified that she was present. I also asked at passport controls if she entered the country, but they said she was last in Italy in May."

"Good." Garini nodded. "Then we can cross her off." He felt a bit better. It was the first name he could cross off without doubt - if she hadn't used another passport, but that was not very likely. A tiny step forward. "How about about Suzanne Morin? Did the passport controls give you any information about her?"

"Yes." Piedro bit into the oozing cheese sandwich. "She arrived December 20."

"Two days after the murder." Garini wolfed down his sandwich. "So she's out of it, too." He didn't know if he should feel good or bad about it. If he could only cross off non-Mantoni-family members, his relationship to Carlina was doomed. But at least it was a step forward. Two women to cross off the list. "How about Ileana Marani, the one who now lives in Rome?"

Piedro lifted both shoulders and made a face. "She's got an alibi."

"But?"

Piedro opened his eyes wide. "Why do you say but?"

"Because you don't look as if this was good news."

"Well . . . ," Piedro wiped a drop of grease from his chin. "The alibi is from the minister of education."

Oh, no. Garini suppressed a sigh.

Piedro made an unhappy face. "Or maybe it was the minister of economy."

"Quite a different person." Garini had trouble keeping his voice level.

"Or . . . or the minister of finance." He lifted his gaze to Garini. "I can't recall exactly."

"But you surely made notes?"

Piedro scratched his head. "I tried to, but they talked so quickly that I--"

"Who's 'they'?"

"The police in Rome."

"Will they send a written report?"

Piedro shrugged. "Maybe."

Garini suppressed an exasperated sigh. "Did you ask for one?"

"Yes, I did." Piedro hung his head. "But they mumbled something and hung up."

"All right. But until then, we know at least that Ileana Marani has an alibi from some minister or other who was with her during the crucial time. That much is sure?"

"Yes." Piedro nodded. "But . . ."

Garini held his temper back with an iron hand. "But what?"

"But it's a government alibi."

Stefano lifted his eyebrow. Why did every conversation with Piedro feel like a cross-examination? "So?"

"You told me you can never believe anything the government says." Piedro looked up with earnest eyes. "They are all bribed, you said."

II

At the Christmas fair, the hours flew by, and they sold the new lace collection as if someone had told every woman in town to stock up on underwear - with one exception. The dressing gown seemed to be invisible, and customers kept ignoring it, even if Carlina drew their attention to it.

"I'll put it on myself in a minute," she said to Ricciarda when it was past five o'clock and they had not sold a single one. "Just to make them notice it."

"It's strange." Ricciarda frowned. "I was so sure it would sell."

From this moment on, Carlina changed her strategy. When yet another woman slid her gaze over the dressing gown without a spark of interest, she asked them right out why they didn't like it . . . and she was delighted by the way her customers replied. The ladies loved to be asked and felt like designers. They criticized pretty much everything, from the fall of the lace to the seams at the side and the pattern in itself, but when they had collected the answers of more than ten people, the major problem became apparent - the ladies didn't like the uneven tails. Apparently, it was too bohemian. "Funny." Carlina shook her head. "I'd never have thought that our customers would be so traditional."

"Me neither." Ricciarda shrugged. "You always learn."

When the Christmas Fair finally closed at a quarter past ten, the sales people collapsed. Carlina heard the popping of champagne corks and smiled. They still had to dismantle everything and pack it into boxes, but that was less exhausting than standing and talking and smiling.

As they had to hand over the room in pristine condition early the next morning, Carlina had decided to ask her cousin Sergio to bring his small transporter and help. Uncle Teo had the job of accompanying him and helping him pack. The apartment of her deceased grandfather on the ground floor of their house had not been rented out yet, so they had agreed to store everything there for the time being. It was dry, safe, and free.

The timing worked well - they had just finished wrapping up the mannequins when Sergio appeared. In his wake trailed not only Uncle Teo but also Signor Morin, the Frenchman.

Carlina lifted her eyebrows in a mute question.

"I've asked him to come along and help," Uncle Teo said with an airy move of his hand. "Every pair of hands is welcome, I said."

"Of course." Carlina suppressed a grin and nodded at Signor Morin. Obviously Uncle Teo had adopted him into the family. Well, why not. They both had sad memories to deal with this Christmas, and if it helped, she was all for it.

Half an hour later, the exhibition room was as empty as it had been two days before. The other women had all left, wishing each other "Buon Natale" with tired faces.

Carlina closed the wooden door of the exhibition room with a relieved sigh. "That's it." She smiled at Ricciarda. "Thank you very much. You've been a great help."

Ricciarda's long ponytail hung limp on her drooping shoulders. "I'm exhausted."

"Me too." Carlina went down the staircase next to her assistant. Each step made a hollow sound, echoing through the building. With a feeling of shock, Carlina realized they were the last in the empty building, in the middle of the night. It didn't feel good. The memory of Sabrina's murder made her shiver, and she threw a surreptitious glance over her shoulder. "It's a bit eerie, isn't it?"

"Yep." Ricciarda hurried forward.

They burst through a small side door that led to the silent street. The air met them like liquid ice, and in the yellow light of the street-lamp, a maze of tiny snowflakes trundled to the ground. The green metal posts that dotted the street already sported white caps. For once, Florence was silent and empty.

"Oh, look, Ricciarda!" Carlina pointed at the metal posts. "It has started to snow! How pretty!"

Ricciarda turned her head. They were still underneath the arch that formed the ground of the exhibition room above them. In the shadow of the massive wall, her foot missed the last step that led down to the street, and she fell onto her knees with a sharp cry of pain. Her handbag banged onto the ground, gaped open, and the contents exploded over a radius of several meters.

"Gosh, I'm sorry!" Carlina hurried to her side. "Are you hurt?"

Ricciarda shook her head and picked herself up. "I'm fine."

Carlina helped her to collect her belongings. She started with the things that had ended up furthest away, on the street, to save them from the snow.

Ricciarda remained underneath the arch and gathered the things around her feet with hurried moves.

Carlina picked up a small frame and wiped the snow from it. When her glance fell onto the picture, she froze. Her breath came out in a soundless gasp, forming a white cloud. The woman looking at her from the frame was the first lady of Trevor's album - Snow-White. Suddenly she knew why Snow-White had seemed so familiar. Her chest constricted.

"She was my mother." Ricciarda's voice was expressionless.

Carlina looked up, straight into the mouth of a gun.

Chapter 16

Piedro burst into Garini's office. "A woman wants to see you urgently."

With one swift move, Garini covered the picture of Piedro's mother with a piece of paper. Once again, he had gone over the pictures. Something about them made him uneasy - he had the feeling that he should have recognized some faces, but the more he looked at them, the more elusive they became. "What on earth are you still doing here?" He checked his watch. "It's past ten." The winter night had long ago blackened out the last lingering light of the weak sun. Garini frowned. Usually, Piedro made sure he left the station the second his shift was over.

Piedro made a face. "My father asked me to drive him home, but then the mayor came, and they're still in his office. Dad said it would only last a few minutes, and now they've been there for hours."

The mayor. Sabrina's husband. Garini felt a prickle of unease go up and down his spine.

"Will you see the woman?" Piedro asked.

"Who is she?"

"She says it's urgent."

Garini suppressed the urge to snap at his subordinate. "That wasn't the question. What's her name?"

Piedro looked at the floor. "I forgot to ask."

"Piedro." Garini forced himself to speak without lifting his voice. "I am in the middle of a complicated case, and I don't wish to talk to some woman who wants to see me urgently if you can't even tell me her name or what it's about."

Piedro pressed his lips together. "But I know what it's about."

"You do?" Garini's voice sounded dry. "That's good. Will you share it with me at some point during this night?"

Piedro swallowed. "She says she has important information."

"Yes?"

"Important information about the case."

"Which case?" It took an iron hand not to lose control when talking to Piedro.

Piedro wrung his hands. "The strangled charmer. The American."

"Ah." Garini lifted his head. "Now we're getting somewhere. This is interesting. Did she tell you more?"

Piedro nodded, then shook his head, then shrugged.

"I beg your pardon?"

"She kind of said she knew who killed the American."

Garini jumped up. "What?"

"Yes, but she said she only wanted to talk to the investigating officer, not to anybody else, so I came to ask you about it."

Garini went to the door. "Then let's go and talk to her immediately."

Piedro had installed the unknown woman in the interrogation room on the ground floor of the police station. With a wistful feeling Garini remembered how he had once talked to Carlina there. How long ago it seemed. He waited until Piedro was also inside the room, then closed the door and looked at the young woman sitting next to the rickety table.

Her hands were clutching a shiny handbag, and she looked at him with fear in her face. Her dark-brown hair was parted in the middle, and her brown eyes looked huge due to the deep smudges underneath. One eye was a bit out of focus, just like Mona Lisa's.

Garini recognized her immediately. For an instant, he didn't move. *What on earth had Piedro been thinking?* Then he went to the table and nodded at her. "I'm Commissario Garini. I'm in charge of the case of Trevor Accanto's murder." Stefano took in every detail of the woman's face. Her mouth trembled, and the lines around her eyes made her look older, but even her obvious exhaustion couldn't take away her beauty. *Carlina is convinced that this woman strangled Trevor.* He was not so sure. "You came in answer to our newspaper announcement?"

The woman gave him a small smile and nodded. "Yes."

"That was courageous of you. Thank you." Garini took a chair next to her.

Piedro created a maximum of noise by scraping another chair

over the floor and dropping into it with a thud.

"Please tell me what you wish to share," Stefano said.

The woman gave Garini a nervous glance. "I will only talk to you, to nobody else. I don't want my statement to be typed or recorded or anything."

Garini looked at Piedro and made a move with his head toward the door.

Piedro lumbered to his feet and shuffled from the room.

"He's not very bright, that one, is he?" The woman frowned.

"Signora," Garini met her gaze, "I can't talk badly about my colleagues."

The woman inclined her head. "Fair enough." Then she faced Garini. "The newspaper said you needed to talk to me. I--" She swallowed. "I was afraid of coming, but I . . ." Her voice petered out, and she started to fold her fingers into an intricate pattern without releasing the handle of her handbag.

"Yes?" Garini didn't take his gaze off her. She seemed intelligent and strong, and he could tell that she thought out things before she acted on them.

"I will not give you my name or tell you my address."

"I understand." *Time enough for that later.* Garini decided to give her a long leash and to let her tell the story in her own way. Intensive questioning would only frighten her off.

"I know who killed Trevor Accanto." Her voice was quiet and determined, even though fatigue etched deep lines into her face.

She has no idea how convincing she is. "Please tell me more."

She took a deep breath. "It's a long story."

He nodded. "We have time."

She gulped. "I went out with Trevor two years ago, during Christmastime. He dropped me afterward. I resented him ever since, but I . . . I didn't kill him." She bit her lips. "I was at that store, Temptation, on the day when he was killed. I bought a pair of those nylons."

"I know."

Her eyes widened. "You know? Are you . . . why didn't you arrest me?"

"I didn't know where to find you."

She grabbed her handbag and jumped up. "I'd better go."

He didn't twitch a muscle. "Please remain seated. If you say you didn't kill him, I'll believe you."

Her mouth dropped open. Without taking her gaze from him, she dropped back onto her chair. "I'd not have thought they have men like you on the force."

"Men like me?"

"Men who listen."

"Thank you, Signora." He inclined his head. "Will you trust me with whatever information you have?"

She nodded. "When I saw my picture in the paper, I was afraid. I knew Trevor, I had no reason to love him anymore, and I had bought the nylons." Her face twisted. "I knew I was in a difficult spot. At first, I wanted to leave the country, but I knew that would draw even more attention to me."

"Yes?"

"So I hid at home. When I went out, I put on sunglasses and a big scarf, so people wouldn't recognize me." She took a trembling breath. "But of course, many people know me, my neighbors, my colleagues . . . Thankfully, I have changed a bit since the picture with Trevor was taken, but still, it was dreadful. Every second, I expected a knock on my door, the police coming to arrest me. I could not prove anything. I could not prove that I had been far away from the Basilica when Trevor was killed."

"Where were you?" She had one hundred percent of his attention.

"I walked around the city, but I didn't go into any store. It was Christmastime again, and as I saw the decorations in the streets, I remembered my time with Trevor." A muscle twitched next to her mouth. "I first wanted to have an early lunch at the Garibaldi Hotel, in the restaurant of their roof terrace, to recall the good time we had." Her gaze dropped to her clenched fingers. "I was also hoping I might see him, but then the thought unsettled me too much. I doubt they enjoy crying guests." Her pale cheeks looked pinched in. "If only I had gone there. The waiter might have remembered me, and I would have had an alibi."

Anger boiled inside Garini. The charming American with his unusual magnetism had managed to destroy so many lives, living by one rule only - how to get the maximum of pleasure for his own life. "Please go on."

Mona Lisa hesitated. "I felt I was going crazy, waiting to be arrested, like a trapped mouse, unable to do anything." She lifted her head and stared at him. "In the end, I couldn't stand it anymore. I felt I had to DO something."

"Yes?"

"So I went back to that lingerie store."

He stiffened. "You went to Temptation?"

"Yes." She nodded. "This morning, at ten."

This morning. He knew Carlina had been at Temptation at ten, having come straight from the setup of the Christmas Fair. Had it been only this morning? The day had been so long. "Why did you do that?"

"I felt I had to retrace my way, had to find someone who might be able to confirm that I had been far away from the church when Trevor was killed. I didn't remember where exactly I had been going, so I figured I'd start with the lingerie store."

His mouth was dry. He didn't take his gaze off the woman in front of him.

"I stood in front of the shop window of Temptation and looked inside, and that's when I saw her."

"Who did you see?"

"The murderer."

"What?" He bent forward. It cost him all his self-control not to shake her.

She eyed him with trepidation but continued to speak in the same calm way as before. "I saw her through the window, standing behind the sales counter. She was talking to a customer, and when she smiled, I knew it for sure."

He forced himself to remain calm. "What did you know for sure?"

Mona Lisa frowned. "That she was his daughter, of course."

He thought he'd misunderstood. "I beg your pardon?"

"She has his mouth, and there's something about the line of her cheek that immediately reminded me of Trevor. I saw it in a flash." She nodded in thought. "And while I was standing there, I suddenly knew the truth. She was his daughter, and she had killed him."

She's mentally deranged. Did Trevor have that effect on all the women he discarded? "I happen to know for sure that Carlina Ashley is not Trevor Accanto's daughter." He tried to put a certain calm authority into his voice.

"Who?" Now it was her turn to look confused.

"The owner of Temptation," he explained. "She has green eyes and brown curls." Had they been talking at cross-purposes? Maybe she wasn't mentally deranged after all. "Aren't you talking about her?"

"Oh, no." Mona Lisa shook her head. "I saw her standing in the background, talking to another customer. She was the one who sold the nylons to me on the day of Trevor's death. I don't mean her. I mean the younger one, the one with long, black hair."

Garini froze. For one crazy instant, he again heard Fabbiola's voice "Beware of children. They will harm you." Could it be? Was Ricciarda Trevor's daughter? *But Ricciarda has an alibi. She was at Temptation during the time of the murder.* He took a calming breath. A voice inside him sneered. *Was she really? What if she left the store unattended?* He'd never considered the thought, misled by the total trust Carlina put into her assistant. *How stupid.* The pictures twirled in his mind as if he was looking into a kaleidoscope. Ricciarda, restrained and composed during their first interview at the café. Her quiet face while she looked at the pictures of the women involved in the case - and her calm statement as she denied all knowledge of them. Could it be? His whole take on the case shifted and re-arranged itself at such speed that he felt dizzy. Could it be possible? It gave her a direct link - a father who had never been there. But that wasn't a sufficient reason to kill him. He had never seen a likeness between Trevor Accanto and Ricciarda, but then, he'd only seen Trevor once, after his death, and later in pictures. Quite often, a likeness came through a tone of voice, a way of moving, not through the physical traits alone. He shook his head. The whole idea was fantastic, created by a desperate woman who wanted to point at someone else to get herself out of trouble. Garini narrowed his eyes. "Why do you think she killed her father? What makes you so sure?"

Mona Lisa pressed her lips together. "I don't think he was much of a father if he went gallivanting around town with another woman every Christmas."

"That would be true for quite a few fathers and yet, they have not found themselves killed." His voice was dry.

Mona Lisa shook her head. "You check into her. I'm sure I'm right." She straightened and slipped forward on her chair. "I have told you all I know. I have to go."

"One moment, please." He held up his hand.

Her eyes widened in fear. "You said I could trust you."

"I'm not arresting you." He made sure he kept his distance, so she wouldn't be scared into flight. "Why are you coming to me now, in the middle of the night, at--" He checked his watch, "At ten thirty? You say you went to Temptation in the morning. Why didn't you come to see me right away?"

She squared her shoulders. "I didn't want to come. I thought you wouldn't believe me. But when it got dark, and when I was at home, waiting once again, waiting for you to come and arrest me, waiting until I thought I would go out of my mind, I realized it would make a better impression if I came of my own free will."

"You were right." He searched her face. Was she telling the truth? Here was a suspect, serving herself on a golden platter, with a perfect motive, the murder weapon newly purchased, and no alibi for the time in question. He was a fool if he let her go. "Do you still have the nylons?"

"I do." She opened her handbag and pulled out the tights. The soft material shimmered in the harsh light of the interrogation room.

That doesn't prove anything. She can have purchased another pair at any later point of time. Garini nodded. "Thank you. May I keep them for the time being?" He wanted Carlina to inspect them and to confirm that it was the right model. "I'll give you a receipt."

She looked at him without blinking. "I can give them to you, but I don't want a receipt. I won't tell you my name."

He held her gaze. "I promise I'll check out every detail, and I do appreciate that you came here and told me what you think. But how can I get in touch with you if I need to ask anything else?"

"You won't." She got up. "That's it. I will go home now and sleep for the first time in days. You do your job and arrest the daughter."

He let her go. Cervi would have his head if he ever knew about it, but that didn't matter. He had to see Ricciarda. His heart stopped. She was with Carlina at the Christmas Fair. He checked his watch once again. They would be busy pulling down the booth. A feeling of fear pooled deep down in his stomach. What if Mona Lisa was right? Carlina all on her own with Ricciarda, Ricciarda who, if she was the murderer, would have no hesitation at all to defend herself with drastic measures if Carlina should stumble upon the truth.

Nonsense, a calm voice inside him said. *They are working together peacefully, and you can still interrogate Ricciarda tomorrow. Even if she is the American's daughter, it doesn't automatically follow that she killed him.*

Garini clenched his fist. Before he had taken a conscious decision, he had already grabbed his coat and pocketed the gun he didn't often take. His body seemed to act with a life of its own even while his mind still grappled with the thought. *She'll laugh at you.* He shook his head and grabbed the Christmas gift he had planned to give to Carlina tomorrow at Temptation. *Ha. You think you need an excuse to see her?* The voice inside him sneered. Without noticing it, he started to run.

Chapter 17

Carlina stared without blinking at the gun in Ricciarda's hand. Everything inside her froze in shock.

"I'm sorry I have to kill you." Ricciarda's voice sounded normal, as if they were discussing which bra to put on display this evening. "I really enjoyed working with you."

"Ricciarda." Carlina cleared her throat. "I . . . I don't believe this. You killed Trevor? You? But why? How . . . ?"

Ricciarda's face changed into a mask of hate.

Carlina had trouble recognizing her. A feeling of horror swamped her.

"He was my father." Ricciarda's hand shook as she spat out the words. "My father. Who left my mother for another woman before I was one year old."

"Your father?" Carlina couldn't take it in. "But--"

"What?" Ricciarda snapped.

"I . . . I can't believe it." The look on Riccidarda's face frightened her. She looked like another person, someone she had never seen before.

"It's true, though." Ricicarda's voice was bitter. "Though he doesn't deserve to be called my father. He left us as soon as he could."

Carlina glanced down the street. Nobody. It was as if they were all alone in the world and not in the middle of Florence. *Make her talk.* "That wasn't your fault." She tried to make her voice sound soothing in spite of its being pressed down by fear.

"No, it wasn't my fault." Ricciarda agreed without emotion. "But it was my responsibility to make him pay."

"Nonsense."

"Don't you say nonsense to me!" Ricciarda's voice rose. "My mother told me to bring him to justice. When she died, she said I should do it."

Carlina shook her head. "That's crazy."

"I'm not crazy!" Ricciarda narrowed her eyes. "He had it coming." She sounded almost hysterical now.

"But . . . but you were at Temptation when Trevor was killed. The waiter gave you an alibi for the full time!"

"I wasn't at Temptation," Ricciarda said with disdain. "I'd never left the store unattended before, but I felt the need to pray, to clean myself, so--"

Carlina thought she'd misunderstood. "To clean yourself?"

"Yes." Ricciarda pressed her lips together. "I had met my father," again, she spat out the word as if it was an insult, "for the first time that morning. He tried to flirt with me." Her face twisted. "With me."

Like a flash, Carlina recalled Trevor and Ricciarda, laughing together at Temptation, before Ricciarda knew who he was. She had thought they looked like an advertisement for family shampoo. No wonder. They had the same blue eyes, the same black hair, even the same way of looking over their shoulders. *How could I have been so blind?*

"He flirted with me, with his own daughter. It shocked me." For an instant, Ricciarda's eyes wavered aside, as if looking for direction.

Carlina held her breath. Would she dare to jump at her? No, she was too far away. Better make her talk. "He didn't know you were his daughter."

"Of course not!" Ricciarda's face was distorted by hate. "He didn't even recognize his own daughter, instead, he planned to add me to his harem. How sick is that?"

Carlina bit her lip. She didn't recognize her calm assistant anymore - the woman in front of her was ravaged by emotions. Helpless, she glanced at the empty street. The snow muffled all sound. Maybe someone would come before Ricciarda worked herself up to pull the trigger. But would that change the situation? What would happen if an innocent citizen should really come up the street and discover Ricciarda with her gun deep within the shadow of the arch? It would not help at all - Ricciarda was safe underneath the arch, with plenty of time to kill anybody coming closer from the street. *Damn.*

Ricciarda focused again on Carlina. "He was Satan."

"What?" It sounded like a croak. Icy tendrils of fear sneaked up and down Carlina's back.

"He seemed like the angel of light, oh, so charming, so delightful, but he was all black underneath."

"And that's why you killed him?" Carlina shook her head in utter disbelief. She had never seen it coming, had never suspected the boiling feelings beneath Ricciarda's cool surface. She had never met the real Ricciarda.

"I didn't plan to kill him." Ricciarda's face twisted. "But when I came to church, to my church, my sanctuary, to pray, to find peace for my troubled mind, just five minutes, not more," the words were tumbling over each other now, and her chest was heaving "There he was, right in front of me, praying!" Her voice rose. "Praying! Satan, praying inside my church. He was soiling it." She looked at her hands. "I had to do it. It wasn't right." She lifted her head. "You should agree. He was busy destroying your cousin."

Carlina gasped. "You can't kill people because they destroy others!"

Ricciarda was unmoved. "An eye for an eye. The scripture says so."

She's crazy. Carlina had trouble with her breathing.

"I bought another pair of stockings that looked very much like ours – though they could get runs, of course - and wore them instead, so you wouldn't notice that mine were missing."

Carlina wasn't interested in the stockings. "What about Sabrina?"

"Sabrina took him away from my mother. When I got your call--"

"My call?" Carlina frowned. "What call?"

"You called me last night, during the reception at her house."

Carlina's knees went weak as she recalled how she had fumbled with the phone in her pocket, trying to reach Garini. "You mean I called you when--?"

"You didn't say anything, and I was about to hang up when I heard your voice, and then Sabrina's. The things she said . . . ," again, the gun made an erratic turn, ". . . they made me see red. She stole him from my mother and me, and she had the gall to say it was his own, free will." She pressed her lips together. "She deserved to be shot."

Carlina's head turned. "Ricciarda, please listen to me. I think it's time we both go to Garini and discuss this with him."

Ricciarda's harsh laughter interrupted her. "No way. He'll lock me up."

"He'll find out anyway." Carlina hoped her voice sounded more confident than she felt. "And it'll be much better if you talk to him before that happens."

"Nonsense." Ricciarda shook her head. "Now stop talking and--"

Before she could finish her sentence, a white blanket dropped from above over her head, following by something heavy and dark. With a muffled cry, Ricciarda fell down.

Carlina threw herself aside.

The gun went off with a soft sound. *A silencer.* Carlina crawled on her knees through the thin layer of snow to find a bit of cover behind one of the green metal poles. She could make out some movements in the dark, a shadowed person shuffling around, but not enough to understand what was happening. Did she have enough time to run away before Ricciarda fired her gun again?

"Are you all right, Carlina?"

Garini! Carlina's heart skipped a beat. She peeked around the pole.

"Come here and help me." His voice sounded different, not quite as cool and ironic as usual. "There's no danger anymore."

She went forward with care, hunched over, a watchful eye on the unmoving bulk next to Garini.

He sat on the ground as if he was having a picnic, a white blanket underneath him. "I handcuffed her," he said. "On hands and feet. She's unconscious right now. It seems I landed right on top of her." He made a move with his chin to the side. "Would you pick up the gun and hand it to me? Just use your fingertips, will you?"

Carlina blinked. Her gaze followed the direction he had indicated and came to rest on the gun, lying in the deepest shadow of the arch like a toy. Without a word, she picked it up and handed it to him.

He placed the gun inside his jacket, then turned to her. "Look at me." He lifted his eyebrows, then patted the white blanket. "Sit down."

Carlina didn't move. "What on earth--?"

"It's your Christmas gift. The quilt you admired at Lisa's booth." He gave her a lopsided smile. "I hope it's not ruined, but I had nothing else on hand to soften the fall."

His smile warmed something inside her. "Garini."

"I would really appreciate if you could sit down." He sounded amused. "At this distance, I can't judge the exact shade of green of your face, and I feel an urge to do that."

She held out her hand. "Why don't you get up?"

"Some slight problem with my leg," he said. "I'd rather sit."

Carlina lowered herself onto the blanket next to him. It felt good not to depend on her trembling knees anymore, but everything still felt surreal. The snow continued to come down in tiny whirls, innocent, white, as if the world was a pure place.

They sat in the shadow of the arch without moving. Slowly, the world stopped shaking.

When she lifted her gaze to his face, the tenderness in it made her breathless. To hide her feelings, she looked up at the trapdoor gaping open above them. "A true Deus-Ex-Machina maneuver, Garini." She made sure her voice sounded light and ironic. "Quite impressive, this drop from the sky."

He smiled, understanding deep in his eyes. "I'd hoped you would appreciate it."

"I do." She managed a wobbly smile. "How did you manage to arrive so spot-on?"

"Long story. I'll tell you later." He pressed his lips together. "I was almost too late. When I came through the back door into the building, the exhibition room was empty. I thought I'd missed you, then I heard your voices downstairs. The second I opened the side door, I saw Ricciarda with the gun. Thank God she was so intent on you that she didn't notice me. I had no clue how to get close enough to her without putting you in danger."

Carlina shivered. "You could only have stopped her with a gun."

"I had a gun." His voice was calm. "But if I had shot at such a close distance, the bullet would have ricocheted off the stone walls, beyond my control. Then I remembered the trap door and rushed upstairs. It took ages to open it." He put his arm around her shoulders and pulled her close. "I was almost too late."

Carlina relaxed against his shoulder. For some reason, she wanted to cry.

He put his finger underneath her chin until she had to lift her face to him. "It's over, Carlina."

She started to tremble.

His lips brushed hers.

They were cold and yet, a sudden flash of heat soared through her.

A car turned with squealing tires around the corner and raced down the street. It slid through the snow, and while it was still moving, the doors opened and several people tumbled out, landing right in front of them.

"Carlina!" Fabbiola surged forward, her golden jacket glittering underneath the street-lamp. "Are you all right?"

Carlina blinked. "Hi, Mama. Where are you springing from?"

Uncle Teo advanced with care through the snow, closely followed by Leopold Morin who slithered forward on his slippery leather shoes. "We were worried about you." Uncle Teo winked at Garini. "But it seems that wasn't necessary."

"Why are you huddling against the Commissario like that?" Fabbiola's tone implied she didn't approve. "Couldn't you find a more romantic place than a freezing arch?"

"We didn't have much choice." Garini's voice shook with suppressed laughter. His arm tightened around Carlina's shoulder.

A smile spread across her face. It felt strange, as if she had forgotten how to smile properly and had to start learning it again from scratch, but it was a beginning.

"What's that?" The Frenchman pointed a trembling finger at Ricciarda, still lying without moving on the ground. His thin face quivered.

"It's Ricciarda Fazzolari."

"What?" Fabbiola started forward. "Is she dead?"

"No," Garini said. "She's unconscious. She's also the murderer of Trevor Accanto." His voice was sober.

". . . and of Sabrina. She shot her." Carlina's voice shook. "She told me so herself."

For once, her mother was robbed of speech.

With his free hand, Garini flipped open his cell phone and pressed a few buttons.

"Who are you calling?" Fabbiola sounded accusing.

"Reinforcements," Garini said. "I have to tie up this case, and

Ricciarda and my leg both need to see a doctor before we freeze into permanent position here."

Fabbiola narrowed her eyes. "How come she's unconscious? What did you do to her?"

"Oh, it was nothing." Carlina replied for Garini who had started to speak into his phone. "He just jumped down several meters from the trapdoor up there," she pointed at the arch above them, "because otherwise, Ricciarda would have added me to her list of victims."

Fabbiola looked stunned. "I didn't see that in the cards." She shook her head in dismay. "How is that possible?"

Chapter 18

Fabbiola nestled a slip and matching bra into the small folding box Carlina had ordered in bulk for the first time this Christmas. It opened up into a tiny box all by itself if you pulled at one end, and it was the quickest way to create a charming gift package.

Carlina watched her mother from the corner of her eye and gave a silent prayer of thanks that she had decided to order the boxes in spite of the cost. She would not have made it through today, short one staff member, if her mother hadn't jumped in to do the gift packaging, and to watch her mother wrestle with scotch tape and slippery wrapping paper would have stretched her taut nerves beyond a point she could endure.

Carlina glanced at her watch. Ten more minutes, and she could close the doors of Temptation. The high Christmas turnover was a boost that helped her to go on, but this year, she felt more tired than ever before. Well, no wonder. She still couldn't take it in that Ricciarda had been the killer, Ricciarda, who had worked next to her for months.

Garini had sent her a text message this morning, telling her that he had sprained his ankle and torn a ligament. He had also noted that Ricciarda was physically well and that he would be in touch later on. His last sentence had helped her through the day.

The store was packed full, and both Marianna and Annalisa were busy with customers. Carlina felt she never wanted to approach a customer again, but she forced herself to address an elderly man who stood in front of the display with his hands folded at his back, detached and cool, as if he was admiring a painting in the Uffizi gallery. "Can I help you with any advice?" She smiled at him from the side.

He turned and looked at her.

Her eyes widened. She knew those light eyes, the penetrating gaze. *Garini's father!* "You must be Signor Garini." She held out her hand. "I'm Carlina Ashley. I know your son." She would never again overlook family traits. Never.

He took her hand and shook it. "Glad to meet you."

"Is . . . is Stefano all right?" She searched his face. It was thin and deeply lined, but she thought she could detect a friendly shimmer in those strangely familiar eyes.

"Yes." He nodded. "He's at home, recovering. He sent me here, to look after you."

Carlina smiled. "To look after me?"

"He told me the full story this morning." His voice was softer than his son's. "You've had a nasty experience."

"Yes." His friendliness made her want to cry, but then, she was so tired that even small things managed to push her out of her equilibrium, things she would usually have put away with a laugh.

"You are the Commissario's father?" Fabbiola appeared behind them, her golden jacket gleaming.

Carlina winced. She'd wanted to make a good impression. At least her mother had left her trusted cushion with the stars behind the counter. Probably she felt safe inside Temptation. What a farce.

"Yes, I am his father." Signor Garini said it simply and with pride.

A rush of warm feeling filled Carlina. *He has reason to be proud.*

Fabbiola grabbed Signor Garini's hand and pumped it up and down with enthusiasm. "I congratulate you." She continued to shake his hand as if it was part of some exotic fitness program. "From the bottom of my heart. I often say that your son is an odd man . . ."

Carlina closed her eyes.

". . . yes, a very odd man, and rather cool and disturbing at times, but I will forgive him everything," she now added her second hand to her first and pressed both around Signor Garini's hand, " . . . everything, I say, because he has saved my daughter from that lunatic."

"Mama." Carlina gave her mother a strained smile. "I believe there's a customer waiting for a gift wrapping."

Fabbiola looked over her shoulder and waved at the elegant

woman who stood with a tapping foot in front of the sales counter. "I'm coming, Signora!" Her voice was loud enough to be heard in the whole centro storico, the historical center of Florence. "But I first have to congratulate this man for his son. He saved my daughter from death by jumping through a hole in the floor."

The woman looked at the door as if measuring how long it would take her to escape.

Carlina went to the counter and started to chat with her in a low voice while quickly placing her purchase into the gift box. At the same time, she strained her ears to follow the conversation between Signor Garini and her mother, but she couldn't make out the words. Her mother seemed to do all the talking. *Oh, God. Whatever will she do next?* People say that if you want to judge a woman, you have to look at her mother. *Heaven forbid.*

Signor Garini, however, seemed to weather the avalanche of motherly gratefulness with a stoic smile and shortly afterward left the store with a friendly nod at Carlina.

She turned to her mother. "Mama!" She spoke low enough that the others couldn't hear them. "Couldn't you have been a little bit less . . . ?"

"Less what?" Her mother looked surprised.

"Less . . . exuberant?"

"My dear." Fabbiola picked up her cushion and traced the pattern of one golden star with her finger. "I am certainly not willing to be less . . . exuberant, if you want to call it that, when it comes to praising someone who deserves it."

"*He* didn't save my life." Carlina stressed the first word. "It was his son."

"I haven't forgotten that." Fabbiola gave her a satisfied smile. "And you don't need to worry. I will express my gratitude to Stefano Garini in no uncertain terms tomorrow."

Carlina suppressed a shudder. "You won't see him tomorrow." *Thank God.* "Tomorrow is Christmas." Maybe her mother's gratitude would have cooled down by the time the holidays were over. What a nightmare, to imagine that Garini would join them for the Christmas meal, to experience the complete family at full blast, a hyper-grateful Fabbiola, reading the future in no uncertain terms for all of them - if they wanted to listen or not - her aunt Benedetta in a frenzy of cooking, Uncle

Teo distributing hopping money-frogs left and right, probably aided by the shattered Frenchman this year, if she knew anything about it, Annalisa in tears because of her dead lover, with her brother Ernesto mercilessly teasing her, Emma self-righteous as if she had never made a mistake in her life, and she, exhausted beyond everything . . . oh no. It was much better if she kept Garini at a distance until their friendship was strong enough to withstand the pressure of her undiluted family.

"You are mistaken." Fabbiola patted the cushion as if it was a well-behaved dog. "We will indeed see both of them tomorrow because Signor Garini has just accepted my invitation to our Christmas meal. And I will crochet them two extra large stars tonight."

Epilogue

Emma leaned across the festive table, her eyes glistening in the candle-light. "He gave you a quilt for your bed. You know what that means, don't you?"

Carlina pressed her lips together. "Shut up, Emma." Thank God the others were all busy in conversation, and for once, Emma had spoken low enough so nobody had overheard them. She looked around the table. The Mantoni family had just finished eating the *secondo piatto*, the main course, and Carlina already felt as if she would explode if she added another morsel.

It was warm inside the crowded room, the air heavy with the aroma of the opulent Christmas lunch. Thank God her sister Gabriella had decided to spend this Christmas day with her husband's family, or Benedetta's kitchen would have been too small.

To Carlina's left, her mother and aunt Benedetta were focused on explaining how to prepare a savory roast recipe with thyme and rosemary in the true Italian way to Leopold Morin. He seemed to enjoy himself, judging by the faint flush of red on his thin cheeks.

Uncle Teo had pushed his plate aside and showed both Garinis how to fold money into leaping frogs. From their impassive faces, it was hard to tell if they found it riveting or only pretended to do so.

At the far end of the table, Carlina's cousins were sitting, their red-haired heads together. For once, Ernesto and Annalisa weren't fighting. Ernesto was checking out his brand-new telephone while Annalisa looked over his shoulder and commented on his progress.

Good. Carlina took a relieved breath. At the moment, nobody was thinking of their losses, of the people missing around the table tonight, of loved ones lost. Christmas was such an emotional drain, and she had feared that it would be awful this year. Instead, everybody seemed to be intent on making the best of it. Maybe her mother had been right to invite Leopold Morin and the Garinis. With only family present, people were apt to forget civilized behavior much sooner.

Emma touched her arm. "Hey, earth to Carlina. What are you thinking?"

Carlina turned her gaze on her cousin. "I was thinking that families exert more self-control if comparative strangers are present for Christmas. Did you know that January is the busiest time for divorce lawyers? The discrepancy between Christmas expectations and reality is so hard that many crack under the pressure."

Emma opened her eyes wide. "What strangers are you talking about?"

Carlina blinked. "I'd say that's pretty obvious, isn't it?"

Her cousin grinned. "Uncle Teo told me this morning that Leopold will ask for a sabbatical at his university. He'll move into grandpa's apartment on the ground floor, so from now on, you can quite count him as one of the family." She giggled. "Isn't it perfect? Leo and Teo. It sounds like a book for children, about a pair of happy mice or something."

"That's great!" Carlina smiled. The Frenchman seemed to get along so well with everyone, and he would be company for Uncle Teo. Besides, the apartment downstairs would not be so painfully empty anymore. "But why wasn't I told together with you?"

"Because," Emma shrugged, "you were still asleep by eleven o'clock, when Teo and Leo broke the news, and Fabbiola made us all go around on tiptoes. She said you had escaped the clutches of death by a hair's breadth." Her voice rose as she uttered the words in a dramatic way.

"So I have." Carlina's answer was dry. She did not want to think of Ricciarda.

"Well, and as to the Garinis, it's the same," Emma made an airy move with her hands. "They're almost family. Which brings me back to my original thought." She gave Carlina an exaggerated wink. "What did you give Garini for Christmas? It's not a secret, is it?"

"You'd better tell me what Lucio gave you for Christmas."

Carlina knew the answer, because Lucio gave Emma a ring - every year a different one. Carlina had already predicted that Emma would have to grow some more fingers to accommodate them all as the years passed.

However, Emma wasn't fooled. "You know he gave me a ring, as every year, so stop dithering." She glanced with pride at the new ring on her thumb. "I see you don't want to tell me. Is it a secret, then?"

Carlina did not want to discuss her gift with Emma, who would not understand it in a million years, so she shrugged and turned her back on her cousin. "Let it go, Emma."

Across the room, she met Stefano's gaze. She had managed to give him a voucher when nobody had looked. A voucher for a full day off, just the two of them, by the sea. Walking along the wintry coast, with the wind in their hair, and no family or murder within fifty kilometers. Taking the time to stop by a nice restaurant, to warm up and eat at leisure, to talk, to get to know each other with time to spare, with nobody else around. *Heaven.*

Even now, a feeling of warmth pooled deep inside her as she remembered the slow smile spreading over his face when he had read her voucher.

She looked up and met his gaze resting on her. Her smile deepened, and the babble of family conversation melted away, leaving just the two of them. *I'm looking forward to next year.*

About the author
Mischief & Humor from Page 1

Beate Boeker has been a traditionally published author since 2008. Several of her novels were shortlisted for the Golden Quill Contest, the National Readers' Choice Award, the "best indie books" contest, and the RONE Award 2014. Her mystery Delayed Death, the first in the series "Temptation in Florence", hit the Amazon bestseller list "international mystery & crime" in 2013.

By day, Beate is a marketing manager with a degree in International Business Administration, and her daily experience in marketing continuously provides her with a wide range of fodder for her novels, be it hilarious or cynical. Widely traveled, she speaks German (her mother language), English, French and Italian and lives in the North of Germany together with her husband and daughter.

While 'Boeker' means 'books' in a German dialect, her first name Beate can be translated as 'Happy' . . . and with a name that reads 'Happy Books', what else could she do but write novels with a happy end?

Learn more about Beate at www.happybooks.de. This is also the place where you can contact her directly, and where you can sign up for her newsletter.

Alternatively, you can also find her on
Facebook (Beate Boeker Author)
Twitter (@BeateBoeker)

Cozy mysteries
by Beate Boeker

Delayed Death – Temptation in Florence #1

What do you do when you find your grandfather dead half an hour before your cousin's wedding? You hide him in his bed and tell everyone he didn't feel like coming.

Charmer's Death – Temptation in Florence #2

What do you do when your best customer seduces your beautiful cousin? You try to save the situation, but it becomes a little harder than planned when he's found strangled.

Banker's Death – Temptation in Florence #3

When Carlina's attractive cousin Valentino returns from Dubai to Florence, he quickly becomes the most unpopular member of the wide-spread Mantoni family. When he is murdered, only Commissario Garini is sorry because he has to investigate the Mantoni family once again.

Expected Death – Temptation in Florence #4

Coming soon: The family patriarch Uncle Teo has fallen in love – and the whole family hates her with good reason. Nobody is surprised when she's killed, but this time, the Mantonis are in for it, and one of them ends up in prison.

Contemporary romances I
by Beate Boeker

<u>Mischief in Italy</u>
A father-son conversation leads to unexpected results and manages to turn both their lives upside down.

<u>A New Life</u>
How often have you wondered if A New Life wouldn't be fun? Circumstances force Anne to start again in Florence, Italy – with totally unexpected results . . .

<u>Rent a Thief</u>
Can you fall in love with a thief?

<u>Stormy Times</u>
Joanna is lost in a blizzard on her way home from a difficult foaling. Just one man can save her – but he's strangely reluctant to come to her help. A Christmas romance.

<u>A Little Bit of Passion</u>
How much independence do you have to give up when falling in love?

<u>Take My Place</u>
A single mother sets up her own company and tries not to fall in love

<u>Wings to Fly</u>
Cathy tries to land the job of her life but an accident changes all her plans.

Contemporary romances II
by Beate Boeker

It's Raining Men (co-written with Gwen Ellery!)

Four cousins inherit one bedraggled umbrella, and each of them has to keep it for three months. Join them during this magic, amusing, touching and romantic year, and you'll finish this novel with a happy feeling deep inside.

23215256R00136

Made in the USA
Middletown, DE
19 August 2015